ETHAN
JUSTICE
ORIGINS

SIMON JENNER

Ethan Justice: Origins

For my wife, Julia

Prologue

I remind my captive of the need for obedience by stubbing out my cigarette on his forehead. The smell of singeing skin is exquisite. He is tightly gagged to prevent the noise levels permeating his detached home. His screams are merely loud groans that die inside these walls. The bouncing wooden chair settles as his energy levels deplete, welts red and angry where rope has rubbed against ankles and wrists.

"Are you ready to talk?" I ask.

He nods his head urgently. The pain has done the trick. Compliance will spare him pain. He understands.

"Tell me everything you know about Bradshaw and his invention," I say, pulling up a matching chair and sitting opposite him, taking hold of the spittle-soaked material wrapped tightly around his mouth. "If you make a noise, you will die."

He nods his understanding, and I unwind the makeshift gag.

"Talk," I say.

He is a pen-pusher and doesn't understand the science behind Bradshaw's invention, but my breath quickens at the power he describes. I see vengeance unfolding before my eyes as he continues, without further encouragement, to stammer out Bradshaw's address. I sense truth behind wide-eyed fear, but I need an angle.

"What's Bradshaw's weakness?"

He jerks back in the chair. "What?"

"Little boys, little girls, drugs ... What's his poison?"

"I've ... heard ... he gambles heavily," he splutters. "Owes more than he can pay."

Perfect. It's enough, and I should be moving on. I pat him on the head and reapply the gag. He begins to fidget as he ponders my next move. I walk to my black gym bag and remove the hatchet, slapping it against my free palm. It is cold and heavy. I need to know for sure that he has spoken the truth.

"Place your little finger flat on the arm of the chair," I say, pointing to his left hand.

The chair jumps, and the groans return, his eyes fixed on the hatchet. I twist his balled fist sideways so his little finger is against the arm. His mind will not allow his hand to open up and release the finger.

"It's a finger or the whole hand," I tell him, raising the hatchet. "Your choice."

The finger creeps out, and I bring down the axe before he has time to retract it. His eyes close as the cutting edge meets the digit halfway down. The small axe buries itself into the hard wood beneath. The chair shakes and creaks, like it might fall apart, as he thrashes from side to side, tears streaming from his eyes and leaping from his cheeks. I doubt he has ever experienced real pain before. He is lucky I can't hang around to educate him.

I place my foot between his legs, pressing down on the chair, keeping it planted to the floor. "When I come back, I want you to nod if all you have told me is true. Shake your head and you will have a chance to correct your mistake without further pain." I lean down until our faces are close, and I smell the cold sweat that drips from his brow. I feel his shakes travel into the chair and up my leg. I smile. "If I doubt your nod, then I will take another finger, and we'll try again. Understand?"

He nods, red eyes blinking, face slack and drooping in defeat.

In the kitchen I open up the gas valves of the hob and oven, setting the boiler to spark in fifteen minutes. It is an easy adjustment, one that will not survive the explosion and subsequent fire. A deliberate nod greets me as I walk back into the lounge.

I exhale through pursed lips, sorry to be leaving so soon, but I have taken too much of a risk already. There will be other opportunities. I collect my *things and leave, confident that fire will cover my trail and darkness my departure.*

It is time to start the dance with Bradshaw.

1: Sunday 18th September, 13:30

John Smith was sitting alone in his parents' dining room, a shrine to designer opulence. What was taking so long? Where were his parents and sister? Where was the delicious smelling roast lamb?

Three loud raps at the front door aroused his curiosity. Adelaine House was at the end of a two hundred yard gated driveway which required authorised entry. John would have heard if the intercom system had been operated and so it had to be somebody with the code - Uncle Michael or ... his best friend Mark Bradshaw.

Thank God. Now he would have an ally at the table, and his parents would lay off the subject of his career, or more correctly, the lack of one.

John heard his father greet Mark at the door.

"Good to see you, Mark. How's the world of finance treating you?"

"Pretty good, thanks, Adam. Is John here?"

"Yes but..." his father's voice descended into a whisper. As still as he could be, John strained his ears but was unable to hear. He had an uneasy feeling that he was being kept out of the loop on something.

"Got it," Mark said finally, in a failed attempt at whispering in baritone. "We'll put him straight."

John's stomach sank and his appetite plummeted with it.

*

Thirty minutes later, a thick and heavy silence blended with the smells of the steaming cuisine laid in front of John. He had so far parried every attempt at small talk with short sharp, not to be followed, answers. The others shared knowing glances when they thought John's attention was elsewhere. He had hardly touched his starter and was equally unable to appreciate the main course.

John rested his head on his hand as he guided a roast potato around a lamb island and through a moat of gravy with his silver fork. He raised his eyes from his plate.

"Come on then," he said. "Let's get on with it."

City whiz Mark, wearing a dark power suit as always, was sitting opposite John and next to Rachel, John's sister. Rachel had left home over a year ago when she was twenty-two. She had purchased her own property with an obscene mortgage, met by a more obscene salary at one of the larger prestigious fashion houses. For the life of him, he could never remember which one.

Mark looked to his left, past Rachel to John's father at the head of the table. Adam Smith nodded, and Mark cleared his throat as if addressing a board meeting.

"Listen, John, we're all a bit concerned about you."

Here it was. It was time to duck out. John stood up and tossed the embroidered napkin onto his plate. He glared at Mark. "Not you too. I thought you were my friend."

"That's why we asked him here." His mother, sitting to his right, tugged his shirt and he half expected her to tell him to tuck it in - but she didn't. "Don't blame Mark. He took a great deal of convincing to come here today."

His mother was such a drama queen. "Look, Mark, forgive me if I don't want to be a super-preened city stiff like you. I can't believe you've let them rope you into this."

Rachel, dressed in a figure-hugging, high-fashion, pink dress of her own design, dabbed her matching lips with her napkin. At least she wasn't wearing a ridiculous hat today. "Jonathan, Mum and Dad just want the best for you. For Christ's sake, you've got a maths degree from Oxford, and you're working as a clerk in an office."

"Don't call me Jonathan." Pretty and successful, Rachel had it all. Why did she have to be such a huge pain in the arse? "What the hell use are your services to the world? Created any new designs for the third world recently? Let's give the starving some street cred, why don't we?"

John's father raised his hand. "John, leave your sister alone, and sit down, please."

"Forget it, Dad. I know I'm a disappointment to you all, but it's my life, and I'm living it my way." John turned to leave.

"If you don't sit down, Son, we're taking your flat back."

John froze. "You'd do that?"

"It's in our name."

"You'd really take my home?"

"Jonathan," his mother said. "You're thirty-two, and you dress like you're seventeen. We have given you every advantage. Why can't you just use them?"

John turned back to face his detractors. "I support myself," he said at no one in particular. Why had he said that? He braced himself.

His father made fists with his hands as they sat by his plate. "We pay your rates and utility bills and don't charge you rent. Just how is that supporting yourself?" He gestured to Mark whose pock-scarred face, the result of acute teenage acne, looked decidedly uncomfortable. "Mark here lives in Kensington and makes a seven figure salary. You, on the other hand, make ... I don't know? Are you into five figures yet?"

Yes, of course they thought Mark was wonderful, but they didn't know of his out of control gambling problem or his fondness for high-class prostitutes. He wasn't the saint they thought him to be. Boy, could he tell them some stories, and by coming here he would deserve it - but he wouldn't do that. Besides, it changed nothing. What they were saying was all true. John was a waster. He knew it, Mark knew it and his family knew it.

"Another banker, that's just what the world needs," he said under his breath as he returned to sit at the table. He had lost. It was time for damage control.

John nudged at his potato with his fork, but it had taken on too much gravy and fell apart. "What is it you want?"

"We'll give you six months," his father said, again gesturing to Mark. "We were going to make it three but Mark told us six was fairer. It's the eighteenth of September. Why don't we agree to a deadline of the end of March?"

Mark had his uses after all. How would John celebrate Christmas properly if he had a proper job to hold down?

"How about twelve months?"

"Not a chance."

"And who's going to turf me out?" John poked his mother's shoulder. "What would the neighbours' say, Mum? Just think of all the gossip."

His mother's cheeks reddened, and she shifted in her chair. "Adam?"

His father banged his fist on the table, shaking the cutlery. "I'll sell it for next to nothing to a slum landlord if that makes you pull your finger out."

"Calm down, dear." His mother took hold of his father's hand. "Remember your heart."

John jerked back in his chair as if someone had pushed him. "What? What about your heart, Dad?"

Adam Smith shook his head and squeezed his wife's hand. "It's nothing. You know how your Mum fusses."

Elaine Smith snatched her hand back. "You call quadruple bypass surgery fussing?"

John turned to Mark who shrugged. He looked over to Rachel who nodded. His attention returned to his father. "Dad?" His father avoided eye contact by looked over to Rachel. This was all becoming too much. "Will somebody please tell me what's going on?"

"Your father needed emergency surgery after a massive heart attack two months ago," began Mrs Smith. "If we hadn't been able to pay for the operation privately, he'd be dead."

John couldn't believe what he was hearing. "But Dad's always been so ... healthy? He's only fifty-four."

Mrs Smith continued, ignoring her son's interruption. "Anyway, ever since the operation, he's been worried sick about what's going to become of you if he dies. He wouldn't tell you, but he lies awake at night trying to come up with ways of getting you back on track. The stress will eventually kill him..."

"Really, Elaine, please..." his father complained, eyes wandering around the room, anywhere but on John.

"No, Adam, it has to be said." Nobody could do disappointed better than his mother - not even Rachel, although she was catching up. "You're killing your father, Jonathan." Her hand rose to her forehead. "Can't you see that?"

Despite the added drama, the message hit home hard and deep. A heart attack - Jesus Christ. "Why didn't you call me?"

Elaine Smith looked her son squarely in the face. "Because seeing you might have killed him."

*

On Monday morning John called work to tell them he was sick. He feigned a weak voice as it seemed only proper to play the part. It was his first instance of sickness in the two years he had been with the company, and regardless of his lowly position, he had always performed his clerical duties to the highest standard. At least he was his father's son in one regard.

Discovering a new vocation within six months sounded relatively straightforward for a man with an honours degree from Oxford University. He needed to brainstorm his options, and as he always thought better with a drink inside him, he sat in his, no, in his parents' flat, with a notepad and a half bottle of cheap Scotch whisky.

By Friday lunch time, his notepad contained one underlined word:

<u>Ideas</u>

His bin contained seven empty scotch bottles. For the last five days, he had not shaved, hardly eaten and slept on the sofa, certain that inspiration was only another drink away. At that point, he decided there was a serious flaw in his reasoning and called Mark for assistance. Mark suggested that they meet at a sports bar named 'Dribbles' in Soho, where they always went when Mark had a large bet on a football match. Didn't Mark see the irony in not even liking football? Maybe he could convince Mark to give up gambling to support him in his career launching endeavours. It was as likely as the long odds his best friend insisted on chucking his offensive salary away on.

John spent the remainder of the afternoon preparing to go out, dragging himself through all of the necessary recovery procedures until only his eyes displayed the toll his body had paid for the week of worthless brainstorming.

*

At eight o'clock 'Dribbles' was already overflowing outside with customers who had arrived prepared with thick coats and scarves. The idea of drinking cold beer outside in the dark, beneath overcast skies, was lost on John. Fortunately Mark was a regular big spender, and there was always a table made available to him.

Ten large television screens were intermittently spaced and tuned in to various silenced sporting events. Katy Perry was singing her lungs out about kissing a girl and it tasting of cherry Chap Stick. Tonight the VIP table was in a private corner of the massive, wooden-floored bar and their waitress was an attractive Spanish woman in her mid-twenties with shoulder-length black hair and smooth olive skin.

"Como estás, Mark?" she said, as she guided them to their bar-height table with two high wooden stools.

"Muy bien gracias, Carmen, y tu?"

"Yo tambien, gracias. Buscas mujeres?" She patted Mark's behind as he mounted the stool. "Quieres que llamo a Christos?"

Mark smiled. "Quizás luego."

John had witnessed the ritual many times before, but this was the first time he had met Carmen. John took his seat and ordered a Corona beer. Mark suggested whisky chasers, but the thought of more Scotch made John feel nauseous.

Mark was six feet four inches tall and had nearly four inches of extra body to house the abundant alcohol they would undoubtedly consume. Mark scrutinized Carmen's bottom as she ambled away to collect their beers, chatting to other regulars as she went, some taking advantage of the overcrowded floor space to make 'accidental' contact. She didn't seem to mind.

"Is she ... you know?" John asked.

Mark grinned, "Available for hire?"

Despite his skin blemishes, Mark was handsome and had plenty of women chasing after his affections. He was slim, tall, dressed in expensive Savile Row suits and had the most important criteria in bundles: he was rich. However, Mark detested the act of romancing and figured it a complete waste of his valuable time, preferring one night stands with gorgeous high-class escorts. John could see the attraction but unfortunately found the unknown history of their abundant clientele too much to stomach. Besides he didn't have the funds to pay for such indulgent and risky treats.

"Yes. Is she one of your regulars?" he asked, as Carmen disappeared into the thick of the Friday night crowd.

"No. I think she might be available, but she's not my type. Too short for me."

John thought about that for a moment. Five feet two versus six feet four. He had never considered height as an issue between two potential mates, but as he unintentionally pictured Mark and Carmen in his mind, the likely problems became clearer. He grimaced.

"It's a sixty-nine thing, old boy," added Mark, in case John hadn't quite cottoned on.

"I get it. Please don't say another word. I already swallowed down some sick."

"Are you interested?" enquired Mark, eyebrows raised, mouth stretched into a smirk. "My treat. You're worse with women than I am. Call it a celebratory gift to start your new life."

"No, you're all right, thanks. I promised my hand that I wouldn't cheat on it."

Mark laughed and snorted in that way that only came with old money.

"Mark, pack that racket in or you'll get us into a fight. Some of us peasants don't appreciate the Sloane Ranger snort.

Embarrassed, Mark stopped abruptly and pointed at John. "Listen here, Smith. I know for a fact that your father sold his firm for upwards of fifteen million."

"It's got nothing to do with the money. My Dad's the first in his family to have any. Besides, I won't get a penny unless I join the professional classes."

"So have you anything in mind?"

"No. I've wasted a week trying to think of something that interested me. All I managed to do was feel sick, grow a beard and develop chronic B.O."

"Sounds like a Civil Service job might suit you."

"Very good." John took his bottle of Corona from the outstretched hand of Carmen. She had beautiful brown eyes. "You should tell my Dad that one. He hates Civil Servants."

"I think he told it to me."

Ice cold Corona ran from the corner of John's mouth as he failed to laugh and keep his lips together at the same time. "You bastard," John said, brushing the liquid from his blue polo shirt before it soaked through. "This is my best shirt."

"Now I know why they call this place 'Dribbles'," Mark said. "Anyway, what's this about best shirt? I thought that was your *only* shirt."

"Like I said. You bastard."

John looked up from his beer-dampened shirt to see that Mark was whispering into Carmen's ear. A moment later she was gone, but there was more of a purpose to her stride. What was he up to?

John grabbed his friend by the suit lapels. "I hope you haven't done anything stupid."

Mark raised both hands from the table, palms facing John. "Me? Never." A look of triumph spread across his face, like he'd won one of his ludicrous bets. "I've got it."

Pulling his arms back, John shook his head. "Go on," he said.

"Do you remember when Spunk Eyes Spencer attacked me in the playground, when we were about sixteen?"

"Yeah, wasn't it because you called him Spunk Eyes?"

Mark considered this for a moment. "Yes, I suppose it must have been. Anyway, you took him down like you were born to it."

"What's your point?"

"I'll never forget the look in your eyes as you faced off. It was like you were on a roller coaster ride, caught up in excitement and exhilaration, not a flicker of fear to be seen."

John took a swig from his bottle and swallowed, enjoying the memory of pulling Anthony Spencer from on top of Mark as he swung fist after fist into his best friend's face. He had enjoyed seeing the fear in the bully's eyes. "I'm a bit old to be a boxer."

"What about the police?"

"Are you serious?"

"I don't mean the boys in blue. I'm talking about your secret service types. They earn six figure salaries, and you could get that look back."

"And they don't exist."

"Believe me, John, they exist all right. I can't believe I never thought of it before. Leave it with me, and I'll see if I can set something up."

Mark raised his bottle and John did the same, toasting to resolving his future. Like Mark knew anyone in a secret police unit. The thought of telling his mother he carried a gun and shot people for a living did widen his grin somewhat.

"So we've sorted out my career path, what do we do now?"

"Let's get absolutely fucking trollied." Mark's suggestion threw him into a fit of posh snorts, so loud that a few disapproving stares gravitated their way. John stared them all right back.

"I'll drink to that," he said.

2: Saturday 24th September, 06:30

John Smith lay on his back in his bed, staring into the blackness. No light had appeared through the cigarette hole in his thick velvet curtains signalling it wasn't even seven o'clock yet. He closed his eyes and tried to remember the events from last night. A week on Scotch and a night of God only knew how many Coronas had taken its toll on his cognitive powers. Oh yes, he was going to become a secret agent, and then they got pissed. Not too much then.

"What time is it?" said a sleepy, female voice.

John shot up, grabbed the duvet with both hands and pulled it to his chest. His heart pounded, and his skin tingled with goose bumps. Movement had not been kind to his head. He looked over to his left but the room was still pitch black. Anyway he worked it, his head came back to the same conclusion. There was a woman in his bed.

"What the...?"

"Heh, stop stealing all the covers, chummy," said the silky voice. "That's no way to treat a guest." A soft hand slid under the duvet and onto his bare chest, stroking him in slow circles. "I'm yours till eight if you want to go again."

John felt around and banged on the lamp at his bedside. The room lit up and John blinked rapidly as he fought to focus his eyes on the warm, wriggling body that was attempting to clamp on to him. Her words percolated in his brain while he gazed down at the slender, naked frame. She was truly spectacular: hardly twenty, long dark hair, pale smooth skin and the mischievous face of a wayward angel. She was way out of his league. The soft hand crept towards his crotch just as his brain caught up with reality.

"You're a prostitute?" he exclaimed, sliding off the bed, taking the duvet with him and wrapping it around himself like makeshift armour. With a few feet between them, the young woman's beauty was blatant and decidedly distracting. "You're a prostitute," he repeated, not sure what else to say.

Chocolate brown eyes glistened and tears formed in their corners as his guest crossed her legs, folded her arms and bent awkwardly over in an attempt to cover her newly found modesty. "I'm an escort actually, not a prostitute, and I don't do anything I don't want to."

John could not handle a crying woman: prostitute, escort or otherwise. For Superman it was Kryptonite, for some it was fingernails on a blackboard, but for John it was a woman's tears. The more tears, the more John fell apart.

"Don't cry,' he started. "I don't care what you do. I've got every respect for prostitutes." He saw the corners of her mouth drop further, and the tears began to flow. "I mean escorts. Please... Please... Please don't cry." But cry she did and how. He racked his brain for the right words to stem the tide and end his pain. Any lie would do. "My sister is an escort. It's in my family, why would it bother me?"

Her eyes narrowed and lingered on him, perhaps testing whether his statement would crumble under the glare of her teary vision. He held her gaze. His lie was working. "You're only my second client," she said, wiping her eyes and looking around the room for her clothes. "You seemed really nice."

With the pounding in John's head relegated to a low priority, the memory of the night before surfaced. Mark had lost his bet on the football match and had seemed somewhat dejected until Carmen, the Spanish waitress, had arrived with a friend - Samantha or something? John had hit it off immediately with Carmen's friend which should have been a clue the size of a skyscraper. But he had been drunk so he should cut himself a little slack. She had come home with John - the same woman who was crouching on his oversized bed as her eyes continued to scour the room for her clothes.

Taking care not to drop the covers, John knelt and retrieved the woman's clothes from under the bed. She would never have found them without moving, and she wasn't going anywhere until she could adequately cover herself. He passed the items to her with a trembling hand. Was that the whisky or the fact he had a beautiful, naked woman on his bed? Most likely the latter. He turned his back to her, allowing her some privacy to dress. He noticed the light appearing through the hole in the curtain. Seven o'clock had been and gone.

"We seem to have gotten off on the wrong foot," he said. "I remember that we chatted and kissed and that Mark took off, but I honestly didn't know about..." How did he say this without eliciting further histrionics? He needed to mind his choice of words. "I didn't know about ... you know?"

"Forget about it," she said, dismissively. "You were off your face. Your buddy thought you could do with cheering up. Do you even remember my name?"

"Samantha is it? Sorry," he said. "I can barely remember my own."

"You can turn round now," she said.

John turned and was surprised to find her standing in front of him with her hand held out. She stood about an inch above him in black high heels and a black mini dress. The mischievous look had gone, leaving just the face of a dark-haired angel.

"I'm Savannah," she said.

"Yeah right," John said. He extended his hand to meet hers. It really was the softest of hands, and he felt a pleasant tingle shoot up his arm when they touched. "I'm John Smith," he said.

"Yeah right," she said. "Look, if you could just pay me the thousand pounds ... John Smith...," she gave a huge grin like there was something funny about the name, "... then I'll be off."

John caught his breath. "Didn't Mark take care of that?"

"No, he said you were loaded and wouldn't hear of it."

"This is a joke, right?"

"Am I smiling?"

She wasn't, but she was still stunning. It must be a con. Mark was the City Financier, the money man, Mr Fat Wallet. He was a joker but not of the practical kind. He was way too sophisticated for that.

"I'll call Mark," he threatened.

"Well make it quick," she said, looking around the room. "I need to go."

John grabbed the cordless phone from the bedside table and speed-dialled his best friend.

"Yes," the voice was sharp and edgy. It didn't sound like Mark at all.

"Mark?" John said.

"Oh it's you. What is it? I'm in the middle of something."

"Good morning to you too."

"John, I don't have time for games," said Mark. "What is it you want?"

"You set me up with a pro ... a girl." Phew, that was close. "Now she says I owe her a thousand pounds."

"Yes. Your parents are right. You're a waste of space. I thought this might give you the kick up the arse you so badly need." Mark hung up.

John's head thumped like his heart was inside it. He stared at the handset open mouthed. Mark had never spoken to him like that before. Yes, he'd made fun of John's adversity to success and yes, he'd turned up at his parents' house last Sunday in an intervention style attack on his lifestyle - but this? The voice was Mark's, but the behaviour was not that of his best friend.

"Told you," she said.

John shook his head and exhaled. His head didn't appreciate the movement.

"Arghh! This can't be right?" What was up with Mark? He let out a huge sigh while he held his head with one hand ensuring that it didn't move. Mark could wait. He had more immediate issues. "How much do I really owe you?"

Her eyes registered frustration. "A thousand, like I already said."

John shook his head slowly as he looked her up and down, sizing up the threat. She seemed way too nice for this situation. It was all just a big joke. Had they even had sex? He had been way too drunk to remember, and he'd never managed legless and penetration at the same time. She was something else though. In her case, he may well have just gone the extra mile. None of his thoughts made any difference because he didn't have a thousand pounds, and what could she do about it anyway?

"I don't have it," he said. He held out his upturned palms as if this proved how poor he was. The duvet fell to the floor leaving him totally exposed.

"Nice," she said, taking her time to look John up and down, "but I'll still need the cash."

He fell to the floor and pulled the duvet up to his waist. "I really don't have it," he said, trying to appear unruffled as he looked up at her. He hesitated before saying, "You really liked what you saw?"

She bit her bottom lip and rolled her eyes. "Look, John Smith, I don't do the threatening, I'm just the talent." She reached into a small black purse which John hadn't noticed against the matching dress and passed him a business card. "Call me within forty-eight hours when you've got the cash, or my boss will break your legs."

John stared at the card blankly. "But...?"

Before he could form a coherent sentence, Savannah Jones of Aphrodite's Angels had left the building.

3: Saturday 24th September, 08:00

John Smith could not get back to sleep. He was not good tired, but his spinning mind prevented a return to slumber. What had Mark got him into?

For three hours he paced around the spacious flat in a pair of black boxers, swearing under his breath at his predicament, kicking anything in his path. Damn Mark. John never lectured him about the thousands he blew on gambling, so what gave Mark the right to interfere with his life? Some bloody friend. Where could he get a thousand pounds in forty-eight hours? He wouldn't be paid for another six days and there was a salary advance and an overdraft to cover, leaving a few hundred over for essentials at best.

Recent events with his family meant they were unlikely to assist without a good explanation, and no matter how many ways he played out the scene in his head, it didn't end well. Besides, the thought of begging his parents or Rachel for money turned his stomach. His sister was Daddy's girl through and through. The voice might be shriller but the message would be the same: you got yourself into this mess, so you find a way to get yourself out of it. No, it had to be Mark or a local money lender, and as a loan shark would put him effectively back to where he was, he reckoned he was stuck with Mark.

His huffing, puffing and expletives were scarily interrupted by the occasional thought of the long-legged Savannah. He couldn't recall being so taken by a person's natural beauty before. And those eyes! Had she really liked what she saw, or was it all part of the service? Why had he asked? He must have appeared so lame. She had seemed incredibly nice for a prostitute. He guessed people expected a lot for a thousand pounds - and why shouldn't they? Some of them might even work hard for it. He wondered how long it would take him to save up for another night and whether she would agree not to sleep with anyone else until then? Probably not, he concluded.

At 11.00 A.M. he gave up thinking and headed to the wet room for a shower. After ten minutes of sixteen individual jets of hot pressurised water massaging his every muscle, he was a new man. He admired himself in the full-length mirror. Not bad for thirty-two considering he hadn't exercised since university. A little muscle mass had deserted him, but at least it hadn't turned to fat. He jumped on the scales which measured him at just over twelve and a half stones with eighteen percent body fat. At half an inch over six feet, he reckoned they were pretty good stats. Savannah could do worse.

John changed into a pair of tatty old blue jeans, a red t-shirt, baggy green GAP hoodie and a pair of Nike black Air Max trainers bought recently on his credit card. They had been a steal at just under a fifth of a night with Savannah. As usual he skipped breakfast.

*

Two tubes later he was standing outside Mark's apartment block in South Kensington. The streets were bustling with the rich and the even richer. Most pedestrians carried designer umbrellas of varying lengths and colours despite the predictions of the weathermen for a late summer. Not surprisingly, the sky, grey and overcast, threatened rain or worse. Did anyone believe the weather forecast anymore? John glanced along the line of neatly parked residents' cars which followed the curve of the avenue, and as usual, didn't spot a car that cost less than fifty thousand pounds.

Doormen in various uniforms, complete with hats, many like the trained monkeys sat on top of the barrel organs of yesteryear, stood outside blocks of exorbitantly priced apartments. This wasn't the most expensive post code in London but it was right up there. Of course, Mark's apartment was the penthouse. How much did a flat have to cost to be considered an apartment? Wasn't an apartment just an Americanism for flat? The rich and their obsession with labels, John mused as he dialled Mark's mobile. The pickup was immediate.

"Where are you?" asked Mark.

"Outside," he said. "Can you tell the concierge to let me up? Last time he refused and told the doorman to never let me back in."

Mark sounded pissed off. "Why are you here?"

"Come on, you posh bastard. You owe me after that stunt you pulled." John put on his best aristocratic accent. "Tell Parkes that Lord John Smith is here."

"You're such a child. I'll instruct him when I'm done."

"Or you could say, 'let my friend in'. Try talking like the rest of the human race, why don't you." John disconnected the call. They were like chalk and cheese all right. Sure they'd gone to the same elite school, but they were worlds apart in every other way. And yet the tie between them was strong, and neither one had ever managed to explain it. It was what it was, and despite the possibly bone-threatening position Mark had left him in, John would do just about anything for him. Once he'd coughed up the thousand pounds, of course.

John watched yellow leaves fall from the oaks, beeches and silver birches which were prevalent along the exclusive avenue. The light breeze seemed distinctly autumnal, carrying a chill which his hoodie failed to deflect. As the leaves fell in a lazy, pendulum-style motion, he was reminded of his failure to take hold of his own life which too seemed on a downward path to nowhere.

Five minutes later, Parkes emerged from the building and headed towards John at a brisk pace. This didn't bode well. He wore the same bus-red uniform as the doorman but had a more elaborate hat. Perks of the job, John supposed. As he approached, he opened his mouth to speak but John beat him to it.

"All right, Parker?" John said.

"It's Parkes," he said. "My name is Parkes."

He was a tall, muscular man of about forty years old with a pronounced black widow's peak which he hid beneath the hat. The head gear was a half-height, black top hat with a bus-red band to match the uniform, giving him the appearance of a circus ringmaster. Parkes had been a thorn in John's side since Mark had moved into the block fifteen months ago, always making entry to his friend's apartment difficult for him. Mark had told John that Parkes was ex-military, but he didn't believe a word of it. John had never taken to orders well: at school, at home and especially from a steroid-pumped attendant.

"Wasn't that what I said?" asked John.

"No."

"Nice hat. Got enough saved for the hair transplant yet? Can I come in now?"

"Mr Bradshaw is unavailable."

"No, he isn't," John said. "I spoke to him less than ten minutes ago. You were supposed to be telling the doorman to let me in. What the hell is going on?"

Parkes rubbed his mouth with a white-gloved hand and leaned forward so his face was close to John's.

"Don't take that tone with me, Smith," he said through clenched teeth. "I could break you like a twig."

What's with all the threats today? Parkes seemed overly nervous and antagonistic. John pushed Parkes away, both palms thumping into the bigger man's chest. Parkes grunted as the air left his lungs and stumbled backwards to keep from falling, arms rotating like two erratic windmills as he sought balance. Passersby turned their heads as they continued to walk, interested, but not wanting to be involved. While the concierge considered his next move, John called Mark once again - it went straight to voicemail - strange.

He redialled Mark's mobile again as Parkes cursed under his breath at the numerous passersby with nothing better to do than stare. Voicemail again. John considered taking a run at the entrance to the apartment block, but Parkes was built to block, and it didn't appear an even contest. But Mark could be in trouble, and John needed the money to keep his legs intact. Looking into the concierge's eyes John shrugged, turned on his heels and started to walk away.

Five short paces later, John spun round and charged.

The diversion had worked. Parkes was already heading back to the entrance. Unfortunately, Parkes's colleague, the doorman, had spotted John and screamed. John reached the concierge at full pelt, just as he turned in reaction to the warning. Dipping and turning his left shoulder, John caught Parkes full in the chest sending him backwards for the second time, only this time directly into the doorman. Both figures tumbled to the paved ground beneath the maroon cloth canopy of the apartments in a tangled heap. Onlookers gaped in astonishment, but John didn't hang around to explain, continuing forward from the collision, on and into the apartment building.

John ran through the overly large reception area where Parkes should have been on duty and launched himself into the single lift which was open, waiting like a sideways mechanical mouth to swallow him. He stabbed the top red button for the penthouse several times, and after a few 'come ons', the doors closed smoothly and the lift began its ascent. He bent over, hands on his knees for support, gasping for air as his cardiovascular system struggled to provide his muscles with sufficient oxygen. Perhaps he should have taken a bit better care of himself.

The lift chimed and opened revealing Mark's solid wooden doors directly opposite. John immediately picked up the cylindrical bin from inside the lift and placed it between the doors, just like he had seen in a movie. He rolled the cylinder sideways into position so it sat in the crack between the lift and the adjoining floor. Anyone who followed him would be forced to take the stairwell. As expected, the lift doors chomped repeatedly on the bin and failed to close. John jumped over the obstruction and made for Mark's doors. He rang Mark's bell with his right hand and banged on the doors with his other fist.

"Mark... Mark... Are you there, Mark?" John shouted, not caring who heard him. He paused and put his ear to the cold wood of the door. There was a definite sound of a door closing. With a two-step run up, he rammed the same shoulder he had hit Parkes with, into the doors. Pain shot through his shoulder as his bone collided with the hard wood, and he rebounded from the impact. God that hurt. He wasn't going to get through the door as easily as he had gone past the concierge.

He looked around for something heavy enough to use as a makeshift battering ram, but there was nothing but a fire hose in the tall, narrow corridor, and the lift's bin was in use and far too light. While searching, he noticed the red 'break in case of fire' box to the left of the lift which he promptly smashed with his elbow, sending an ear-piercing, two-tone wail throughout the building.

Resisting the urge to cover his ears, John charged the door once more, again bouncing back in pain like a rubber ball off a brick wall. He leaned with his back against the door, panting from exhaustion and the adrenaline rush. Jesus, what was he supposed to do? Where was an axe when you needed one? He felt rather than heard the click from the locking mechanism behind him, and the right hand door twitched slightly inwards. John kicked the door as he turned and rushed into the spacious entrance hall. Empty.

"Mark, where are you?"

As John eased his way along the high-ceilinged hall, nothing looked out of place. The Chinese art from several dynasties, which John disliked, was perfectly hung on maroon walls. As always, the place looked spotless and smelt of disinfectant. This was clearly no robbery. All of the doors were shut, which again, was not unlike Mark. Maybe he'd left by the fire escape. But why?

John ran straight ahead to the far end of the hall and flung open the solid oak door to the lounge. An instant draft hit John, telling him that the window to the stairs on the outside of the building was open. He dashed to the window and leaned out. The metal staircase vibrated with the sound of hurried footsteps.

"Mark, is that you?" John called. He stuck his head out further but the staircase hindered his view. Rather than wait to see who appeared at the bottom, he decided his time would be better spent checking the rest of the flat. If it was his friend descending the outside stairs, then Mark was safe and if it wasn't, then John was safe. He didn't give it another thought and took one quick look around the lounge before heading for Mark's study.

It wasn't rocket science. The study was the place where Mark would work or place bets online - therefore he almost lived in there. He strode to the second door on the left, turned the ornate handle and pushed it open. The windowless room was dimly lit by an overturned desk lamp, and it was impossible to make out any detail. John's heart banged like a bass drum as he reached behind him to turn on the main light. The sight in front of him brought foul-tasting bile to his throat.

*

In a small coffee house on Kensington High Street, Herb Johnson was regretting his decision to allow his partner to return to work so soon after injury.

Four months earlier, in a botched raid on a suspected terrorist's residence, Max Wilson had taken a bullet meant for Johnson. Wilson had subsequently declined psychological counselling and requested immediate return to work after his release from Earthguard's private hospital. While Wilson was physically mended, it was clear to Johnson that the mental side of recovery was lagging far behind. The guy had always been a rock and

Johnson owed him, but they were off mission and he needed to get Wilson back to current business.

He looked his stocky, pug-faced partner in the eyes.

"So what are we doing here, Max? We're supposed to be keeping watch on Bradshaw."

Wilson looked like a well-dressed boxer and spoke like a BBC newsreader. Johnson could never get his head round the anomaly. "Bradshaw's one of us. I've known him for years. I'd be less surprised if HQ suspected you," Wilson said.

"That's not the point. It's what he's developed that makes him a risk. Answer my question. What are we doing here?"

"I just got the feeling that you weren't happy with my work since my return," the stocky man said.

Johnson clenched his teeth. "And that's why you took us away from our observation points? We could be canned for this."

"We couldn't talk face to face from fifty yards apart."

The thought of messing up on the job was tying Johnson's stomach in knots. "Other than staying in contact while we observe, we shouldn't be talking at all. Tell me what's on your mind, and let's get back to work."

Wilson shrugged. "I miss my old job."

Johnson shuffled his chair forward and lowered his voice to a venomous growl. "For fuck's sake, Max. You know we can't talk about our pasts or our personal lives. Are you trying to put us out of work?"

Shoulders a body builder would have died for slumped. "My wife died last week while I was in hospital."

The senior Earthguard agent looked around the bustling coffee shop. Nothing. It wasn't unusual for an agent to be kept under surveillance after a considerable period of inactivity. He felt for the big fool, but his hands were tied. He had to follow procedure.

"Don't say another word, Max, or I'll be forced to report in to the controller." Johnson leaned in a little further. "Look, Buddy, I owe you big time, but this is my livelihood you're messing with. We work together, not play together. You know the rules. If you've got problems, then take the counselling on offer."

Wilson rubbed his flat nose, the result of many blows, most on the job since they had been paired up a month over five years ago. London guard was one of the most sought after agent posts. A paltry two operatives covered a sprawling city rife with infinitely varying beliefs and an abundance of high profile targets. Most in the international field considered it second only to Washington, and Johnson was the first American to land the post. The pay and benefits were substantial. And his bull of a partner was about to blow it for them both. Wilson's bottom lip trembled.

"My daughter..."

Johnson reached inside his thick dark coat for his phone. "One more word Max..."

"All right. You can't help. Forget it. I should never have tried." Wilson stood up and threw a ten pound note on the table. "Back to work then."

As Johnson rose, a good ten inches further than Wilson, his phone vibrated ominously inside his jacket. He had a bad feeling.

"Johnson," he told the caller.

"We're getting some activity on the satellite from your subject's location. Is everything okay, Agent Johnson?"

Johnson's worst fears had been realised.

*

John doubled over as if hit in the stomach by an invisible force. He couldn't breathe, and his empty stomach searched for content to eject. Retching dryly, he fell to his knees.

Mark was slumped forward in his chair, his upper body resting on the surface of the desk. The side of his face was sitting in a pool of blood. A Chinese letter opener skewered his left hand into the top of his head like he was patting himself. The end of his little finger and half of his thumb lay in front of Mark's open eyes in their own small pool of thick red body fluid. The ivory handle of a huge dagger, which John recognised as one of Mark's collection, protruded from the centre of his friend's back. There was no life evident in the eyes. John didn't need to have seen a lifeless body before to know that his best friend was dead.

Documents were scattered all around Mark's body, some sat in the spreading pool of blood which crept towards the front edge of his expansive antique desk. John looked on, unable to take his eyes away, unable to fathom the scene in front of him. His eyes remained glued as Mark's blood flowed over the desk's edge like molten lava, splashing freely on the sixteenth century Persian rug. Knowing Mark's fondness and unreasonable over protectiveness of the rug, John's first instinct was to stop the blood flow onto the almost paisley-like, patterned carpet.

He noticed Mark's outstretched right arm with hand still clutching the door entry remote control like he was trying to hand it to somebody. Pointing it at the door like a TV remote perhaps? No, John remembered Mark explaining that it didn't work like that, although he couldn't remember exactly how it did work. Mark was always boasting about his high-tech security system. Fat lot of good it had done him.

John pushed himself upright and steadied his shaking legs by grabbing the edge of the desk, taking care to miss the parts wetted with his friend's blood. Intrigued by the pointing arm being at odds with the rest of the body, John gently took the hand and began to pull away the fingers around the remote. He expected a cold and vice-like death grip, but each digit was still warm and came away easily. John removed the remote and laid it on the desk. In Mark's palm was a small, folded piece of paper stuck to the skin. John peeled it away and began to unfold it when he heard footsteps entering the apartment. Instinctively, he slid the paper into the waistband of his underpants, hoping that it wouldn't slip down. Why did he wear boxers?

John turned slowly round to see two dark-coated men and a fireman, who had presumably responded to the alarm which had now ceased. The policemen appeared remarkably composed considering a dash up eight flights of stairs. Despite their matching attire, the two officers could not have been more different. The short one was in his late forties with the face and build of a well-battered heavyweight boxer. The other man was basketball-player tall but solidly built and most definitely in charge.

Parkes, eyes shiny with indignation, hand raised, forefinger pointing accusingly at John, as if there could be confusion should he lower it, spoke first.

"That's him," he said, panting like a dehydrated dog. "He's the one I was telling you about."

"This isn't what it looks like," said John, knowing that it didn't look good but nevertheless wondering exactly what it did look like.

4: Saturday 24th September, 12:42

Savannah Jones sipped at her cup of lukewarm herbal tea in a booth of a small Pizza Hut in Shepherd's Bush, wishing she'd changed clothes before arriving. She had thought her small, damp-ridden bedsit would not provide the uplift in spirit she so longingly craved. Instead she had spent the last four hours at Hammersmith tube station on a fixed stool making a tall 'Americano' coffee last well beyond its intended lifespan. The pimpled teenage boy, who worked the concession stand, had seemed glad of the company and hadn't pressured her to order more or to move on.

Savannah sipped again at her tea. It truly was disgusting. She allowed the liquid to fall out of her mouth and back into the cup without swallowing. Why hadn't she ordered a coffee?

The red plastic, high-backed double seats gave her some protection from the eyes of the few other customers who, sitting down for an early lunch, could surely tell how she made her unsavoury living. She looked and felt like a whore. God damn it, she was a whore, or prostitute as John Smith had called her.

John Smith! She wondered why he'd withheld his real name. Maybe he'd known the bill for her services was his and blamed his friend to escape payment. Perhaps he'd rumbled her lack of confidence and figured she was easily cheated out of her fee. His place was big, and she knew that a Chiswick address didn't come without a big price tag. No doubt she'd screwed up. She had much to learn.

Savannah had known the world of escorting would be seedy, but her friend Amy, who had recommended Aphrodite's Angels, said it would soon pay off her debts and give her the chance she badly needed to work her life out. Work for a month and then jack it in, she had told her. One day and two clients later and she had collected the grand sum of fifty pounds, fifty percent of which she owed to her new boss, Christos the Greek, who was already over ten minutes late. Not much of a living from an hour and a night's work.

She banged the cup down harder than she meant to, splashing straw-coloured liquid over the red paper tablecloth. It smelt worse than it tasted.

"What's up Sweetie?" said a voice from behind.

Savannah went rigid but somehow convinced her muscles to relax before Christos seated himself against the wall, directly opposite his latest employee. She needed to appear calm, collected and unruffled.

As always he was dressed completely in black: jeans, sweatshirt, trainers and brand new leather bomber jacket. For a forty-five year old, his look was not cool. He was of average height, stocky but not fat, with dyed black hair slicked back with a wet-look hair care product. He had a large broad nose on a chubby face, which along with his irregular shaving habit, had given rise to the 'Christos the Greek' moniker - at least that was Amy's version.

Apparently, his real name was Christopher, born and bred in East London and had never been overseas. He had a faint but distinctive smell about him which Savannah guessed was the hair gel, but could equally have been a deodorant failing to mask a hygiene issue.

She needed her wits about her, to act like it had all been a walk in the park. So far her boss had been nothing but kind, full of helpful advice, and she had no reason to think he'd changed overnight. After all, she was new and had to learn the ropes.

"So how'd your first night go, Sweetie?"

She looked into his eyes. They were dark slits on a face which yesterday, had radiated red-faced joviality like an out of season Santa. Not today. Even the high-pitched, cheeky boy, Cockney patter had lost its previous charm and carried with it an element of threat.

"Not so good," she said. "I'm sure things will get better though."

Christos didn't move, his hands remaining under the table, his eyelids closing further until the slits were almost gone. "Helen told me you had two clients. I ain't great at maths but I reckon that makes two grand. A grand for you and one for me."

It was no wonder the clients never saw behind the scenes at Aphrodite's Angels. A high-class escort agency needed a 'smooth as silk operator' on the front desk. In this case it was Helen, Christos's wife. On the rough diamond scale, Christos was at the far end of the rough. Savannah was rapidly suspecting that his diamond side had also been a facade. She cursed at Amy under her breath.

"What was that?" snapped Christos, his shovel-like hands slamming down onto the table sending the condiments momentarily airborne. "You giving me shit?"

Damn. This was all going to Hell and fast. Placate him Savannah, placate him. She dug into her small purse and handed him three ten pound notes across the table. "That's over half of what I earned."

His big, clumsy hand reached out and grabbed the money and tucked it into the inside pocket of his jacket. Moving quicker than Savannah could have anticipated, the same hand grabbed her wrist and yanked her closer to him. He leaned in the rest of the way, and she felt the warmth of a breath so rancid she swore she could taste it in her mouth. "Explain yourself," he said.

Savannah tugged her arm, trying to get free, but his grip was too tight.

"You're hurting me," she said, looking around, hoping that someone else might notice her plight. She thought about screaming, but her need to see the matter through outweighed her distress - just.

"Explain yourself," he repeated with added spittle which travelled the short distance onto her face.

"Okay, okay. I screwed up. What can I say?"

"I want details."

"The first one at the Dorchester, short and skinny, over from Italy for business..."

"Ricardo," Christos elaborated. "Go on, what happened?"

Savannah felt her face flush. It was bad enough she had to go through last night, let alone tell this foul-breathed bully about it."

"He didn't have any condoms, and I wasn't having sex without protection."

"You didn't take condoms with you?"

"I'm new to this," she said, trying again to pull away. "Get off me, will you?"

Christos didn't budge an inch. "Carry on darlin'."

She wanted to cry, but she would not let this bastard have the satisfaction. She clenched her teeth together, dug deep for unused resolve and hissed back at Christos hoping her breath stank as bad as his. "He wanted to do it without, but I said no, so I agreed to get him off by hand as long as he put a sock on it."

Christos laughed in her face, long and loud. It was a laugh that contained genuine humour, and for a few seconds Savannah believed she had diffused the situation. "He looked so miserable while I was doing it I didn't think I could accept the fee," she added.

Christos stopped laughing, his face settling into contemplation. "He's Italian. They always look miserable when they have sex. They think it makes them look macho. They should wear black like me and smile when they fuck, those miserable bastards." He pulled her closer so that his nose pushed hard into her cheekbone. "So he offered to pay you?"

"Y...y...y... Yes, but I only took fifty for my time." Don't cry Savannah, she told herself. You'll never do this again or have to talk to a piece of filth like this again. You can wait tables or clean floors, but you'll never have to be treated like this ever again. Get it over with, and get on with your life. This had all been a huge mistake. What filthy, sordid and violent world had she entered? What had she been thinking?

She didn't know if he suspected that she was about to scream or break down, but he released her and she sat back as far as the seat would allow. He shook his head when she wiped off his saliva from her face with her bare arm.

"Okay, so that's one," he said, a little less tension in his voice. "What happened with the other you picked up in the sports bar, the yuppie?"

"He said that it was his friend's idea and that he had no money."

Christos chewed on a thumbnail a while before responding. "You gave him the talk?"

"Yes, that I was just the talent and he had to pay or you'd break his legs." She could still smell the saliva on her face. She shuddered.

"What's his name?"

As she spoke the name, she braced herself for the backlash. "John ... Smith, he said it was."

"Are you fucking kidding me?" he roared. "Do I look like I won't break your legs right here, right now?"

He didn't. He looked like a snorting bull about to charge, like he knew no other way to deal with the situation that confronted him. Savannah bit down on the soft inside of both lips and concentrated on the pain. She felt a trickle of blood inside her mouth and the taste of metal. If she ran, Amy would tell Christos where to find her. She had a few words for Amy of her own, if she made it out on unbroken legs.

A uniformed waitress in her mid-twenties with long blonde hair and blue eyes walked up to their booth and stopped. She was pretty but not so pretty that she'd turn heads, and the way she savagely chewed gum did nothing to enhance her looks. She appeared most unimpressed with their behaviour.

"My boss says to be quiet or leave," she said in an East European accent, 'leave' sounding more like leaf.

Christos gave the waitress a menacing stare, all slit eyes and snarling teeth. "Mind your business."

"It is ... how do you say ... your funeral?" replied the waitress, seeming even more unimpressed, if that were at all possible.

Christos stared at the woman in disbelief, his mouth agape and his eyes wider than Savannah had seen before. She noticed the edge of a contact lens as she watched his eyes, now side on as he looked up and faced the waitress. She wondered how he managed to get them into those tiny openings.

"We'll be done in two minutes," Christos said, almost politely and entirely devoid of his Cockney accent.

"Good." The waitress turned and walked away.

Christos exhaled. "Did you see that? That bird's Russian, part of the Russian mob over here in London. You mess with their bitches and they'll cut off your dick and ram it down your throat. You either suffocate or bleed to death. Either way your last taste before you die is your own blood and piss."

A joke about his penis size not being sufficient to block his airway popped into Savannah's head, but she thought better of sharing it with him. Although the thought of him dying that way did bump her resolve back up a notch. "Are we done now?" she asked.

Christos leaned over once again, and she backed up so much she almost stood up.

"Don't worry darling, I'm not going to make a scene in front of the Russians."

She slid back down into the seat. "So what now?"

He glanced around him before lowering his voice to a whisper. "Our business will be over when you pay me my grand. If I don't have it in two days, I'll sell you to the Arabs who will fuck your tight little arsehole until you can shit melons without wincing. Are we clear?"

Savannah's lips trembled and, unable to speak, she meekly nodded her head. Christos got up and left.

The East European waitress returned to the booth, a concerned expression on her face, no sign of the chewing gum.

Savannah was glad of the company. The young woman had unnerved Christos, and that gave Savannah a sense of security. "Please sit down," she said.

The waitress sat down exactly where Christos the Greek had been. She placed her hand on top of Savannah's. "You work as whore for this man... No?"

Savannah said nothing. Her stomach sank.

"I can get you better rates. We meet later... Yes?"

Savannah jumped up and ran out of the Pizza Hut, sending her herbal tea cup crashing to the floor. She needed to find John Smith - like now.

5: Saturday 24ᵗʰ September, 13:15

Outside the Kensington apartment building, the cold breeze had dropped and a few gaps had appeared in the cloud cover giving the day a brighter feel. However, as John Smith could attest to, there was still a definite chill in the air.

He sensed that all was not as it should be.

Perhaps his initial reaction at being found at a murder scene had rose tinted his perception of the two men who escorted him outside. In retrospect, they had been very keen to remove him from the scene of the crime. He was glad he hadn't divulged his name or carried any identification.

"Aren't you supposed to read me my rights?" he asked, hands cuffed behind him, an officer on each side guiding him along the crowded street at a steady pace.

"We'll take care of the paperwork back at the station," said the taller of the two, on his right side, in a thick American accent. Since when did the Metropolitan police force take on yanks? He shoved John hard in the back with the palm of his hand.

The message carried with the shove was clear: shut up and walk. But John didn't feel compliant today. A part of him hurt. The pain was geographically obscure, deep in a place where pain carried emotions as well as physical symptoms. There was a monster ball of grief inside him which swelled and yearned for release. But now was not the time for self-pity. He pushed away the thoughts that fed the ball and swallowed the pain back down.

He regarded the two men in turn, from head to toe. The long, thick, navy blue coats covered everything from their shoulders to their knees. Beneath the knees, both men wore black suit trousers and black shoes. Stooping to look more closely, John realised that the spotless shine came from boots, not shoes, and tell-tale stitching indicated steel toe caps. Were they standard issue for the police? The man on his left was the eldest, and John placed him in his late forties, a good ten years ahead of his partner, who he reckoned was a year or two older than himself.

Both men had short mid-brown hair. Neither man wore a discernible expression, but the taller man had a look about him, a glint in the eye perhaps, which exuded job satisfaction. He also had a Bluetooth device in one ear, which he occasionally pressed as if he was straining to hear something. If these guys were CID, John was next in line for the throne. Thoughts for his own safety suddenly occupied his mind.

"Nice clothes," he said to no one in particular, looking forward again, smiling warmly at those who had the nerve to look him in the eye. Pedestrians parted like the Red Sea, nervous that he was a threat to their safety. "How come you didn't park nearer? Surely, they give you a special permit to park anywhere when on the job?" John said.

"Shut up and walk," the shorter one said, without a discernible accent, tonally similar to Mark but without the exaggerated drawl which belonged to those with a privileged lineage. John felt an elbow in his back. That hurt. Elbows from the left, hands from the right, he noted. MI5, CIA, Mafia perhaps? No, not stylish enough for the mob. There was something almost military about their behaviour. He needed to push a few more buttons.

John turned to the captor on his right. "Your partner's not very tall, is he? Have they relaxed the height requirements for entry?"

Another elbow thudded into his back, sending John stumbling forwards.

"I'm not sure you can do that," he complained, as they quickly caught up to him. John looked down to his left, where the shorter man's head bobbed along a good five inches below his own. "You've got some serious shoulders on you. Did they allow you to add your shoulder width to your height for entry purposes?"

Another dig in the back from the left but this one was sharper and harder, and it remained pushed roughly into his spine just above the waistband of his jeans. A gun! Instinctively, he froze, almost bringing them to a standstill.

Fear for his life mixed with the grief lodged in his gut created a moment of purest clarity. His life had been a failure. No, that wasn't it - he had been a failure. His life was flashing before his eyes as the moment before death demanded, but there was nothing to show him. Other than his desire not to be dead, what was there to live for? At the precise moment he closed his eyes expecting a bullet to sever his spinal column, he felt the concealed, folded paper free itself from the waistband of his boxer shorts, and the thoughts of imminent death disappeared. His father had always said that he had no sense of priority.

"Keep moving kid," the tall man whispered in his ear. John guessed the man was from New York or somewhere close. "Head for the tube station." The word tube was pronounced like 'toob'.

John looked ahead and saw the entrance to 'High Street Kensington' approaching on their right, just past a lingerie shop. Would they kill him in such a busy place? Surely not? He shuffled along in an effort to slow the downward progress of the loose paper which had escaped the shorts completely and now tickled his right thigh about four inches above the knee. If they were escorting him to his death then he reasoned that his last sight would be the underneath of a speeding tube train. He had to run before they reached a platform.

Still sandwiched by the two men of unknown employment, they reached the entrance whose sign canopied out in an arch above the pavement, beneath a large double-faced clock. Like a mini mall, there were shops inside, perfectly situated for maximum exposure to possible purchasers. The long, pillared corridor, which led to the ticket machines and stalls, was swarming with activity as a mixture of shoppers and travellers fought for the space to move. Once they were deep amongst the throng, John would scream and run. Panic would ensue, and he could escape in the belly of the bolting crowd.

"Go on kid," said the American. "Keep walking."

"I'm thirty-two," John snapped. He wouldn't face death being talked down to.

A few shuffles later, about twelve feet into the station, the paper brushed past his ankle. He stopped. It was out of his jeans. It was now or never.

"Guns, they've got guns," he bellowed, dropping to his knees. He saw the note on the ground. He needed to retrieve it before the stampede began. His hands were useless to him. There was nothing else for him to do. Without thought of hygiene, he leaned over, pressing his open mouth to the smooth tiled floor and closed his lips around the folder paper. Then using his prone position like a sprinter, he pushed off from the ground to enhance his acceleration and took off. His purchase was good, and had it not been for the knee of a particularly large lady connecting directly with his chin, he might have given himself a head start. He collapsed face down on the cold floor, like a floored fighter. He had lost.

"Are you all right?" asked the large lady.

John lifted his head from the floor and waggled his jaw from side to side. He felt a click from his handcuffs as they fell away behind him. He turned, expecting to see one of the two men with keys in their hand, but they were nowhere. He pushed himself up, grabbing the fallen handcuffs as he rose. He was still giddy from the blow that had stopped him in his tracks. He shook his head like a dog shook off water, hoping to clear his thoughts.

He looked deep into the crowd in all directions for unusually rapid movement or a tall man with short hair. Nothing. What he did see made some sense of his sudden freedom. Two armed policemen stood near a pillar about thirty feet from the entrance. They were part of the build-up to the London Olympics, John recalled - on full display to the general public and would be kidnappers. He should be grateful. Without their obvious presence, he could well have been the latest addition to the growing number of tube suicides. They were also the reason that his firearm alert went completely ignored. The crowd had assumed that he meant the armed police.

"Are you all right?" repeated the lady of around fifty years of age, hands full of carrier bags. She wore baggy black tracksuit trousers, trainers and a huge purple overcoat. Her hair was expensively coiffured, perhaps for a later engagement. The bags in her hands were from every designer shop imaginable. Obviously she didn't dress to shop. "You've got something caught in your mouth," she added.

John removed the note along with some hair and dirt from the floor. He placed it safely in the pocket of his jeans. The woman was clearly expecting something more as she made no move to carry on about her business.

"I'm fine thanks. Sorry about bumping into you," he said, assuming the lack of an apology was the cause for her delay.

"Think nothing of it young man." She smiled and raised her eyebrows. "Those for your girlfriend?"

"I'm sorry?"

Her eyebrows rose. "The handcuffs. You got someone in mind for those?"

He'd forgotten about the handcuffs. He tucked them into his hoodie pocket. He needed to be alone to look at Mark's note and to plan his next move. What he didn't need was an old, fat lady with a handcuff fetish coming on to him. Before he could answer, she continued in a voice that trembled excitedly.

"Anyone who'll lick a tube station floor and carries handcuffs about town is someone I want to know."

Jesus. What did he say to that? "They're for my boyfriend," he tried.

"I can work with that," she said, after way too little consideration.

A small group of onlookers, lured in by the initial collision, had by now realised that this vaguely interesting encounter was developing into something a little steamier. One girl, late teens in a pink anorak, was lifting her iPhone above heads in their direction. Tomorrow, he might well be on YouTube.

John, certain that nothing he said would aid his cause, stepped to his left and entered a fast moving stream of bodies bound for the trains.

"I'm here most Saturdays around this time," the woman called after him, but John was on his way home.

*

Wilson turned to his partner after both men had watched John Smith disappear into the crowd. He was still churning inside from Johnson's refusal to listen to his troubled thoughts. Sure there was protocol, but he had taken a bullet in the chest for the ungrateful bastard and surely that had to be worth five minutes off the record. Now he'd allowed Bradshaw's murderer to flee, remotely releasing his keyless handcuffs into the bargain.

"Why did you let him go?"

"Because we know where he lives, and that's where we'll catch up with him."

"We do?"

"Yeah, he needs to believe he shook us off or he won't lead us anywhere."

The tall agent was starting to piss Wilson off. "Are you going to let me in on your little secret?"

Johnson pulled out the Bluetooth device from his ear. "I sent his picture to HQ, and they have confirmed his identity as John Smith. He's a friend of Bradshaw's, but they cleared him nine years ago when Bradshaw first started working for us."

"An alias?"

"Not according to HQ. Until we prove otherwise, we have to assume that he's the killer or in league with the killer." Johnson ran his hand through his short hair. "But we've got a bigger problem."

"What?"

"The latest prototype of Bradshaw's invention is missing from the lab."

Wilson's breath caught in his throat, and he felt his world begin to crumble. They should have been there, and all of this could have been cleaned up quickly and easily. Now things were a mess, and it was his fault. Johnson had been right. He shouldn't have come back so soon. Or maybe it was Johnson's punishment for not listening. "Well Smith didn't have it. It's too big to conceal. Maybe it's still in Bradshaw's apartment?"

Johnson said nothing, his eyes locked on Wilson's face. Wilson began to fidget, stretching out his fingers and cracking his knuckles. The silence was unbearable. "You think it's my fault. Come out and say it."

Johnson's stare never wavered. "The clean-up team have reported back to HQ. The item was not found." He grabbed Wilson by the shoulders. "If we don't sort this, then we're both out of a job. If I lose this job, I'll end your life. You need to get your act together and help me clean up this mess. Are we clear?"

There was no malice in the words, but the threat was genuine. Who did he think he was? The man, whose life Wilson had saved, was threatening him. Johnson had agreed to talk off mission. Sure, Wilson had insisted, but it was Johnson's call. He was the senior officer, and he'd signed off on his return to duty. Blame could not be delegated. Why didn't he get his bloody hands off?

"Are we clear?" repeated Johnson, raising his eyebrows and squeezing his partner's shoulders tightly.

"Clear," answered Wilson through tightly ground teeth. This was not what he had signed up for.

*

I drive along Kensington High Street putting out my Marlboro Red and lighting another. The harsh smoke catches in my throat in a pleasing way. Common sense dictates that I should put more distance between myself and the scene of my second illegal kill. Who am I kidding? Second murder, I mean. Well, actually my fourth murder, but the first two were before I was legally responsible so they don't count. Bradshaw reneged and had deserved to die. Torture had been failing, and the pounding at the door necessitated immediate evacuation. Loose ends are never an option. Ten more minutes, maybe less, and he'd have told me everything. I need to think and driving helps. I can't bring myself to drive straight ahead and on to relative safety.

To my right, at the tube station, I see a short, burly man being gripped at the shoulders by another man, about a foot taller. Both are dressed in thick navy blue coats. Johnson and Wilson. These are the Earthguard agents Bradshaw spoke of yesterday. Bradshaw's description had sounded suspect but here they are, literally larger than life. This is a stroke of luck, perhaps? Instinctively, I duck my head as the tall one's gaze wanders close. Idiot, what am I doing? I bear little resemblance to the man who entered Bradshaw's apartment and snuffed out his worthless life.

I look in the mirror and tug at the battle scar on my bottom lip with my fingers. Could it have given me away? It is only noticeable when I smile, causing both lips to skew in a lopsided grin. Not a chance. I am safe.

The agents look like smartly dressed clowns in a circus, their disparate shapes adding comedy to deadly serious faces. Such pompous idiots wouldn't survive a month in the SAS. I suspect their presence at the tube station is not for my benefit. So why are they here? Why aren't they at Bradshaw's apartment sifting through papers on the blood splattered desk? Could the agents be charged with recovering Bradshaw's invention? Perhaps they were headed to its location.

An urge to run down the agents overcomes me. I need them alive for now but ... one twitch of the steering wheel and a burst of acceleration and these fools would be mulch. Heads would be crushed and bones snapped like twigs. Blood and brains would be spread across the pavement. My breathing quickens as my excitement grows. My thoughts unconsciously turn to Sasha. Later she will whisper down the phone to me, filth that she wants me to force out of her, and I will come like a train, thinking of her spread-eagled under my weight, unable to escape. The little bitch would love it too, she just doesn't realise it yet. But no, failure does not deserve reward and so the call will wait until success is mine.

I follow the agents up a side street. They are too busy ignoring each other, eyes fixed dead ahead, to notice I am just a few yards behind. There is no doubt in my mind that I will kill them once I recover my prize. The agents get into a top-end, black Mercedes. Overpaid as well as overrated. I might tie them lying down and facing each other, securing them so that their positions are inescapable. With delicate twitches of a scalpel, I could nick the major arteries in their necks. I could watch as their faces pale, blood spurting in fine jets across each other's bodies. The art will be in making the wound small enough to make death slow but not so small that the wound clots. Too big and the fun ends before it really starts. I am no surgeon but I am willing to learn. I can feel prickles of pleasure on my arms.

Anticipation is a wonderful thing. I can't wait to talk with Sasha afterwards or maybe even during. Her reluctant whispers will complete the day's satisfactions. It's so nice to have a sister.

6: Saturday 24th September, 14:05

The District Line tube train was mostly empty and yet it seemed like all eyes were on John.

Like a hot piece of coal, the unopened piece of paper bothered John every second of the short journey home. He had thought about pulling it from his jeans on the tube and once again when he exited the train at Stamford Brook station. Each time his fingertips wandered into his pocket he was overcome by the feeling that strange eyes watched his every move. But it was more than that. He had the oddest feeling that if he ignored the paper, maybe it, and the scene in his best friend's apartment, would turn out to be figments of his imagination.

The five minute walk from the station went some way to allaying his fears that he was being followed. As he examined every person he overtook or met, he realised that he still didn't know where Stamford Brook became Chiswick and vice versa, or if Stamford Brook was just part of Chiswick. His head was full of rubbish.

The closer he got to home the more space appeared between him and the next man. By the time he had turned two corners and reached the converted Victorian building, where he occupied the ground floor flat, there was barely a soul in sight. He leapt up the steps to his building, three at a time, taking one last look around him before entering.

He doubted that the two men he had evaded at High Street Kensington tube station could have stayed on his tail. And his home was the last place they would expect him to go - wasn't it? Besides, they hadn't asked him a single question before or after snapping the handcuffs on - not even his name which meant they couldn't know who he was or where he lived. Who the hell were those guys? They sure as hell weren't regular police. Regular police did not turn and flee at the sight of their colleagues - armed or otherwise.

As he closed the main building door behind him with a shove from his heel, a veil of comfort tumbled over him like a warm, familiar blanket. At his own entrance, to the left of the stairs, he turned the key and barged open the door of his home, letting out a long sigh of relief. It was good to be home. A hand tapped his shoulder from behind. Without thinking he lunged forward into his flat, turned and slammed the heavy door shut right in the tear-striped face of Savannah Jones.

John gasped for air. That was the second time today she had sent his heartbeat into orbit. Feeling somewhat foolish, he recovered his breathing and composure and opened the door again. She was in the same slinky mini dress as before, holding her high heels in her left hand and gripping her purse in the right. So that's how she crept up behind him. Her face was troubled, and her shoulders slouched. He should get rid of her quickly.

"I thought I had forty-eight hours." John looked at his Rolex Daytona. "It's quarter past two which means so far I've had about seven hours."

"I need it now. I can't wait any longer. It's a matter of life and death."

John put on his sternest face. "I still don't have it, and to be honest, it's no longer my priority."

John watched as Savannah's mouth drooped and tears welled up in her dark eyes. Her tall, slender frame seemed to shrink in front of him. How often did this girl cry? She closed her eyelids as if to halt the flow but instead sent a tear racing down each cheek. Part of him wanted her gone and another part of him welcomed the delay to his own, more serious concerns. When she wasn't crying, she was a pleasure both to look at and be around, and for someone so miserable and unwashed, she certainly looked incredibly good. For one of the few times in his life, he welcomed the company.

He took a step back and opened the door wide. "Come in."

Clearly not expecting the invite, Savannah needed a couple of seconds before the offer hit home. Once the penny dropped, she was quick to scurry inside. Savannah followed John through the second door on the left of the small entrance hall into the 'L' shaped lounge, diner and kitchen area.

"Can I get you a tea or coffee," asked John, hoping he had at least one or the other to offer.

"Either would be cool," replied Savannah, sinking into the soft old sofa against the wall.

John filled the kettle, found his last remaining tea bag, and pulled out two red mugs from a cupboard above the sink. Although strangely glad of Savannah's presence, his mind was still filled with the shock of his friend's grisly death. Images of the severed digits and the letter opener pinning Mark's hand to his head flashed between moments of normality. The grief was now wavering on the surface, and he wondered for a second just how Savannah would cope if he broke down in front of her.

"Christos wasn't too pleased that I only made him thirty quid from two appointments," she called out from the sofa, where she lay back deep into the big, comfortable cushions.

John poured hot water into the mugs before sharing the tea bag between them. He gazed vacantly into one of the mugs as he added milk, watching the liquid become lighter the more milk he tipped in from the half-full carton. And then it overflowed, but he just kept on pouring until the liquid spilled onto the black granite worktop and then the floor, like Mark's blood had spilled onto his favourite rug. John turned the carton further until it was perfectly upside down, speeding up the flow of milk into the mug and producing a 'glugging' sound.

"Are you nuts?" said a voice.

John jumped, dropping the milk carton onto the worktop, sending milk and diluted tea all over his hoodie. He turned to see Savannah staring at him with her hands on her hips in disbelief. He shrugged his shoulders. How long had she been standing there? How long had he been in another world? He wasn't doing so well.

"Mark was murdered this morning," he said. "My best friend in the whole world. My only real friend, stabbed through his head and through his back."

Savannah frowned as she studied John. Her mouth was open, and her eyes explored his, searching for something, something to tell her he was not messing her about perhaps? She approached John with her arms held out to him. He tried to back up, but the kitchen was small and there was nowhere to go. As she reached John, she grabbed him with both arms and pulled his head down onto her chest.

"Let it out," she whispered in his ear.

John let it out. And out it came in guttural wails, many times the volume of Savannah's in the early light of day. She guided him to the sofa, like a Good Samaritan helping an elderly person across a busy street, stroking his head as they moved, constantly whispering, reassuring, and keeping his head pressed to her.

"It's okay, let it out."

For fifteen minutes John lay, face buried in the sofa, as Savannah stroked the back of his head, over and over. Despite considerable effort, he was unable to stop. And then as suddenly as the grief had taken him, it went. He lay quiet for a while feeling weak and foolish, his embarrassment preventing him from turning over. Eventually, he spoke into the cushion.

"I think that the police may be after me," he said.

"What for?" she said, still stroking the top of his head.

John was beginning to feel like a pet dog, but she had been there for him during his moment of need and he didn't want to make light of it. His need to unload overcame his dented ego, and he flipped himself over to face Savannah. For the next ten minutes, he recounted the details of his trip to Mark's apartment. She remained silent, lips slightly parted throughout, shaking her head as if she was listening to something that couldn't be true. Thankfully, she rested her hand on his calf while he spoke.

"So you'd have to assume that the real police would have come along later, interviewed Parkes and made the assumption that I was the murderer."

"But you're not ... right?" she asked.

"Of course not," John said, sitting upright. "Why would I want to murder my best friend?"

"Because he tricked you into owing me a thousand quid?"

"You think I'd commit murder for a thousand pounds?"

"It would be my luck to get stiffed by a murderer."

"Stiffed?"

"Cheated."

"I never cheated you out of a thousand pounds. That was down to Mark."

"So you said. Why don't you call the police and tell them what happened then?"

"Because they'd just tell me to come in."

"So?"

John exhaled. "So they might not let me out again. In fact, there are probably police on the way here now."

Savannah pinched her bottom lip between a thumb and forefinger, rolling the soft flesh around, face scrunched up in thought.

"Give me the thousand pounds, and I'll help you," she exclaimed.

John didn't know why but trusting this weird and wonderful girl seemed preferable to being alone. Was he being stupid? Probably. But other than go to his parents where he'd just be the failure causing more bother, he didn't have much choice. He wasn't going to be responsible for his mother's break down and subsequent enrolment into a psychiatric home.

"I don't have it, I told you."

This place must be worth a fortune." She stared from wall to wall. "Don't you have any decent possessions?"

"Not really. The place is in Mum and Dad's name. I just live here." He lifted his hand towards Savannah. "As for possessions, the only thing worth anything is this watch."

Savannah grabbed his hand and twisted it, giving the watch a good looking over. "Rolex Daytona. How much is it worth?"

"It's the dual-metal, champagne-faced model. They go for around ten thousand new, but this was bought nine years ago as a graduation present. I might get two or three thousand for it if we can find a watch dealer.

"Or a pawn shop."

"We won't get such a good price at a pawn shop."

"No, but I know one nearby who won't ask any questions. The guy's a sleaze, but we don't want to attract any extra unwanted attention, right?"

"Right." He flicked the safety clasp on the gold and silver bracelet and slid the watch off. "Just out of interest, before I hand over my only asset of any real value..."

"What?"

"Did we actually have sex?"

"No, but I would have, and it would have been the best you'd ever had."

"To be honest, that's not saying much." John cleared his throat, wishing to a superior power that he'd never said that. "So are we agreed that you still owe me sex once I hand this watch over?"

"No, but if you're nice to me I might kiss your cheek when all this is over, on one condition."

"Fair enough," agreed John. "What is it?"

"Tell me your real name."

John laughed. "Let's get out of here before it's too late. I'm sure I'll get more than a kiss if I get locked up. I'd be the equivalent of a supermodel in prison."

She laughed. "You wish."

7: Saturday 24th September, 15:30

I am fifty yards behind the black Mercedes on a narrow road parallel to Chiswick High Street. Most of the old buildings here have been converted to flats. Rents must be high, and even the less fortunate on this street are wealthier than most. I am parked on double yellow lines. It is impossible to park here unless you are an agent who has no need to be concerned with traffic violations. I don't want a record of being here and so watch all sides as well as the Mercedes. What are the fools waiting here for? I light a cigarette.

My attention is focussed as I watch Wilson, the short and broad shouldered one, leave the car. He must be two hundred and fifty pounds of solid muscle. I can take him, stealth is everything, but they haven't got the weapon yet and he is too close to his partner. He appears to be stretching his legs. Someone taps at my window. Shit. I have no disguise and do not turn as I lower the window and speak.

"Yes," I say, my peripheral vision recognising the large frame of an elderly man. I reach to my ankle and pull on the handle of my stiletto blade.

"This is residents only parking. You'll have to move on," he says, much louder than I care for. The agents must not be alerted.

I keep my eyes ahead and take my voice down to a whisper. "I'll only be here a little while and I'm on double yellows so I'm not taking anyone's space."

The man's voice rises. "Look at me when I'm talking to you."

I have no choice. I put out my Marlboro Red in the ashtray and turn to the man. He is bigger than I first expected. In one motion, I pull free my knife and thrust the four inch narrow blade through the man's throat. I get in three lightening stabs before he has time to raise his hands. He looks at me wide eyed as he clutches his throat and begins to stagger. I look him up and down and smile at him. Once upon a time he might have been a tough guy. His vocal chords and airways are damaged beyond repair, and his screams are barely audible gurgles that won't betray my position. I open the car door and help the man down to the ground behind my van. He will die quietly. Illegal kill number two is less fun than number one. I return to my post.

Twenty minutes pass before the Mercedes pulls away. Why are they crawling along? They must be following someone on foot. Eventually we reach Stamford Brook tube underground, and Wilson jumps out. I have to make a decision. Johnson is the man in charge and I stay on his tail. It feels like progress. I may get to call Sasha before the day is out. An exquisite shudder runs right through me.

*

Johnson's phone vibrates. He answers.

"Where are they, Wilson?"

"We're at Shepherd's Bush underground station. Do you want me to take them out?"

The tall agent stared at his phone like it was an alien artefact. Everything he said to Wilson had fallen on deaf ears.

"No, keep on them, and I'll be with you soon."

Johnson ended the call and pulled away. He tapped a few buttons on the steering wheel, and Ave Maria erupted from the impressive sound system. It was his favourite stress reliever. It was the first time he'd listened to it in five years.

*

At four o'clock Savannah and John exited Shepherd's Bush Market underground station, turning right along the Uxbridge road.

Traffic was bumper to bumper and pedestrians jostled to get in and out of the market opposite. Savannah had once worked in the well-known market, and she would have enjoyed saying hello to a few of her friends who still worked inside the thronging centre. But she needed Christos off her back more than she needed to catch up with old pals. Other than Wales,

Shepherd's Bush was where she had spent most of her life. She had never liked it enough to consider it home though, even when her mother had been alive.

John's black waxed Barbour jacket was several sizes too big for her narrow frame. The shoulders were loose and the jacket was heavy but it kept the cold afternoon drizzle from her skin. John had thrown an old, dark blue, Marks & Spencer's anorak on top of his hoodie. They must have looked quite the pair.

"We'll sell the watch and then go to my bedsit so I can change," she said, her arm linked through his as they walked beneath the street lamps which had already started to flicker into life, despite the official sunset being three hours away.

John had responded well to her kindness, especially having his head stroked, but she had to keep him focussed. He was her ticket out of the escort business, and the sooner she paid Christos the Greek, the sooner she could start over. Once she'd handed over the grand, she'd call the emergency services and get John taken into care. He needed psychological help, and probably quite soon, but not before she paid Christos. There was no other way she could help Smith, and she would be keeping her end of the deal, even if it wasn't what he believed he had agreed to.

What sort of person goes round calling themselves John Smith and making up crazy stories about gruesome murders? At least he hadn't shown any threatening behaviour, and somehow she sensed that he was more danger to himself than to her. It was best to be on her guard, though.

"John, are you okay with that?"

"Sure." he said, "Sell the watch, go to your bedsit."

Savannah sensed he was going into himself again which could well mean another outburst was on its way. She had to stop his imagination from taking him over the edge. She wondered if he was on any medication and if he carried anything with him?

"Do you take any pills?" she asked. "For anything?"

"Like headaches, you mean?"

She wasn't sure how to word her enquiry without arousing suspicion. "Yes or anything else?"

"I suppose the same as the next man. For hangovers and suchlike."

"Nothing else?"

John's eyebrows shot up. "You mean recreational drugs?"

"No. I don't know what I meant. Just ignore me." God, he seemed so normal sometimes. No wonder he'd been off the radar for so long. If she hadn't witnessed the dramatic breakdown, she'd have thought him saner than her.

They spent the next five minutes in silence as they followed the straight stretch of the Uxbridge Road with its mixture of ethnic food takeaways and everything else from pharmacies to cash lenders, drycleaners and off licences. It truly was a world of its own, seeming like one of the few places where you could buy almost anything legal or otherwise.

As they neared their destination, a sense of unease overtook Savannah. She had never felt comfortable around George Tibbett, a well-established dealer in stolen goods. But desperate times demanded that she must suffer for her freedom. Lewd innuendo and personal space invasion would not kill her, and John, despite his mental state, would make it all the more difficult for the old man to intimidate her.

"Here we are," Savannah said, as they reached a small shop with the shop face windows painted out in what once might have been a brilliant white emulsion. There were no words above the shop, and it appeared almost derelict with flaky brown paint falling from small, old-fashioned, wooden window frames. Parted, concertina-style, metal security gates were the only indication that there was something worth protecting inside.

"Are you sure?" John asked. "Looks closed to me."

Savannah knocked on the glass of the wooden door causing it to rattle loosely in its frame.

"I doubt they have anything of value in here," John said, putting his hand above his eyes and attempting to peer through the opaque window. "I can't see anyone inside."

The window rattled again, and a cloth blind behind it lifted. George Tibbett's wrinkled face peered at them before he undid several bolts and pulled open the door.

"Savannah, my dear," he said, brushing his thick white hair back with his hand. He glanced at John and sneered before returning his attention to her. "Come to rob me again with your beauty?"

The spindly old pervert's eyes flashed up and down her oversized jacket which thankfully hid her feminine curves from his gaze. It wasn't the fact that he was in his seventies that made his lecherous behaviour so appalling, but it did make him all the more pathetic. His attempt to dress younger only made him more so. Designer jeans and trainers did not go with craggy, old, sagging faces. He brushed up against her. She forced a smile to override the need to cringe. "Hi George," she replied, putting her mouth to John's ear. "Let me do all the talking, okay?"

John nodded but appeared more interested in his new surroundings. The small shop was around ten feet from front to back, fifteen feet wide and dimly lit by a solitary low-powered bulb hanging by a grubby wire from the ceiling. Shelves, from the floor to the ceiling, adorned the left and rear walls. Thick wire caging sat two feet in front of the shelves, allowing access to the valuables solely via a door at the far right of the room.

Another door to the right of the shelves, directly opposite the cage door, gave access to a back room. The area in which they now waited contained a small wooden table and chair where Tibbett must have idled his time away waiting for customers or just as likely, the police. A light blue metallic cashbox and lamp sat on top of the table.

Savannah recalled that there were separate lights above each shelf which Tibbett could operate to allow prospective buyers a better look at his mostly contraband stock. He clearly didn't waste electricity on non-purchasing customers. Savannah handed Tibbett the watch. He felt the weight and took it to the table, turned on the lamp and examined it closely.

"How much are you after?" he asked.

"Three thousand," John said, not looking back as he leaned against the cage wire, straining his eyes to examine a shelf of necklaces.

Tibbett looked over to John and then to Savannah. "Your friend has quite a sense of humour."

"Don't mind him," she said, rolling her eyes. "He's a bit simple. What can you give us for it, George?"

Seemingly bored of staring at badly lit jewellery, John shot Savannah a playfully offended look. She smiled back, grateful he wasn't exhibiting any signs of anxiety.

"I thought he'd got a touch of nutter about him," Tibbett said, tapping his forehead. If only he knew, thought Savannah. "I can give you seven fifty. It's my special friend rate."

"I'd hate to get enemy rates," John said, looking at an array of mixed gemstones.

"I don't sell to my enemies," Tibbett snapped. His patience with John was running out. "Can I speak with you in private please, Sav?"

It was the last thing Savannah wanted to do, but it had to beat what Christos had in store for her. John was not behaving too strangely, but Tibbett was obviously not comfortable with him around, and she could not let this deal fall through. She walked over and stood by John at the caging. "Is that okay?"

John lowered his voice. "Are you sure you want to be alone with that creep? He looks like a child molester or something."

"Well I'm no child so I'll be fine," she whispered, squeezing his shoulder. John looked unconvinced.

"Sav?" Tibbett said.

Savannah could sense the agitation in Tibbett's tone. This transaction was turning sour, and she couldn't let that happen. "Sure, I'm coming," she said. "John, I'm going in the back to talk with George. Will you be okay?"

"I'll be fine," he replied. "Just be quick will you please? I doubt there's much in here that hasn't been stolen, and I don't want to be here when he gets raided."

Savannah wasn't sure if John was just messing or if he was stressing for real. She couldn't let him continue to wind up Tibbett and she couldn't risk him melting down. He just had to hang in there for a few more minutes.

"Just stay here, and don't touch anything. I'll only be five minutes max. Are you sure you'll be okay?"

John looked at her like she was the mad one - the nerve of crazy people.

"Yes, go and be quick," he said.

Savannah followed Tibbett to the cage door where he took down a large bunch of keys from a hook. It took him two minutes and five keys to unlock the gate and another two minutes to lock it back up, his attention constantly switching between the locks and John.

Savannah willed the old man to speed up the proceedings. Finally, she followed him into an empty box room barely six feet square. Tibbett pulled on a hanging light cord and an old-fashioned fluorescent tube, the width of the ceiling, flickered into life. He closed the door behind them.

"Jesus, you need sunglasses in here," she said, protecting her eyes with one raised hand.

"You get used to it my dear," Tibbett said, stroking Savannah's hair. "I'd forgotten how beautiful you were."

Savannah drew back. He'd been creepy before but had never laid a hand on her. "Get off me George. I need the money for the watch. What's with you today? I thought we were friends?"

He reached out once more forcing Savannah to step back to avoid his touch. "We are friends my dear. But Christos has plans for you."

"What are you talking about?"

"He says no one is to help you - or else. Seems he has some foreigners interested in you. They'll pay big money for prime stock like you."

Savannah went rigid and whiter than the brilliant light that forced her to squint. So Christos *was* planning to sell her. Her mind travelled back to the elaborate photo shoot at a respected studio in Hampton Hill. He had explained the occasion away as a promotional exercise for the internet, promising her that her face would be pixelated to protect her identity.

The experience had been fun, no nudity and at no point sordid in any way. The penny dropped - stupid girl, Savannah. Her face became clammy, and she gasped for air. That bastard had never wanted her to repay the money. He had expected her to fail. The photographs had been for marketing her sale. Her only chance was to get the cash and prove the sleazebag wrong.

"I won't tell him, George. Just give us a grand, and he'll never know."

Tibbett looked at the watch dismissively and put it into the breast pocket of his jacket. "Like I said, I can only give you seven fifty." A sickly smile formed on his lips, his green eyes wide and leering as he studied her. Out of nowhere, his hand shot out and grabbed the zipper of her jacket, tugging it down before she could react, revealing the black mini dress beneath. If real people's eyes came out on their stalks, then Tibbett's would have jumped out of their sockets.

"Oh yes," he said, his breathing rapid and warm on her face. "Now that you're in the business, let's do some business." He reached for her breasts with trembling hands. "Two fifty for your mouth and seven fifty for the Rolex. We all go home happy."

Savannah backed away, but soon her back was tight against the wall, and she was limited to sideways movement only. Tibbett followed her step for step until she reached the corner. Planting his hands on her breasts, he gripped the flimsy material and pulled it down, snapping the two slight shoulder straps and exposing Savannah's breasts. His hands shook uncontrollably, and his mouth was open wide. The look in his eyes wasn't human but that of an animal taking what was his, savagely. She screamed and clawed at his face.

"Savannah?" John called out. "Are you okay?"

Savannah brought up her knee but missed her attacker's testicles by an inch, instead catching his inner thigh. The hard strike bought her a second or two, allowing her to shove him hard in the chest, but he was still between her and the door, and she was still cornered. Tibbett quickly regrouped and lips parted in a snarl, eyes locked on her brightly lit flesh above the torn, dangling dress, he closed the gap between them. Savannah saw the madness return to his eyes.

"I'm calling the police," shouted John, rattling the cage over and over.

"You've got no phone," said Tibbett panting, a look of extreme annoyance replacing the one of madness. Without zipping it up, Savannah closed the Barbour jacket to cover her exposed skin and folded her arms tightly to keep it from flapping open. "I have a detector in the shop which tells me if a mobile phone enters the shop, so don't try to bullshit me. Just wait there like a good boy, and you and Savannah will leave with a grand when I'm done."

"It wasn't on when I came in, would that make a difference?"

Tibbett grabbed Savannah by her narrow neck and shook her with a force that belied his frame and age. "Does he have a phone?" he demanded.

"Hello, police please," John said. Savannah had no idea what he was up to, but Tibbett's eagerness to attain sexual gratification was clearly wilting. Had he brought a phone with him? She hadn't seen one. She tilted her head and shrugged, hoping it looked convincing.

The bony fingers around Savannah's neck tightened. "I said does he have a phone?"

"I don't know. He could have."

"Put the phone down kid, or I'll break her neck."

"I don't think Christos will be too happy."

Savannah felt the circulation return to her brain as Tibbett's grip relaxed. She threaded her hands upwards between his arms, forcing his hands to leave her neck. Bloody hell. John had been listening all the time. Mad as a hatter and as smart as a button. She could have kissed him right there and then. Tibbett pulled out a thick bundle of fifty pound notes from his inside pocket. There had to be at least five thousand in his hand. John's voice returned.

"Yes, I'd like to report an attack at a shop in Shepherd's Bush."

"I'm not touching her kid. You can hang up. I'm handing Savannah the cash now. Tell him Savannah."

Savannah zipped up the Barbour jacket and held out her hand as Tibbett counted out twenty, fifty pound notes. It was his turn to feel fear. "Tell the kid to hang up, Sav," he begged. "I'm sorry. I need help. Please tell him."

A stiff kick in the balls was the least he deserved but she was baking under the thick coat and her need to get outside into fresh air was greater than her need for payback. "It's okay John. He's handing over the money."

"Tell him to make it two thousand and to stop calling me kid. I'm thirty-two for God's sakes."

"Thirty-two," exclaimed Savannah. I thought you were about twenty-four." She looked at Tibbett and nodded, her confidence flooding back like a wild, untamed river. "You heard the man. Keep counting." Fresh air could wait a few extra seconds.

"Put the phone down first kid... Sorry, I mean, Mister, and I'll pay two."

"I should hurry. I think that they're a bit agitated. It wouldn't surprise me if they weren't trying to triangulate this call already. I'll just tell them where we are, shall I?"

"No. I'm counting. Just don't say another word." He peeled off a bunch of fifty pound notes from the stack and slapped them into Savannah's outstretched hand. "There, there's more like two and a half there. Tell him to hang up the call."

"Not until you open the gate, let out Savannah and lock yourself back in," John called out. "That gives us a head start."

Tibbett stuffed the remainder of the cash pile back into his pocket. He tapped his bottom lip with his forefinger.

"You think I'm fucking stupid, kid?"

"Messing with Christos sounds pretty *fucking* stupid to me." A pause filled the air before John's voice returned. "Sorry about that," he said. The attacker was threatening me but I've shut myself in a cupboard now. I think he may have killed someone. We're in Shepherd's Bush, I'm not sure of the exact address but I can give you directions."

The vicious animal that had terrorised Savannah was beaten and sulked like a reprimanded puppy. "Okay. I'm doing it, Mister. Savannah and I are coming out. Just please don't say any more."

"Speed it up then, Georgie boy. I can't hold this call up much longer."

Savannah tucked the bundle of notes into one of the big outside pockets of the jacket. She walked out of the back room and went to the gate, closely followed by Tibbett. John was not at the gate and the light was out. Tibbett flicked a switch but the darkness remained.

"John?" she called, straining her eyes to see.

"I'm in the corner. I removed the bulb. I don't want this bastard getting a good look at me and sending somebody after me later."

In the left corner of the shop, aided by the light escaping from the back office, Savannah could make out John's back. His head was bowed and he was leaning into the corner as though he was about to urinate. Son of a bitch. He was heading into another pretend world. She prayed that he wouldn't break down. Not now when they were so close to getting out, not when she was a hair's breadth away from getting Christos off her back forever.

"Look, Mister. I don't want any more bother." Tibbett began unlocking the gate. "I just want you two out of here. If Christos finds out about this, I'll be as dead as you're gonna be."

"I'll pay him his money," Savannah said, walking through the open gate and into the front of the shop where John remained stooped in the corner. "A deal's a deal."

Tibbett entered a key into the top of the door's locks. "You're his ticket to the big time. He won't give that up easy. You should run for it. Get as far away as possible. The bottom and last lock snapped shut. "There, I'm locked in. Now hang up the phone and get the fuck out of my shop."

John turned around with his hands held out. With her eyes now accustomed to the darkness, Savannah could make out that both were empty. "You want to revisit the discussion about your stupidity?" John said.

Tibbett fumbled through the massive set of keys. "You bastard," he screamed, forcing a key into the top lock.

"Come on, Savannah. Let's go," John said, taking her by the hand.

John hadn't been acting strangely at all. He'd been hiding in the dark so that it looked like he could be on the phone. She pulled him to her and kissed him full on the lips. "For a loony, you're bloody brilliant."

"What?"

"Forget it. Let's get out of here before the sick old pervert gets free."

8: Saturday 24th September, 16:45

Fifteen minutes later John and Savannah were standing in Savannah's East Acton, first-floor bedsit. John couldn't believe that anyone lived like this. It was damp, cramped and in need of complete refurbishment.

While Savannah changed, he used the communal toilet in the hall. Abundant mould grew around the window frame and ceiling and the air was thick with the smell of stale urine. Evidence of the residents' eating habits was engrained on the sides of the toilet bowl. With a concerted effort, and breathing only through his mouth, John forced his aching bladder to empty. The soggy, stained towel, which hung beneath the cracked washbasin, had more dirt and germs on it than his hands had ever experienced. He rushed out without washing his hands.

"That toilet is disgusting," he said, re-entering Savannah's shoebox of a room. She wore tight blue jeans, scuffed white trainers and a thick red Adidas hoodie. She had tied her hair behind her head revealing her small ears. If you stuck a point on them, she'd look just like a sexy pixie.

There was a small, rickety wooden bed with a four inch mattress in one corner, a small two-ringed stove next to a sink in the other and a wardrobe against the opposite wall which took up a quarter of the floor space. A two feet square window was covered by a single green curtain hung via a threaded steel wire. John noticed a clean-looking towel next to the sink and took the opportunity to wash his hands.

"I don't use the toilet here," she said. "I use the cafe toilet fifty yards down the road. They don't seem to mind."

John was glad to hear it. The thought of Savannah using the toilet made him uncomfortable. Even after washing his hands he still longed for his wet-room back at home. It would take a good ten minutes of steaming hot jets to make him feel clean again. It was a shame it wasn't safe to return there.

"Grab a few clothes and put them in a suitcase," he said, looking above him at the bare forty watt bulb that hung from a worn white cable. He couldn't wait to get out of there.

"It's all I could afford," Savannah said, giving him the piercing eyes, hands on the hips treatment which was becoming her trade mark. John didn't want to be judgemental, but surely if you lived like this then you did something about it. He'd hardly set the world alight with his achievements but then he didn't need to because he didn't live in squalor. If he'd been put in a place like this one, he'd have soon pulled his finger out. He must remember not to have that conversation with his parents.

"Let's get out of here," he said, unable to take the scowl of disgust from his face.

"Screw you," she grumped. "I can't find my passport. I think Christos must have had someone swipe it."

"Well let's get busy." John grabbed her by the arm and looked her in the eyes. "If Christos is going to renege on his word, then we'd better not hang around somewhere he knows you might be."

She pulled her arm away from his grip. "Not until I speak to Amy."

"Who's Amy?"

"Follow me."

John followed Savannah up the stairs to the top floor of the converted building. He caught himself admiring the lines of her bottom and legs and felt sort of pervy for a while, especially after the Tibbett incident, but he was only human and she was wearing figure-hugging jeans. Besides, she would never know. It had been a hell of a day and perks had been sadly lacking.

There must have been nine bedsits in all but only one in the attic. It was the penthouse bedsit, so to speak. The cream carpet outside was thick-piled wool and not the threadbare grey synthetic material that graced the rest of the shoddy building. Savannah raced up and banged repeatedly on the metal-skinned door with the side of her fist, a look of grim determination and anger on her face.

"Amy, open up."

"I'm busy," came the muffled reply.

Savannah's lips narrowed and she pounded even harder this time. "If you don't open the door, I'll set the fucking place on fire."

John couldn't believe the change in Savannah, from the girl who always looked like she was about to cry to ... this! The door battering continued until Savannah's arm ran out of steam and she stopped to catch her breath.

"Go away," the voice said from inside.

"Did you sell me out to Christos?" Savannah asked, leaning on the wall, still a little out of breath. John reckoned it was the emotion more than the exertion that was draining her. Her teeth clenched and she drove her fist against the solid surface as she slowly and deliberately spoke with every blow.

"Did you ..." thump, "sell me ..." thump, "out to ..." thump, "Christos?" Double thump.

"You don't get it do you?" The voice, now most definitely nervous and defensive, came back. "I'm thirty-eight. There's no thousand quid punters for me no more."

"What's that got to do with anything?"

"Christos pays me to recruit new talent. Why do you think I got you the bedsit? As long as I bring in new girls, he lets me stay here and throws me extra. Keeps me off me back."

Savannah took long and deep breaths. John could see she was barely holding it together. John considered the extent of Amy's betrayal. This woman had lured Savannah into a world where your word meant nothing and human life was no more valuable than an animal's and sometimes probably less.

Savannah's voice trembled as she spoke. "How much did he throw you for me?"

John shook his head. There was no point to this conversation and they were taking a risk by just being there. Who was to say that this heartless whore hadn't already texted Christos and tipped him off that she was here? Savannah looked away from John, avoiding his eyes and banged on the door with renewed vigour. John could see the knuckle of her little finger had begun to swell. He grabbed her hand and pulled her round to face him. "Let me try something," he whispered.

For a moment she looked like she might vent her anger on John for interrupting her business but the tension leaked from her body like air from a balloon and she nodded, defeated and exhausted.

John put his mouth to the cold steel door and spoke in a deep Jamaican voice.

"Amy, you don't know me but Savannah works for me now. I'll be paying your protector for her services but I need her passport. I'll give you ten seconds before I set light to your walls. Be a good girl and shove the passport underneath the door. Ten, nine, eight..."

A UK passport appeared beneath the door.

"How...?" began Savannah.

John put his forefinger to his lips and shook his head to hush her. "Sensible girl. Now the cash you received for recruiting Savannah. I reckon I'll use it to pay your protector."

No reply. John pressed his ear to the door and swore he could hear beeps from the buttons of a mobile phone. He picked up the countdown again. "Three, two... He's not close enough to save you from burning to death, honey... One."

Savannah stared at John in disbelief. "You could help me out here," he mouthed almost silently. Her eyes lit up.

"No, Calvin, don't burn her. Christos made her do it I'm sure. Put the lighter fluid down, please."

No Oscars anytime soon but it might just work if Amy's already scared enough. There was a shuffling sound from behind the door and the sound of a phone being placed on a table.

"All right," Amy bellowed. "I'm getting it. Don't burn me. It's coming."

John kept his ear pressed to the door. No more beeps. A stream of crumpled notes began to arrive under the door, mainly tens and twenties. John motioned for Savannah to pick up the money and the passport. When the stream dried up John pointed to the stairs and whispered.

"Get going, I'll be down in a minute."

She returned a puzzled look and shrugged.

"Go on," he insisted.

Savannah complied and set off down the stairs. Once John reckoned she was out of earshot he re-summoned Calvin the pimp.

"Sorry darling. Not fast enough. And me don't like leaving talking evidence. Say hello to your maker." John rubbed the carpet where it met the foot of the door hoping the sound was convincing. "Der she blows," he shouted, jumping back for effect.

He ran down the stairs, catching up with Savannah on the way out the main front door.

"Let's get as far away as possible as quick as possible," he said, grabbing her by his own coat, dragging her out of the building and circling them around to the back. John pointed up to the window where the top of the fire escape began. A full-figured woman of about forty backed out of the attic window and onto the platform. She was screaming, nothing discernible but as loud as a banshee's wail. She wore a bright pink dressing gown and matching fluffy slippers with bunny ears attached to the front.

Savannah looked bewildered and turned to John. "What's she doing? What did you do?"

"She thinks the place is on fire," he said, grinning from ear to ear. "I figured after what she did to you, it was the least she deserved."

Savannah burst out laughing and wrapped her arms around John again. "You might be crazy but I promise I won't tell the authorities."

"What?" said John, enjoying the experience, putting his own arms around Savannah. This girl was a couple of cogs short of a full mechanism but being around her made him forget about all the bad stuff that had happened. He felt the best he had felt all day, sort of exhilarated, high on adventure perhaps? He pushed back a pang of guilt. Mark had always told him to stop wasting his life and his friend's murder showed him how precarious life could be. "How much money have we got?" he asked.

"Three thousand one hundred with the five hundred we got from Amy."

"Great. Flag down a taxi. We're off to Knightsbridge and then Piccadilly."

9: Saturday 24th September, 18:00

Herb Johnson and Maxwell Wilson were watching proceedings from seventy five thousand pounds worth of sleek black Mercedes saloon.

"You've got to be kidding me," Wilson said, pointing to John Smith and Savannah Jones diving into the back of a London cab. "Those two are laughing and smiling like little children. Smith's no murderer. I think he was just in the wrong place at the wrong time and if we follow him we'll end up with nothing."

Just then Savannah's former friend Amy ran past the car, waving her hands frantically in the air.

"Fire," she screamed over and over.

Johnson and Wilson gave her less than a second's attention. Johnson turned back to his partner.

"Smith's thirty-two and Jones is twenty-one. Not exactly kids. Unless you've got a better idea then we stick with them and see what happens." Johnson pressed his foot gently on the accelerator, allowing six point two litres of V8 engine to pull them away with a throaty growl.

Johnson loved the Mercedes almost as much as he loved his job. Sure, it involved killing but he prided himself on his ability to only end the lives of those who were a threat to others. Sometimes this meant going against orders but he always got the job done. He had to live with himself, after all. The job didn't exactly encourage relationships. He could wait until retirement for companionship.

Johnson's priority was to find Bradshaw's killer, which may or may not be Smith, and recover Bradshaw's deadly invention. All this while stuck with a partner who was a shadow of his former self. If Wilson lost him his perfect occupation, he had meant his threat. He would kill him and not lose a moment's sleep. Johnson had kissed too many asses and put in too many hours to see it all flushed away over the personal problems of Wilson. His job was his life and in that regard he was not a forgiving soul.

"If we want to cover our backs, shouldn't we take these two out?" Wilson asked, raising two fingers, pointing out the window and pretend shooting a young woman with brightly dyed blue hair.

"Die," he said, feigning recoil with his hand.

Outside Johnson was unflappable while inside Wilson was seriously pissing him off. He took deep breaths to calm himself.

"Think man, think. Before we take anyone out we need to find out what their involvement is. Where would you have us go instead?"

"Visit Bradshaw's gambling circle. We've checked out all of his contacts and got nothing. Bradshaw must have sold the weapon to somebody one of his high-flying betting cronies introduced him to."

"Checked them out myself last night. Nothing."

"You're not keeping me in the loop here. How do you expect me to help?"

"In your current state you're next to useless and I expect you to help by carrying out every command I give you to the letter. Got it?"

Wilson looked away and aimed his fingers at a pink-haired teenager.

"Got it," he said as he pulled the imaginary trigger.

"Looks like they're heading upmarket," Johnson said, eager to keep Wilson from whatever dark thoughts occupied his mind. The man had been solid for five years. What had Johnson done to deserve this?

They followed the cab to Knightsbridge where the taxi pulled up outside the green frontage of Harrods department store. Smith and Jones jumped out and ran inside.

"Follow them and report back on what they do inside," Johnson said, stopping several cars behind.

"I can tell you now. They are going shopping."

Johnson took another deep breath. "Still, follow them and see what they get up to. I'll wait here. No getting trigger happy. Have you got your Taser? You can use that as a last resort."

"Sorry, lost it."

Johnson scowled. "Isn't that the third one you've lost since we've been together?"

"Sorry, Boss."

"Promise me you won't shoot anyone."

"Yes, Sir."

Johnson was getting tired of babysitting Wilson. Perhaps it would be better to take him to a quiet space and break his thick neck before he did too much damage. It wasn't possible without losing sight of Smith and Jones. He would reconsider later.

Wilson got out and slammed the door hard. Johnson winced inwardly and opened his window. When Wilson passed, en route to the department store entrance, Johnson called him over. Wilson bent down.

"What is it now? I get it. No shooting."

Johnson's hand shot out of the window catching his partner's Adam's apple with measured force. Wilson stumbled back, both hands clutching his throat, short rasping gasps filling the cold air with mini clouds of condensation.

"Don't slam the door," Johnson barked at his subordinate, whose eyes were still wide with surprise.

Herb Johnson shut the window and took in a deep breath. If he was going to get any use out of Wilson then he was going to have to scare it out of him. One more screw up and he would bury him. It had already been a long day and it still seemed a long way from the end. If he had to take down Smith then the chances were that the girl would have to die too. What was Smith's agenda? Johnson was convinced that he would lead them to the missing item. If he had to blow his brains out later then so be it. But not before he was sure Smith had killed Bradshaw.

He revved the engine before turning it off. The sound brought calmness to his thoughts.

*

I can't park anywhere near Harrods without a traffic warden pouncing on me in seconds. I can't kill a traffic warden on a busy pavement. I pull down a side street and double park. There is just enough room for other cars to pass. It is a risk I must take. I cannot lose the Mercedes. I grab my equipment bag from the back of the van and run back to Brompton Road. Luck is with me. Johnson is sitting in the car alone. The sky is dull and darkening but it is not enough to cover me. I walk along the pavement until I reach the rear of the Mercedes. I resist the need for a cigarette and I wait.

A stretch limousine pulls up several cars down. It has private number plates. All eyes are on the rear door as the chauffeur reaches for the door handle. I couldn't care less about a pop diva or Sultan but I welcome the distraction and drop to the floor and roll under Johnson's car. There is plenty of traffic noise but I can't be too careful. The undercarriage is reinforced. I will need to make adjustments. I get to work.

10: Saturday 24th September, 19:20

With John pulling Savannah from pillar to post in order to speed her along, they soon spent five hundred pounds on new clothes. A sports jacket and smart black trousers plus white shirt for John and a new black, slightly more conservative mini dress for Savannah. She really was like a kid in a candy store. Every time they came across a new section of clothes or electronics or exotic food or just plain old sweets in a fancy box, she would exclaim, "John, check this out. Can you believe this?"

Having visited the famous store several times in his teens, John could well believe it, and while it had changed somewhat, the general feel of the place remained. Essentially, it was a place where the rich and the wannabees went to waste money. The rich paid there and then while the wannabees racked up heart attack inducing sums of credit by any means available to them. John and Savannah were cash customers today and by the spring in Savannah's step and the delight in her expression, impulsive shopping was clearly a first for her.

At a table in the Pizzeria they shared a Quattro Formaggi pizza. It transpired that neither of them had eaten all day and the sizeable dish lasted less than five minutes. Savannah brushed the cloth of the dress material with the palm of her hand. "It's so smooth," she sighed. Then her eyes became distant, fixed somewhere in the air where there was nothing to focus on. "I loved that old dress. My Mum bought it for me just before she died."

John crossed his fingers under the table and hoped that she wasn't going to cry again. This would not be a good place to have a scene.

"I'm sorry," he said, genuinely. "Was it a long time ago?"

"Three years," replied Savannah. "Her body rotted from the inside out before my very eyes."

"Cancer?"

"Yes, she was a smoker and she never quit, even after being diagnosed, though I begged her day and night."

John remained silent. What did you say to that? Well, wasn't it her own fault? She should have listened to you. True or not, these facts were not what she needed to hear.

"She left me taken care of," she continued, her gaze still concentrated in space. "Left me a small flat in Shepherd's Bush. Nothing like your mammoth pad but two small bedrooms, mortgage all paid off. Even had a small, communal vegetable patch where I grew strawberries every summer. I love strawberries, don't you? My Mum loved strawberries too."

John knew that he would regret asking but he honestly did want to know.

"So what happened?"

"Dad happened, that's what. Turned up two days after the funeral, swore he'd changed and moved in. Six weeks later he'd drunk himself to death, gambled the flat away and I was out on the street."

"Jesus Christ. You must hate him."

"Not really. He couldn't help himself. He was addicted to gambling and alcohol like I'm addicted to lost causes and you're ..." Savannah paused. Either she couldn't think of the words to say or felt the need to temper the ones that first came into her mind. " ... addicted to lying," she finally ended the sentence with. "Mum told me never to let him back, she knew what would happen and she was right. I gave him the excuse to ruin us both. It's my fault more than his."

John pondered on the 'addicted to lying' part of the conversation and what she might possibly be referring to. He made a mental note to ask her later. "I'm not sure that I want to know or whether you want to talk about it, but how did you get involved with a scumbag like Christos?"

"Another lost cause. I worked in Shepherd's Bush market for a Jamaican guy who sold DVD's and a bit of marijuana on the side. Spoke a lot like

Calvin actually. You were pretty cool in the shop and at the bedsits. You're a strange one all right."

"Thanks, I think. You coped pretty well yourself."

John didn't want the conversation brought round to him. He wasn't ready to talk about Mark yet. This adventure with Savannah had pushed his problems to one side and that's just where he liked them.

"So you worked for this Jamaican in Shepherd's Bush market," John nudged.

"Yeah, he paid me in cash, gave me a little weed here and there which I sold on. I got myself a bedsit and I was studying business at night school. Finished the course with merit last June and moved in with Graham during the summer."

John had a sinking feeling when he spoke. "Graham?"

"I met him at night school. Going to change the world he was. Always strapped for cash, always borrowing from me and never paying me back. I should have known as soon as I moved in."

"Go on."

"He was sweet and kind to me and his flat was cool. I figured that he had money. He always went on about how rich his parents were, how he'd take me on cruises and show me how the other half live. After all the crap with Dad and working myself through a qualification, I figured I'd finally landed on my feet."

"Dare I ask what happened next?"

"I woke up one morning and he'd gone. He'd taken my clothes, my qualification, my purse, bank card, jewellery and everything. Even the ring that my Mum had left me, the last thing I had of hers - a simple gold band with a sliver of an emerald in a tiny claw. That sicko Tibbett wouldn't have given me a fiver for it but it meant a lot to me." A tear ran down her cheek but it was alone and John didn't interrupt, glued to her every word. "It turned out that the flat was a rental on which he owed three months back rent and I was chucked out the very next day. I was back on the streets again after nearly three years. He had cleared out my bank account - three thousand five hundred and forty seven pounds. I never saw him or the money again."

"Didn't you call the police? Banks have got insurance against that sort of thing. If you get a crime number the bank has to pay you back."

"Didn't want the hassle. Picked myself up, dusted myself off and started again. Got my job back at Shepherd's Bush market and then met Amy who got me the bedsit about four weeks ago. You know the rest."

John had a thousand questions. Like why didn't she really go to the police? With the three and a half thousand she could have got herself a replacement certificate for her business qualification, got a decent job and put a deposit down on a flat of her own. John could imagine the word 'victim' written in capital letters across her forehead.

She was a sucker for a sob story and she'd been taken advantage of one too many times. Everyone she ever trusted since her mother died had let her down. So what did that make him? He was dragging her into God only knew what, and he couldn't stop himself. A part of him knew it was wrong but he had no one else to turn to. He had no real friends, other than Mark, and his family had already had their fill of him. It was wrong but he couldn't face being alone. He would make it up to her, he promised himself.

"Bad luck all right," he said, glad she wasn't looking at his guilt ridden face. "Rotten bad luck."

"Yeah," she agreed, gaze still in mid-air.

"So ready for Piccadilly?" he asked, as upbeat as his conscience would allow.

"Sure," she replied, snapping out of her trance, looking at him expectantly. "What's in Piccadilly?"

"Why the Ritz, my dear, the Ritz," John replied.

*

Wilson prepared to contact Johnson from a toilet cubicle located in the bathroom close to the Pizzeria eating area. He'd always loved pizza, as had his wife, but the delicious aromas had done no more for him than the smell of disinfectant inside the bathroom, another pleasure that had departed with Julie. Hearing the girl's bad luck story had reinforced his anger at not being able to spend her last remaining weeks together. At least Savannah had said her farewells. He took in a huge lungful of air and it was all he could do not to burst into tears.

Julie's doctor had explained the chain of events to Wilson only eight days ago:

"It was cancer of the most voracious kind I'm afraid. When she came in two months ago she was already in tremendous pain. Why she didn't come in sooner is a mystery. We tried everything but the damage had already been done and the cancer was everywhere. We made numerous attempts to contact you."

"I was in hospital myself."

"Your wife said, but she didn't know where or why? We thought it might be the pain killers affecting her mind."

"It's a long story."

"Your daughter said you were a killer and in prison."

"That sounds like Kate."

"Do you wish to use our chapel?"

"Isn't it a bit late for that?"

"Some people find comfort there."

Damn bloody Earthguard, keeping him in the dark. Dick Burns, another useless yank, had confirmed that his employment did not cover family healthcare and that the Earthguard private hospital was reserved for field agents only.

"I contacted the Ministry of Defence who control the UK budget for Earthguard and asked for a special dispensation to move your wife. I told them that you couldn't leave your bed and that your wife was terminally ill. When I told your controller he visited Whitehall personally. It was the same response. Funds are tight and the money was needed elsewhere."

"Why didn't anybody tell me that my wife was sick," he had said, close to wringing the pen pusher's scrawny neck.

"You were in a coma for the first month and once you woke up, your surgeon said you were not to be put under undue stress. What could we do?"

Wilson pulled out six sheets of soft toilet tissue from the dispenser, wiped away his tears and blew his nose. Bloody politicians. He pressed the top side button on the Breitling Blackbird watch. This wasn't the ordinary model. This was an improvement in timekeeping, complete with two way radio communication and a global positioning system.

"Johnson, come in."

"Johnson. Anything to report?"

A short beep sounded to let Wilson know that Johnson had finished speaking.

"I've been listening in to their conversation. I've got nothing on Smith but he seems to be helping Jones sort out her problems, and by the sounds of it she's been through the wringer and back." Johnson sniffed before he let go of the button.

"Are you crying?" Beep.

The nerve of Johnson. Wilson ignored the remark.

"I heard nothing that links either one to Bradshaw's murder or the missing item."

"Yeah, I've got their files on the monitor now. She's definitely clean and I'd have to agree that the chances of him being a killer are pretty slim. You reckon we could get them to help us?" Beep.

"Are you serious?"

"We're alone in this and you're currently a borderline retard. We could do with all the help we can get. If the girl's in trouble then maybe we could do a deal?" Beep.

Wilson muted his watch while he blew his nose again. The thought of helping the girl out had its appeal. She had suffered at the hands of her father and her boyfriend and her mother had died of cancer. It might give him a purpose for a while.

"No risking the girl's life," he said into the watch.

"Sure thing. Where are they now?" Beep.

"I know where they're headed. We can pick them up there. I mean it about the girl, Johnson." But Johnson had ended transmission. That unfeeling bastard. It wouldn't have surprised Wilson if Johnson rejected his request for time off to attend Julie's funeral. If it wasn't good for his career, he didn't give a damn.

Wilson turned the winder of his watch anti-clockwise to rewind the recording he had made while sat opposite Smith and Jones. The small internal speaker played back part of the conversation surprisingly clearly.

"A simple gold band with a sliver of an emerald in a tiny claw. That sicko Tibbett wouldn't have given me a fiver for it but it meant a lot to me."

Yes, Savannah Jones was all right, he decided.

11: Saturday 24th September, 21:30

It was nine thirty in the evening by the time John and Savannah got checked in to a junior suite at the Ritz. At six hundred pounds it was a little more than they were expecting to spend but John insisted that she didn't worry about it. It was all right for him. He could disappear into another world.

John Smith was a conundrum. On one level he was her hero, rescuing her from the clutches of a perverted sexual predator, and on the other level, he appeared to be a mixed-up creature who needed professional help. Another lost cause - shouldn't she be running a mile?

She couldn't help but realise that the more time they spent together, the safer she felt around him. Wondering what John's thoughts would be on how to best resolve the Christos problem, she decided to see how the night went and make a decision in the cold light of day tomorrow.

With their Harrods' bags filled with their used clothes, they headed for the suite having politely declined assistance from the hotel's staff. John had such a way with words, he was obviously far better educated than Savannah, but for someone with such a privileged upbringing he carried no aura of superiority that many of his kind wore like a royal cape to be twirled in the faces of those less fortunate.

"So how come you didn't bring your passport?" she asked.

"It's at my parent's house. I never use it and I'd probably lose it if they didn't keep it safe."

"Just as well we got mine back or they wouldn't have let us have a room. They will give it back, right?"

"Of course."

"Good."

"You'd have thought that paying in cash would have been enough," John said. "Anyway it's not a room, it's a suite!"

Savannah giggled like a naughty school girl. A suite at the Ritz, it was all utter madness but such fun nonetheless. If she could just get Christos off her back who knew what might happen.

"Yes, a suite," she sang as she twirled along the corridor to their destination. "I could have danced all night, I could have danced all night, and still have begged for more."

"My Fair Lady," John said, twirling round once. "You're a bit young for that, aren't you?"

"My Mum and I used to watch it together on video every week. It was her favourite film. Audrey Hepburn was so beautiful."

"Yes, it's one of my mother's favourites. I think we watched it together when I was young."

"Did she put you in a dress?"

"Very funny," John stopped walking and rubbed his chin between his thumb and forefinger as if in the deepest of thoughts. "You know, I think she did," he said, roaring with laughter and spinning around once more.

This was a corridor to a place so grand that royalty would not feel out of place, a corridor where anything was possible, a corridor where dreams and wishes might come true. This moment was the happiest Savannah had felt since losing her mother. She recollected Audrey Hepburn gliding around the staircase, beautiful big dress swishing through the air behind her, her head giddy with the success of the night - just before her world came crashing down around her. An icy shiver shot down Savannah's spine.

"What's wrong, Savannah?" John asked, as he entered the key card into the electronic lock to their suite. "You look like you've seen a ghost."

"Nothing," she lied. "Just a bit tired I guess."

Savannah's worries evaporated when they entered the suite.

"Oh my God," she said, open mouthed, hands and arms outstretched. "You could fit fifty of my bedsits in here."

It was a vision of lavish taste with luxurious curtains, drapes and crystal chandeliers. Cream walls held elaborately framed original works of art.

Tied-back gold and green striped drapes separated the bedroom from the seating area and a beautifully adorned king size bed invited tired and wealthy visitors to rest their weary heads. An abundance of fine antique furniture completed, but at no time cluttered, the expansive space. Savannah was in heaven. Then John fell apart.

"Savannah, pass me that Harrods' bag," he shouted, holding his head in both hands. "How could I have forgotten?"

"What's the matter, John?"

"Hurry up. Not that one, the one with my jeans in."

Savannah could see John visibly shaking as he frantically dumped the contents of the bag onto the huge bed. He grabbed his jeans, like his life depended on it, and pulled one of the pockets inside out sending a folded piece of paper onto the pale cream duvet. John gently picked up the small object and sat down on the side of the bed and stared at it like he expected it to burst into flames at any moment.

"What is it, John?" Savannah ran over to the bed and sat beside him. "Are you having a meltdown?"

John said nothing and continued to stare at the paper he held in both trembling hands.

Savannah put her arm around his shoulders. "Is that an emergency number you need to call if you feel strange?"

John turned to Savannah. "It was Mark's," he said, ashen faced.

"Is it his phone number? Do you need to call him? Is he your carer?"

John's pained expression turned to confusion. "What are you talking about?" he waved the note an inch in front of Savannah's face. "Mark had this in his hand when I found him. He's dead and I haven't even looked at the note. What sort of friend am I...? I mean was I? I can't bring myself to open it, even now."

"Calm down, John. It's not real. You're having an episode." Savannah began to stroke his back. "It'll be okay," she whispered softly, over and over.

John jumped up from the bed. "It won't be okay," he shouted, stomping his foot repeatedly on the floor like a child in a tantrum. "My best friend's dead. Don't you get it? While we've been gallivanting around, he's still dead and nothing will ever change that."

Savannah's wonderful dream had come to an abrupt halt. Lost cause, she reminded herself. How could she have repeated the formula so soon after the last disaster? Yet, this lost cause had helped her. He wasn't like the

ETHAN JUSTICE: ORIGINS • 74

others. He might need help but he was not just a taker and abuser. Her gut instinct was to make an excuse, go outside the room, find a phone and call emergency services. She had the money to pay Christos. He would abide by their deal and set her free to start over. Savannah stood up feeling like a fraud and a bitch rolled into one.

"I need to get some air," she said, marching towards the door.

"Please don't go," John said, his head and shoulders drooped as he turned and sat back down on the bed. "No more hysterics, I promise."

Go, Savannah, she told herself. But she couldn't do it. Just like she couldn't say no to her father or leave Graham once she knew he was no good. Savannah was just as much a lost cause as John Smith.

"Turn on the TV please," John said.

Savannah did as she was asked, picking up the remote from the ornate table and sending the signal to wake up the television from standby mode. The angle wasn't the best so Savannah twisted the flat screen to allow them to see the picture face on, from the side of the bed.

Without looking up from the floor John said, "Turn it to BBC1 and press the red button, please." He sounded like a beaten man, like someone who had gone fourteen rounds in a boxing ring with a far superior fighter and realised that there was still another round to go and he might not make it to the end.

"There you go," Savannah said, trying to sound upbeat but failing miserably. "What are we looking for?"

"Navigate to the news headlines and see what the choices are."

Savannah entered the news headlines section. "Now what?"

"Read them out please."

"Middle Eastern peace talks fail, Government says it will get worse before it gets better, Arms dealer commits suicide, the Pope denies that the Roman Catholic church encourages homosexuality... Do you want me to carry on?"

"Yes, keep going. Is there something about Mark's murder?"

Savannah sighed deeply and handed the remote to John. "Look for yourself. It's all in your head. I'm going for a bath."

She wouldn't leave him and she wouldn't inform the authorities but she'd be damned if she'd encourage his depressing fantasies.

The bathroom was the loveliest and the biggest she'd ever seen. The twin sinks sat under a swirly brown marble top, hardly contemporary but magnificently impressive nevertheless. A single red rose sat in a narrow-stemmed vase between the two sinks. To the left was a bath big enough for two with gleaming gold-plated taps which delivered cascading waterfalls when she turned them. It was a far cry from her bedsit shower which required one, fifty pence coin a minute, to stay warm even if you could put up with the leftover dirt, smells and body hair from previous users.

She slipped out of the new dress and waited for the bath to fill, in just her newly purchased soft yellow bra and panties. She couldn't wait to jump in the bath and enjoy the free scented crystals provided by the hotel. As she turned the taps off and tested the water, a loud banging started on the bathroom door, startling her. Luckily, she had thought to lock it.

"Savannah, come quickly, you have to see this." John's voice was mumbled through the thick door but the urgency carried through regardless.

"I'm in the bath," Savannah lied.

"Then get out. It's important. Please just look at this and then I promise I won't bother you ever again."

Savannah groaned inwardly, slipped her dress back on and opened the door. John was standing in front of the television, remote in hand.

"Look at this. It wasn't the story I expected but it's him all right."

She moved next to him. The headline on the screen was one Savannah had already read aloud. "Arms dealer commits suicide," she said. "I saw that one already."

"You didn't see the detail." John highlighted the headline and pressed enter on the remote. The screen flashed up a paragraph with a photograph beneath it. It was the man who had introduced Savannah to John in the sports bar last night.

"Jesus Christ," she mumbled through her hand as her mind was jolted like a whip cracking inside her brain. "You're not mad at all... It's all real." She fought to catch her breath. "You're not mad," she repeated. Who and what had she got herself involved with? Taking deep breaths she took control of her breathing. "You never said he was an arms dealer."

"He's not or rather he wasn't." John handed Savannah the piece of paper that had fallen from his pocket earlier. "Now look what I found in his hand."

Savannah looked at what she had assumed was a note, to see that it was a left luggage ticket for Waterloo Station.

"It's just a piece of left luggage. So what?"

"We need to get there before it closes at eleven tonight."

"It all sounds a bit Alfred Hitchcock, don't you think? Left luggage tickets and all that."

"So?" urged John, not the least bit deterred. He regarded her with a newfound intensity. He had never looked so determined, his eyes boring into hers, waiting, demanding agreement to his irrational request.

"I'm sorry I was wrong," Savannah said, turning her back on John.

"What? About Mark?"

"No about you," she said, walking away. "You are crazy."

12: Saturday 24th September, 22:15

John and Savannah debated their next move in the soft-cushioned, mahogany-legged chairs in the sitting area of their suite at the Ritz hotel.

John was amazed that Savannah hadn't headed straight for the hills. In fact she seemed almost pleased that his best friend was dead, as it proved that John wasn't in need of professional help. Her reaction to the reality of John's predicament had given him a much needed dose of testosterone and convinced him to take the trip to Waterloo alone. What sort of man would drag an already troubled girl into even greater danger?

"Look it's just three stops on the Bakerloo line. You stay here and enjoy your bath and I'll be back before you know it."

"Or dead more likely." Savannah threw her arms up. "You've got no idea who could be waiting there."

"Nobody knows that I have this ticket. Knowledge of its existence probably died with Mark. Mark wanted me to have whatever is at Waterloo Station."

"Did he tell you that?"

"Of course not, he was dead, but his arm was outstretched like he wanted to give me something."

"Maybe he wanted to give it to someone else. Besides, they said he killed himself so why didn't he just leave you a note?"

John leaned back on two legs of the chair which emitted an unhappy groan in complaint. He sat forward again before anything snapped. She must understand. She didn't have to come with him, but he still needed her support. "Mark had a letter opener in his head and a dagger in his back. How can that have been suicide? Somebody has either messed with the evidence or the police have issued a lie to keep the lid on this thing."

"What thing?"

"I have no idea?"

"Did you have any idea what Mark was mixed up in?"

"He was a financial wizard of some sort, trading in risky stocks and so forth."

"Have you ever been to his office?"

"No, he worked mainly from home."

"Did he talk about his work?"

"No, never."

"Did you ask him about it?"

"Listen, I know what you're driving at but we've been best friends since school and if he was selling weapons I'm sure I'd have suspected something. Christ we told each other everything. He would have told me."

"Even if it put your life at risk?"

"Shit, shit, shit. I don't bloody well know any more. All I do know is that he knew I was outside when he was being murdered and he wanted me to find the note."

"All right," Savannah said.

"All right what?"

Savannah stood up and slid out of her new dress a few feet away from John.

John's eyes opened wide and his mouth opened wider. She looked soft and smooth and clean and beautiful, despite everything she had been through. John struggled to speak. "I'm not ... sure ... we've got time for that," he said.

"It's got to beat being raped up the bum by filthy Arabs," she said walking over to the bed with great purpose in her stride.

"Well ... I don't know what to say." John stood up and made tentative steps towards the bed. "I'd certainly hope so."

"Well come on then slowcoach." John looked to the tall ceiling and mouthed 'thank you' when out of nowhere his jeans hit him full in the face. Savannah was retrieving her old clothes from the other Harrods' bag. She slid a lithe leg into her jeans. "I'm not letting you get killed alone. Hurry up and get changed."

*

On the Bakerloo Line tube John and Savannah faced each other, hanging on tightly to the ceiling rail by the doors as they debated John's sanity. It was 10:25 on a Saturday night and most of London was apparently using this train. John felt a bead of sweat trickle from his temple, letting it reach his neck before wiping it away. Savannah fanned her face with her free hand and John welcomed the secondary draft he received from her efforts. It was like a greenhouse inside the cramped tube.

Typically, everyone kept themselves to themselves, avoiding eye contact when John scoured his view for suspicious-looking types who might be following them. The problem was that over half of the people he laid eyes on looked suspicious. The rest just swayed along with the rhythmic clackety-clack of the train, like puppets waiting for their master to pull their strings.

"So what you're saying is that if I hadn't been called John Smith then you'd have believed everything else?" John asked.

"Yes, I suppose. When you think about it, it does seem rather stupid. I've never met a John Smith although I know there are more of you than probably anyone else. I think that with the crying at your flat and the not having your passport, I sort of added two and two and got five or maybe even six."

"I'm no expert but I think it's okay to cry if your best friend is murdered."

"I know that." Savannah lurched forward and bumped into John as the tube screeched to a halt at Charing Cross. For every person who left the train, two more got on. John and Savannah fought hard to avoid being pushed back into the aisle. Once the train was moving again, Savannah continued her defence, "Don't make out that I'm heartless. I just haven't had much luck with men and you started off as strange and got weirder by the minute."

"Thanks."

"You're welcome."

For the rest of the short trip John was unable to concentrate on making small talk with Savannah. Instead, he found himself constantly moving his head to view movements caught in the corner of his vision. While he did this, his mind attempted to picture the two men who had escorted him to the underground at High Street Kensington. Unless they had changed out of their big navy blue coats, he should have no difficulty in spotting them.

*

I follow Johnson into Waterloo station. Wilson is not with him. He parks across two other cars, blocking them both in. An official walks over to the car, chest out, radio in hand. He is in for a surprise. Johnson exits the car and talks to the man who is six feet tall but dwarfed by the agent. The official walks away down mouthed and chastised. Unfortunately I don't have Johnson's clout. Several cars rush to a space where a blue Jeep Grand Cherokee begins to reverse. I follow suit, jump out and walk calmly to the driver.

I must not cause a scene. I must not cause a scene. Think of the prize. The man is thirty something with a beard and silver-framed glasses. I offer him ten, fifty pound notes for his space and he happily accepts. Three other drivers complain from the safety of their cars. They don't realise this would be their only chance to confront me directly and live. I saunter to each car in turn and hand the drivers one hundred pounds each. Everybody is happy.

I park and return my attention to the Mercedes. I have followed the black saloon from Knightsbridge to Piccadilly and now to here. Each time the car has stopped, Wilson either gets in or out and does his own thing. I have stuck with Johnson. I am agitated and tense at the lack of progress.

Johnson gets out. He must be meeting up with Wilson at the station. My heart races. The gun must be close. I must calm down but my body is alight with tension and excitement. I am breathing too fast and I can't keep my hands still. I light a cigarette and take three consecutive, long, hard drags into my lungs. It doesn't help. I want to call Sasha but there is neither time nor privacy. If I don't call before midnight she won't answer. I promise myself another kill if I miss my deadline. My mind is wandering. I must concentrate. I put out the cigarette and follow Johnson.

*

Waterloo station heaved with late Saturday night travellers.

The left luggage office was easy to find with a huge blue and yellow sign just to the left of the first platform, with a DHL office on its right. The man on the counter was skinny, mid-fifties and had short hair, greying at the temples. He paced back and forth as if bored out of his mind. John instructed Savannah to wait outside and keep an eye out for the two men he had escaped at Kensington. He gave her full descriptions, right down to the shiny black steel-toe-capped boots. At first Savannah didn't appear to be taking him seriously and so he repeated the request a second time.

"I'm on it, Sir," she joked, standing to attention and saluting.

John went up to the counter and handed over the ticket.

"Is this the original ticket mate?" asked the attendant, inspecting it closely. John suspected the man needed glasses.

"Of course," answered John. "Why wouldn't it be?"

"We get a lot of copies these days," he said. "Wives making copies of their husband's ticket to find out what secrets they store here."

"Well that's the original ticket and I'm not married."

"So who's the gorgeous lady waiting outside for you? I should hang on to that one mate, you'll never do better, scruffy lad like you."

It was hard for John to take offence as the attendant was no picture himself and he felt no need to relieve the man's boredom by allowing himself to be dragged into an inane conversation. Besides, John was anxious to pick up the item and get back to the hotel.

"Do you mind? That lady is my sister," John said.

"I do beg your pardon, mate. Let me hurry your collection up." The man turned and fled into the back with his tail between his legs, returning with a hard-surfaced Samsonite briefcase. "Nice piece of luggage that mate, we don't see many of these." He rapped his knuckles on the side as he passed it over to John. "Fireproof, bombproof, wouldn't surprise me if it was waterproof too."

"Thanks," said John, tugging hard to pull the briefcase free from the attendant's reluctant grip.

The case was surprisingly heavy and John's first thought was that it was filled with gold bricks. Everything about the day felt like a movie. John took a deep breath and braced himself before strolling back out into the station. He tried to imagine he was invisible but his pounding heart reminded him he was very much in full view. He felt like a drug courier passing under the green 'Nothing To Declare' sign at Heathrow airport. John turned to his right where Savannah had waited to keep surveillance. He lifted the case to show her how heavy it was but she was nowhere to be seen.

13: Saturday 24th September, 23:00

I see the agents edging towards the girl from either side. She is half my age. Their backs are to the wall as they casually creep ever closer. To a casual onlooker they are stationary. All this time they've been following a girl hardly out of school? Wilson moves with the ease of a much lighter man. Perhaps I underestimated him. The girl is a real looker. Her dark brown hair shines and follows her gaze as she twists her head from side to side. If I didn't have Sasha, I might be interested. The two giants of men are only feet away and still she is clueless. Why do I itch to call out to her? Instead I take a few pictures with my mobile phone.

Johnson is on the girl, pulling her away from the wall. He is strong, very strong. Wilson's hand clasps around her mouth from behind with a cloth and she is out. They keep her upright from either side as they walk her back towards the car park. Nobody notices that her head bobs like her neck is snapped.

I notice her coat and my heart hammers against my rib cage. The black coat is a man's and is far too big for her build. It could easily contain the briefcase beneath. Why else wear an oversized coat? And surely the agents would not risk an open manoeuvre unless the incentive was known. I am convinced. My time has come and I am prepared. I grab a Marlboro Red and suck on it greedily as I follow the agents. I take up position behind a station pillar. It gives me perfect sight and cover. I dip into my raincoat pocket and feel for the detonator. My hands are shaking.

*

With the briefcase returned to the left luggage office, John Smith ran the length of every platform, peering into train upon train. Breathing heavily, he headed to the car park. Where was she? He didn't think for a second that she'd had a change of heart. If she'd wanted to leave him with the money that she still held, then he'd already given her every opportunity. He wouldn't have blamed her and a part of him might have been relieved that she was safe from further harm. He surprised himself with the strength of feeling he was experiencing over her disappearance. After only one day - and a night - she had become the most important person in his life. He had to find her.

*

Savannah awoke to the pungent smell of leather. Her head pounded like a hangover sent from Hell. She opened her eyes to find herself in the back of an expensive-looking car. Without alerting her two captors in the front to her awakened state, she grabbed at the release handle to her right and kicked the door. It wouldn't budge an inch.

"Let me out of here!"

The aroma from the hide upholstery seeped into her nostrils causing her saliva glands to over produce, bringing on an acutely nauseous sensation. An overhead light lit up the dark interior of the car.

She imagined that John would not be too impressed at her discovery of the two men she had been told to look out for. The truth was that they had found her, although how two such large creatures, complete in navy blue coats, had surprised her was a mystery. Her back had been to the large glass window of the left luggage office and she hadn't dropped her guard for a second. An instant later, the two men were on her and a hand lined with a sweet-smelling cloth was forced against her mouth and nose. How long ago was that? John would be miffed. One simple job and she had blown it. She gave the door another kick.

"Don't kick the car," said Mr Tall, who sat in the driver's seat with his head facing forwards. "It lacks the raw power of the old sixty-nine Boss Ford Mustang, but it has a refined quality that calms me."

"What are you talking about?" Savannah kicked the door again. "Let me out of here. I've done nothing wrong."

"The car is soundproofed and blacked out, Miss Jones. Nobody can hear or see you."

"This is kidnapping."

"Don't be frightened, Savannah. We need your help and in return I'm sure that we can help you," said Mr Short from the passenger seat. "If you'll allow us to talk I'm sure that we'll all be the best of friends."

Five kicks later - enough that John could never accuse her of acquiescing - Savannah gave up. "Do I have a choice?"

"Just hear us out," Mr Tall said. "That's all we ask."

"Go on then," she said. "I'm listening."

"Has Mr Smith mentioned us?" Mr Tall asked, shifting in his seat so that he could face Savannah.

"No, he just told me to keep a watch out for two men with navy blue coats."

Savannah yawned. Whatever they had drugged her with had not completely left her system. She was dead beat. The thought of lying down on that king-size bed back at the hotel was more appealing than ever. "Can we get this over with so I can go?"

"Of course," said Mr Tall, his forefinger on his chest. "My name is Johnson ..." He redirected his finger to the passenger seat. "... and this is my partner, Wilson. We work for an international organisation which, unfortunately, I can't tell you about. I can tell you that we are the good guys but I guess that seems kinda unlikely to you now. We've been following Smith to see if he's involved in Mark Bradshaw's murder."

Savannah shook her head and immediately wished she hadn't. "John reckons Mark was murdered but I know he hasn't got anything to do with it. John says his friend was a stock trader or something like that."

"You believe him?"

She thought about it for a second. At first John had been a client, then a madman and then sane but mixed up in a murder. To be fair she had no evidence to support John's innocence and as far as qualifications to judge character went, hers were non-existent. But she knew, not how or why she knew, but she knew. "I don't know much about men but I know he's no murderer," she said.

"Bradshaw's financial dealings were just a front," Johnson said, leaning over into the back of the car and wiping Savannah's footprints from the window and door upholstery with a wet-wipe. Savannah shuffled to her left to give him more room. "Mr Bradshaw had something of ours and we need to get it back before it falls into the wrong hands."

This was beginning to sound crazier by the second. She was lost in a spy movie. "Are you for real?" she asked.

"Very real, Miss Jones." Wilson shook his head at Savannah as his partner almost disappeared into the back as he scrubbed at the door with a fresh wet towel. "It is a matter of life and death."

Savannah resisted the urge to laugh. The day had gotten more surreal by the minute. If this was a joke then her captors showed no sign of humour. Two expressionless faces regarded her, one flat nosed and attempting to smile, and the other almost handsome but somehow non-descript. Was she supposed to speak?

"What do you want from me?" she said.

Johnson disposed of the used towel in a white plastic refuse bag and threw it to the floor in front of Wilson. "What are you both doing at this station?" he asked.

"John suggested a trip out." Savannah looked out of her window at the steady flow of people entering and departing the station's entrance.

"For what purpose," Johnson pressed.

Savannah could not return Johnson's gaze as she struggled to conceal the reason for their late night visit. She began to count the people leaving the station. One, two, three... "Does there have to be a purpose? Look, I hardly know him. We only met last night." Four, five, six...

"Through Aphrodite's Angels?"

Losing count immediately, she whipped her head round to face Johnson. Surprisingly, her headache had subsided. "You know about that?"

"We know everything about you: when you moved from Carmarthen in Wales to Shepherd's Bush, how your mother and father died, the scumbag you now work for... Should I go on?"

"No." Savannah thought for a moment. Here was an opportunity. "Can you sort people out?"

"Christos the Greek, you mean?"

"Yes."

"So he won't bother me again, not ever?"

"If you help us."

Johnson was a mask and impossible to read but she didn't doubt his ability to help her. It was betrayal, pure and simple. Her fear of Christos outweighed her loyalty to John. No torture had been necessary, the chance of starting out again without a pimp in her life had been incentive enough. Savannah told them everything she knew and hoped to God that she hadn't screwed up.

"So you'll sort out my problem?" she asked, having brought them fully up-to-date. Johnson and Wilson hadn't said a word as they listened intently, hanging on her every word.

Johnson exhaled loudly. "We wondered what took you so long in the pawn shop and why the lady in pink came screaming past us outside your bedsit." She detected the twitch of a starting smile and then it was gone - back to business as usual. "John Smith is clearly a resourceful guy," he added.

"How long have you been following us?"

"Since you left Smith's place."

Savannah cleared her throat. They had promised. "About my problem...?"

The tall man looked over to Wilson who nodded.

Savannah nudged Wilson's shoulder to get his attention.

"What are you agreeing to?"

Wilson twisted his neck round to look at Savannah face on. It was the first time she noticed how completely squashed and spread out his nose was. "Help us out and we can help you. I promise that we won't ask you to take any risks."

Johnson confirmed the situation. "Get Smith on board and help us catch Bradshaw's killer and we'll sort Christos for you."

"That wasn't the deal."

Johnson motioned to the car door next to her. "Then you're free to go."

As if by magic the central locking system disengaged with a soft, smooth click. Savannah didn't move. Memories of Christos' threats echoed in her head.

As she spoke, a world of worry dropped from her shoulders, drowning the lingering guilt at betraying John. "I'll do it."

*

John leaned against a pillar and watched a multitude of drivers as they either parked and exited their vehicle or got in and drove away.

If Savannah was on a train, she was either hidden or already gone. Standing still felt like self-torture but he needed to recover his breath. After a minute he began to wander amongst the cars looking into windows, dashing from vehicle to vehicle like his life depended on it. It was hopeless. He was about to give up when he saw the black, shiny Mercedes with blacked-out windows thirty feet away. It probably just belonged to an Arab dignitary but it warranted closer inspection. What else did he have to go on? He looked around to ensure he wasn't being watched.

Two pillars across from where he had been stood moments earlier, he saw a tall black-haired man smoking a cigarette. It wasn't the fact that it was a no smoking area, as was the whole station, but the fact that the man's face was bright red and he was staring at the black Mercedes with more than a passing interest. This guy was no traveller or train spotter.

John returned to the pillar and continued to watch the unusual-looking man. He wore an old-fashioned raincoat with the collar turned up. When he wasn't dragging on his cigarette or lighting another with the stub of the previous one, his hands were permanently embedded in his pockets.

John fathomed from his new vantage point that one side of the man's face was normal and the right-hand side must have an unusual birthmark or have suffered horrific burns. His hair was so jet black that it was probably dyed. With the face half deformed and the collar turned up, it was hard for John to establish an age but somehow the way he smoked the cigarette and how he huddled in the cold night air, put him in his fifties at least.

*

Do I wait for the girl to leave or enter the code now? I am in control of three lives. To them, I am God. My chest rises and falls too quickly. Calm down. Focus on the prize.

A man in in his mid-twenties wearing jeans and an old blue anorak runs from car to car. His head jerks in all directions. Is he lost? He is drunk or stupid or both. Homeless and looking for hand-outs perhaps? He leaves and I return my attention to the Mercedes.

Minutes pass. What are they doing? I light cigarette after cigarette and breathe cancerous fumes until my throat is dry and raw. I glance around the station at the ignorant public. The thought makes me squirm with pleasure. The explosion will be massive. Others may be caught in the blast. I am their God too.

Bradshaw said that the briefcase could withstand an explosion. Now was the time to test his boast. Hand and detonator leave my pocket. I hold my breath and press buttons as I take cover behind the pillar. Tap, tap, tap, tap. My bladder aches with excitement. It will have to wait. I peer round the pillar. I press SEND.

*

John saw the man's head reappear from behind the pillar and stare at the car more intently than ever. John turned to the car. A huge plume of flames erupted from its undercarriage, engulfing all other cars within a fifteen feet radius, and with an ear-deafening, window-crashing explosion, the car rose twenty feet into the air before landing again, four mini explosions ringing out like gunfire as the tyres burst under the impact. Incredibly, the blacked-out windows remained unscathed.

"Nooooo!" screamed John, running towards the flames.

He got to within five feet but the flames licked upwards around the doors preventing him from getting any closer. He looked around for a fire extinguisher and caught the look of exhilaration on the face of the black-haired man as he watched from behind the pillar. He'd done it. John was certain.

"That's him. He's the bomber," John shouted, pointing at the man. "Call the police."

Aware that all eyes were on him, the man sprinted away from the station, head tucked into his coat as he fled. Based on the man's speed and ability to weave around or jump over obstacles, John reassessed his age. Early thirties, he concluded.

Reluctantly, John's eyes left the escaping bomber as he once again sought the whereabouts of a fire extinguisher. He saw a glint of a red cylinder across the station through the arches and he ran for all he was worth. He ripped the extinguisher from its brackets and supported it on his shoulder as he returned to the fire. There were screams and panic around him but he focussed only on the flames before him. If anything it seemed like the fire was raging hotter or was that just the added heat from his fifty yard dash?

He dropped the extinguisher on its circular base, pulled the pin and squeezed the black plastic handle on the top of the cylinder. Immediately, white powder erupted from the short, flexible nozzle, covering the dancing flames and almost instantly snuffing out their life. John picked up the canister once more and circled the vehicle, keeping the handle squeezed hard so that the spray was continuous. It seemed like forever but yet in under a minute all the flames were gone, leaving a badly charred car body with huge paint blisters and melted tyres, which smouldered with black, acrid fumes.

John reached for the rear door handle but it was still red hot. He pulled the sleeve of his hoodie down so it covered the palm of his hand and he tugged at the handle. It wouldn't budge. What could he do? His heart banged like it wanted to break through his chest. Adrenaline made him stronger and keener but he was still powerless. He rammed the fire extinguisher base into the black window but it bounced off just as worthlessly as he had bounced of Mark's door that morning.

"Oh God, no, no, no," he wailed, tears welling in his eyes, rage building to bursting point. It had been too long. No one could have survived that heat. "Savaaaaannaaaaaah!"

John's body slumped in defeat, his rage requiring redirection. The man in the black coat had killed Savannah. Clenching his fists he banged his knuckles together. This man must pay. His hatred refuelled his tired muscles and he readied himself to chase down the perpetrator of his desolation. What was that sound? It was the click of the car's front door opening. The tall man from this morning pushed open the door fully. He looked completely unscathed.

"We meet again," the tall man said, one long leg following the other as he stepped out of the car. He frowned at John. "Savannah's just fine and will be out in a sec." He moved towards John and patted him on the back. "Great show you put on there. Completely unnecessary but great all the same." His mouth turned down as he gazed at the smoking vehicle. "That car was modified to survive bigger blasts than that one."

John wasn't paying much attention. His focus was fixed on the car and when the back door popped open, he jumped. Savannah exited the smouldering car. She had never looked better. It was like she had just arrived at a world premier and was the star of the show. She looked excitedly at John.

"Did you see that? We went miles in the air and were on fire for ages. We never even felt the heat." She put her hand to her mouth to hide a broad grin. "Oh my God, John. You're covered in soot."

John was so happy to see Savannah he couldn't care less what he looked like. The grief followed by instantaneous relief sent his mind reeling. All he could do was grin like the cat that got the cream.

Sirens sounded and flashing lights approached as the tall man's stocky partner appeared from the far side of the car.

"I'll sort out the authorities, Johnson," he said, motioning to the myriad of blue flashing lights. "They prefer to deal with one of their own. Why don't you get these two back to the hotel and I'll catch up with you there."

John caught a fleeting glimmer of uncertainty in the eyes of Johnson before Savannah tugged at him for attention. He hadn't even saved her so why had he become Mr Popular all of a sudden?

*

I veer into a dark and narrow side street.

My gut churns with acid born of hate and failure. I rip the prosthetic skin from the right-hand side of my face and pull the black wig from my head. They itch like crazy. It's all theatrics to keep under the radar but it works.

A constant stream of Saturday night revellers pass the street's entrance, oblivious to my presence. They laugh, scream and stumble from the effects of alcohol as they go about their pseudo pleasures. I want to kill somebody to vent my frustrations. There are too many witnesses. It is a risk I cannot take.

I throw the skin and wig into a plastic wheeled bin. The raincoat and detonation device follow. I pick up the petrol can from where I'd left it, unscrew the top and empty the contents into the bin. Stepping back I light myself a Marlboro Red and toss in the stainless steel Zippo lighter. I turn in time to feel the heat from the flash of flames on the back of my sweatshirt. I head towards the far end of the street without looking back. The warmth on my back is soon removed by the chill of the air but the heat of festering vengeance burns as strong as ever. One way or another, I will have the weapon.

14: Saturday 24th September, 23:35

My jaws are clenched, my muscles tight. I walk stiffly to a seat in a dingy Bayswater diner, a stone's throw from my hotel. I'm not sure which of the two rat holes smells worse. This place is known only as 'The Pit'. Whoever named it wasn't kidding around. This was the price of anonymity - hanging with the lowlifes. A smell of rancid fat and stale onions hangs heavy in the air. I doubt it will leave my clothes when I return outside.

I look at my stainless steel Seiko watch, a present from my Mother when I joined the Parachute regiment over twenty years ago. I wear it to remind me never to bend to anyone else's will. A lesson she never learnt. It is half past midnight, nearly two hours after the explosion.

Two men sit, side by side, at the table by the exit. Their smiles are wide and their faces close. They are gay. I cannot hear their lewd conversation - probably discussing flavoured lubricants. I don't mind their kind but they should keep it to the privacy of their own homes. There is no need to rub it in people's faces. Failure has made me less tolerant than usual.

I had suspected extra reinforcement underneath the Mercedes and made adjustments accordingly. The explosion should have torn through the undercarriage like butter, but instead the car had risen like a NASA rocket launch.

Perhaps attempting to disintegrate the occupants had not been my best plan. It had been risky, careless and worst of all, unsuccessful. Nobody could have been badly harmed and I am now public enemy number one. But it could have worked and if it had, I would have the gun and the agents would be out of the picture. Missing out on torturing the two fools to their slow and ultimate deaths would have been a small price to pay for the ultimate pleasure the gun promises.

A young girl in an orange uniform requests my order without speaking, simply grunting and displaying a readiness to write on a dog-eared pad of paper. Her plastic nameplate is skewed. It says her name is Olga. She is sixteen, at the most, with short blonde hair and the blank stare of a person without hope. I could snuff out her pointless existence and we would both benefit from the transaction.

I have bigger plans and the temptations that constantly appear must be avoided. I see needle tracks on the inside of her elbow. Her worthless life of drugs, alcohol, and unprotected sex in parked cars will continue. One day soon, one of her indulgences, necessary to dull her inescapable insignificance, will end her wretched being. Self-destruction is inevitable. I order a cup of tea and a salami sandwich.

Who was the scruffy kid in the anorak? I'd written him off as a threat and he'd given me away. He'd been frantically looking for something or someone. I can't picture anything but slim, mid-twenties, shortish hair, ripped jeans and an old blue anorak. Is he with Earthguard or the girl perhaps? Yes, the girl. He had looked harmless. He is a possible danger to my goal. I had let the excitement get the better of me. It is a mistake I will not repeat.

The orange waitress slams down a cracked plate beneath a withered-looking sandwich. An overfilled mug of tea, the colour of oxtail soup, follows.

"Anything else, Luv," she says, hands on hips as if daring me to ask for something else at my own peril.

A smile, a decent plate, bread instead of cardboard, a cloth for the mess of spilled tea? The possible responses are too many.

"Nothing," I reply, looking deep into her tired blue eyes, wondering if I should ask her back to my hotel and snap her neck. I decide against it. She will not get a tip.

I pull out my phone and flick through the photos of the girl. The resolution is good. She has a face and a physique easy to remember. Living amongst the lowlifes has given me contacts and she will be easy to locate. The girl will lead me to Anorak man. Between Anorak and the girl I can extract enough

*information to lead me back to the agents and the weapon. Four deaths to
enjoy along the way.*

*I hold my breath for a moment and close my eyes. I let the pleasurable
tingles overtake me. Sasha pops into my head. It will be past midnight when I
get back to my lousy room. I will not get to hear her voice until tomorrow. The
tingles fade.*

*

Back at the Ritz in their junior suite, discussions were getting heated as John
and Savannah listened to what the two Earthguard agents had to say.

They surrounded a small coffee table in the seating area of the suite.
Through much of the conversation John's eyes had been drawn to the
executive-looking case sitting under Johnson's chair, next to a black Nike
sports bag. It was the case he had temporarily returned to the left luggage
office while he searched for Savannah at Waterloo Station. The most deadly
firearm the world had ever seen, Johnson had said. Designed by Mark
Bradshaw he had said. Other than that, the two men had told them next to
nothing.

John noticed the tall agent's attention was on him from the corner of his
eye. It seemed that the American was reading John like a book.

"Don't ask us anything about Bradshaw or the gun," he said. "We are not
authorised to share this information with you."

John tensed. How many times had he reeled that line off? Mark was gone
and, while insanely curious about the death of his best friend and what he
had invented, his current concerns involved the living, particularly
Savannah and himself. "You nearly got Savannah killed for God's sake," said
John, waving his finger at Johnson and Wilson.

"Like my partner has already explained," began Wilson, "the car was
reinforced to withstand far greater blasts than that one."

"What if she'd hit her head inside the car and got concussed or broken
her neck?"

"I'm fine John," interrupted Savannah who looked exhilarated by the
whole experience, almost glowing from within. John noticed that the two
agents could barely take their eyes from her. She was like one of those
ultraviolet insect exterminator gadgets whose light lured unsuspecting
insects into its deadly centre. John on the other hand was drained, ragged,
and struggling to get a grip on reality.

Savannah, who was seated to his right, grabbed his hand and squeezed it. "We've landed in the middle of something bigger than us and we've got a chance to help. Aren't you keen to bring Mark's killer to justice?"

John raised his eyebrows and looked to the ceiling. He pulled his hand away. "Whoever set off the explosion is not playing games. He didn't blow up the car for a prank. Whatever these two tell you, we're in way over our heads and our lives may well still be in danger."

She regarded him like a star-struck fan meeting her favourite rock star, eyes wide, lips slightly parted, mind searching for the right words to say. "And there you were, putting out the fire and trying to get me out."

"Which you didn't need by all accounts," John reminded her.

"But you weren't to know that. To me, you're a hero."

John blushed and looked away. It was true that a part of him also felt the rush of adrenaline that had so obviously affected Savannah. He couldn't deny that he had felt more alive today than at any time in the last ten years. The difference was that *he* refused to allow it to overtake him. Until today, John's life had been risk free and comfortable and now it was riddled with excitement and extreme danger. Who in their right mind would make that trade?

It was okay for Savannah. Her life was a mess of massive proportions and by agreeing to help these so called secret agents, or whatever they were, her life would be drastically improved. That was assuming that they kept their end of the bargain, of course. Risk your life for a new start. It wasn't a bad deal, although no mention of the odds of survival had been floated by Johnson or Wilson. Savannah would no longer need help, not even from John. And what was John's upside? There wasn't one, but the downside was bleak and permanent.

"I'm just saying that we could take care of Christos on our own." John glared into Johnson's eyes as he spoke. The man remained as expressionless as ever, a great poker prospect if ever there was one. "We've still got enough cash to pay his thousand pounds and if he refuses then we'll take it to the police."

Johnson remained motionless, back and shoulders relaxed, his hands on the arms of the chair, fingers hanging loosely over the ends. "Now that we have the gun, we can make sure that it's returned to safety but make no mistake ..." he narrowed his eyes and they looked right into John's, "...

anyone who will blow up a car in the middle of a busy station is not going to give up real easy."

"I just love that accent. Don't you love that accent, John?" Savannah asked, tugging John's hoodie sleeve.

"Jesus, Savannah, what planet are you on? How can you think this is a good idea?" John tore his sleeve free and addressed the two agents. "You have no idea who this guy is and all you can be sure of is that he wants the gun which you now have. I see no reason why we need to be involved at all."

But Savannah was relentless. "Because, if this guy wants the gun so badly then he's planning to kill with it. We could save lives."

"And end ours."

"Don't be such a baby, John. I didn't take you for a coward."

It was no good arguing. Suddenly, the hero worship made sense. Savannah would do anything to enlist the help she needed to safely end relations with Christos.

Wilson stood up, taking in the decor as he spoke. "I should listen to your friend, Savannah. There are always risks." Savannah sat back in the chair like she'd been slapped down to earth. "But what I should also point out is that if you don't help us ..." his eyes honed in on John, "... then your lives will still be in danger. With or without us this person may well target you. But if you do decide to help, then at least you'll have us to protect you." The stocky agent sat back down.

John retaliated. "He has no interest in us. You're just trying to scare us into helping you."

"He's seen you both and must assume that you're with us."

John didn't like the sound of that. Not one little bit. "Something stinks," he said.

"We can't force you to help us, John," Johnson said. Wilson gave him a curious glance and shrugged his shoulders. Clearly the two were not in agreement on this point. "Sorry," Johnson corrected. "We can force you but my partner and I choose not to." Wilson shook his head but didn't interrupt. "It's a shame, Smith. I saw great things in you. You've helped Savannah here out of three scrapes today: you saved her from being sexually attacked by George Tibbett, a convicted rapist and fence; you recovered her passport by pretending you were about to burn her bedsit buddy alive and you were willing to risk your own life to save her from the burning car. I'd say that showed great promise."

"And I'd say that you know an awful lot about our day," John said.

"Of course we do. You never escaped from us in the subway, sorry ... underground. As soon as we entered the crowd, I remotely unlocked your handcuffs, and we picked you up again back at your flat."

John scowled at Savannah. "Did you know about this?"

Savannah looked away. Johnson continued.

"Come on, Smith," Johnson got up and with one stride was standing over John. "I sense a great deal of sarcasm from you and while my partner tells me that this is a British pastime, I'm getting the hint that you'd rather we weren't around. Now that's fine and dandy and we'll leave you to it but I have to say I'm pretty disappointed in you."

Johnson's remark sounded just like John's mother and the words, although said without malice or his mother's theatrics, stung every bit as hard. It had been a mad day and so much crazy stuff had happened. He needed to sleep on it and, judging by Savannah's outrageous behaviour, she needed to sleep more than he did. In the cold light of day they could make a rational decision. Most of all he needed to talk sensibly to Savannah without their intrusion. Whatever they had filled her head with in the car had done its job. If he could just buy them a little time alone.

"Just give us until noon tomorrow," he said, flexing his hands.

"What for?" the American retorted, still hovering over John where he sat.

A good question that was best lied to or skirted around.

"I want to see if we can sort out the Christos situation by ourselves."

"Why?" Johnson asked.

"Because if we can't deal with a regular creep then how are we going to deal with a cold-blooded killer?"

Savannah stared at John like he had murdered a close family member. Johnson's brow creased, his gaze wandering from his partner to Savannah and back to John.

"On one condition," he finally said, his face returning to its expressionless state.

"What's that?"

"You wear one of our standard issue watches."

"So you can listen in to what we say or track us in another way or ..." John puzzled over the reason behind the condition. He was only half serious with his final guess, "... blow us up remotely?"

John swore that Wilson nearly smiled but Johnson's unreadable stare registered so little it could have been painted on.

"The watch can only be activated by the user," he said. "If you make your decision sooner, activate it, and we'll be with you in less than ten minutes." The tall American dragged the Nike sports bag from underneath the seat he had left and plonked it on the coffee table. Unzipping the black leather bag he said, "Another Rolex Daytona, like the one you sold?"

John leaned forward in his chair and gazed into the bag. There was a selection of fine watches still in their perfect and elaborate packaging. John was lost for words.

"These are the originals but better." Johnson chucked him a green cardboard box just like the one his parents had presented to him after graduating top of his class at Oxford University. "You'll find *that* Daytona keeps far better time."

John's Daytona had always lost about a minute a week. He had returned it during the warranty and it had come back unchanged. He opened the box to reveal another dark wooden box inside. Opening the wooden box, he took the shiny watch from the felt-covered holder and snapped it on his wrist. It was the exact model he had sold to Tibbett, the pervert. If anything, it was slightly heavier than his old watch, which might have kept poor time but had the heft of quality. It was nice to feel the familiar added weight back on his wrist.

"How'd you know it never kept good time?" he asked.

"My own experience. Rolex can sell them regardless and the cost of making them more accurate isn't worth the hassle or investment. We need one hundred per cent accuracy in the field. Our design teams take them apart, improve them and chuck in a few extras while they're at it."

John admired the gold and stainless steel timepiece which had been pre-set to the correct time.

"Just unscrew the start button and press to signal us," Johnson said, zipping up the bag and taking it from the table. "We'll be there in minutes."

"I don't doubt it. Does it still work as a stopwatch?"

"No. Do you need a stopwatch?"

"No."

"All right then." Johnson motioned to Wilson who immediately rose to his feet and collected the case which contained Mark's deadly invention.

"Then we'll see you at noon tomorrow or earlier if you come to your senses."

"I have a condition of my own," John said as the agents headed for the door.

Both men stopped in their tracks. Neither man looked back.

"Don't push it." There was the merest hint of stress in Johnson's words. John wondered if the agent's expression had shifted given that he couldn't see it.

John wasn't going to be fobbed off. "If we agree, I want to know everything about Mark and what's in the case."

The men remained silent and motionless for what seemed like an age. John blew out a slow and constant stream of air until his lungs ached and begged him to inhale. He was certain that, if he spoke next, he would lose the advantage.

Johnson finally spoke. "Okay, you have a deal." Both men recommenced their stride.

Savannah's face was stern and accusatory, her eyes ripping flesh from John's bones. Twenty seconds later, John and Savannah were alone. Twenty one seconds later Savannah spoke. "I hope you know what you're doing, Smith," she said.

"So do I," he said.

15: Sunday 25th September, 01:20

Tiredness enveloped Savannah as she lay in the deep bath covered in citrus and ylang ylang scented bubbles. The bath was so wide and deep that at times she found herself floating and needing to grab the side to steady herself.

She was worried about John. He had been a tower of strength all day. Even when she thought he was truly disturbed, he had continually acted with her best interests at heart. He'd even sold his outrageously expensive Rolex. So what if it didn't keep perfect time? It was a huge gesture all the same. He really was an enigma of the most baffling kind. Could he possibly be right not to trust the two agents? She didn't think so and she didn't understand his reluctance to team up with them. Surely they had a better chance of getting out of this mix-up unscathed with their help than without it.

Savannah fought the compulsion to shut her eyes. Half an hour ago she had been so alert that she imagined sleep to be several hours away, yet the second Johnson had agreed to John's request to deal with Christos by themselves, the familiar lethargy, which accompanied abject disappointment, had returned with a vengeance.

Tiredness won and her eyes closed briefly. Images of Christos and Tibbett flooded her mind, and her eyes popped back open. She pressed the scented bar of soap against the white, complimentary flannel embroidered in gold thread with the Ritz family crest and began to lather up her whole body with suds. She rinsed away the foamy bubbles and repeated the process several times. Each time she pressed a little harder. Not an inch of her skin went unwashed but no matter how much pressure she applied, the feeling of being dirty would not be washed away. She realised that this feeling came from inside and could not be reached with a flannel or even the roughest of brushes.

If she was to feel clean again she would need to come to terms with the events of the day as well as the possible outcomes of the one to come. She would take her own life before letting Christos sell her to the Arabs. Damn John for wanting to take on Christos without assistance.

With two hands on the side of the bath for purchase, Savannah pulled herself upright and showered off the soft bubbles from her body. Her skin was as soft as velvet. No wonder the rich always looked so good. Limitless money could make a princess out of a harridan. If only they had enough money for her to disappear. Maybe they did?

She dried herself with the large, fluffy, white towels but even these hurt when in contact with the places she had scrubbed the hardest. She put on her second set of underwear from Harrods, a soft pink matching set of bra and panties, and stormed back into the bedroom to confront John.

*

"Am I attractive?"

John was on the phone checking his new watch for accuracy against the speaking clock. As he looked up at Savannah, the handset, which had been held in place between his shoulder and his ear, fell to the bed by his side. Savannah stood in front of him dressed only in her sexy underwear.

While John believed the question was delivered with implied ogling rights, the sight of this damp-haired, crazy specimen, who had never looked more beautiful, brought out the bashful in him. Surprised at himself, he turned his head to the right, picked up the phone, put it on the base and concentrated his gaze on the cream-coloured wall.

"Smith, look at me," she bellowed, marching round between John's position on the bed and the wall he was watching. "Am I attractive?" she repeated.

"Jesus, Savannah, what's got into you?"

"Look at me, Smith," she demanded more loudly.

John, concerned that Savannah's volume would only get louder and they would be ejected from the hotel, reluctantly and yet somehow not reluctantly, turned his eyes towards a nearly naked Savannah Jones. Not wanting to be accused of focussing on one particular body part, he attempted to take in the view without moving his eyes but the only way he could manage this was to look beyond her to the wall behind leaving her quite out of focus.

"Very nice," he said. She was doing the hands on her hips thing, obviously waiting for him to continue. "You're a fine-looking woman," he added.

"You're not even looking at me. You're still looking at the wall." She dropped her hands and took two steps closer so that they were only three feet apart.

John looked her directly in the eyes, refusing, however tempted, to be drawn into her game. "What do you want me to say?"

Her hands went back to her hips and he knew that didn't bode well.

"Do you want to sleep with me?"

He spoke before thinking. "I thought I already had?"

"Okay, very clever. Let me put it plainly." She came further forward so that her panties were an inch from his face. He could make out the curls of her pubic hair through the expensive translucent lace. She smelt sweet. John felt his pulse quicken and blood flow involuntarily to his penis. It was true what women said about men being led by their dicks.

She pulled his face into her crotch. "If I have sex with you, will you press the damn button on the watch and get Johnson and Wilson back?" she said.

Each passing millisecond was a giant step closer to the point of no return. John pulled his head back and rolled three hundred and sixty degrees to the far side of the king-size bed in a rapid escape manoeuvre. She jumped on the bed after him, diving and clamping herself around him. She pushed her groin against his. He should have kept his back to her - or should he? There wasn't much by way of a precedent he could draw upon. What a dull life he had led.

"I can feel you through your jeans," she told him. He didn't doubt it.

With one hand she reached behind her back and in a flash her pink lace bra fell away. Suddenly, his mouth was parched, all sign of saliva gone, tongue like a thick-piled carpet. He tried to say 'stop' but the word got caught in the dryness of his throat and came out as raspy groan which may well have given Savannah the opposite signal to the one intended.

Savannah arched her back like a cat making enough room for her hand to slide between them and onto the buttons of his jeans. There was a moment, just a second or maybe even less, when John was no longer in control of the decision and he was at the mercy of one of man's most basic instincts. And then the moment passed.

John pushed Savannah away, rolling off the side of the bed as he did so. Righting himself, he turned and did up the one button of his jeans Savannah had successfully sprung free. He turned back to see her stretched out facing him, on her side, head propped up on one elbow, bottom lip pushed out. Those legs were so incredibly long and shapely, her face so damn pretty, those pert perfectly formed breasts so inviting, her big brown eyes that screamed 'I'm yours go ahead and take me'. What the hell was wrong with him?

"I thought you liked me," she said, smoothing the bed covers in front of her.

"Savannah, what is going on with you?" John grabbed his hoodie, which he had discarded earlier, from a nearby chair and covered her breasts as he sat down next to her. She shuffled over into the centre of the bed, holding his hoodie in place. Her eyes leapt around the room and would not meet his. Her expression reminded him of her look of despair this morning when she had folded herself over to limit her naked body's exposure. Was that really today? No, it was actually yesterday.

John rested his hand on her soft-skinned calf. "I take it that you don't want to see this Christos chap then?"

Her eyes widened in surprise. He was right. He'd hit the nail on the head. "How did you know?"

"From what you've told me so far today, which isn't much, I get the impression that most men have treated you pretty badly."

"So?"

"They promised to help you sort Christos out if we helped them." He studied her face for clues as to what she was thinking and she appeared to be doing exactly the same to him. "You're scared that we can't handle it."

"We can't."

"We've done pretty well so far today."

"Compared to Christos the Greek, George Tibbett is Mother Teresa."

"You think he'd try to kill us?"

"I don't know. You maybe. He wants to sell me to the Arabs for anal sex."

"Is that what he said?"

"He put it a little more colourfully."

John got off the bed and paced around the room. As he walked back and forth in several different directions, he occasionally noticed a faint smell of body odour. After a while, it dawned on him that the heady smell was his. He lifted up his arm and bent his head over to his armpit and sniffed. It wasn't good. Thank God they hadn't had sex. She'd have run for the hills if she'd got a whiff of that. He needed a shower soon, but first he and Savannah needed to agree on a plan of action.

"What if I go and see Christos alone?" he said, stopping at the end of the bed.

"What's wrong with calling the agents?"

"We can't trust them. Think about it. All they want to use us for is bait and if we get killed at the same time, what difference does it make to them?"

Savannah sat up remembering to hold on to John's hoodie just in time. "But Johnson promised that they would sort out Christos."

"And if you're dead, what difference does it make?"

Savannah's mouth drooped and her shoulders slumped as John's blunt remark hit home. She closed her eyes. She looked almost ready to cry. "So what's your great idea?"

"What do you know about Christos?"

"Not much. I'd always thought he was okay until this morning. He was so angry and unstable." She smoothed her eyebrows as she thought. "I know that his wife Helen handles the front end of the business."

"Go on."

"He's racist and he hates Russians, especially." Her eyebrow smoothing became frantic rubbing. "It's more than that... It's like he's in awe of them but at the same time they make him uncomfortable. I'd say he's afraid of them."

"Anything else?" John asked.

"I don't know, Smith. We didn't talk for long. Maybe on our next date."

John returned to his pacing ritual, occasionally pausing and screwing up his face as he sought the solution to their immediate predicament. Savannah watched, waited and at no point interrupted him, replacing her bra surreptitiously while his back was turned. After several minutes John came to an abrupt halt again and waved his hand in the air.

"I've got it," he shouted.

"What?" Savannah asked, jerking her head from the pillow on which it had been resting.

"I've got an idea which if we play it right might just work," he said. "I'm going to take a shower and then I suggest we get a good night's sleep because we're going to need our wits about us."

"Tell me what it is," she demanded, sitting upright, not seeming the slightest bit uncomfortable in her skimpy lace attire.

"After my shower," John said. "I stink."

"Yeah, I was going to say something but I didn't know how you'd take it." She smiled at him and although there was still a hint of a tremor in her voice, she had perked up considerably.

John smiled back. She still looked ravishing. "Very funny," he said.

Savannah's smile faded as another question surfaced. "John?" she asked.

"Yes."

"What if Johnson and Wilson are right and the guy who bombed the car comes after us?"

John's answer came rattling back. "One bad guy at a time, don't you think?"

"Okay," she said, sliding her silky smooth legs off the bed. "You're the boss."

"Yes, I am," John said, his eyes fixed on Savannah as she stretched her arms to the ceiling and then began bending at the waist from side to side in what must have been an exercise ritual of hers. His ethics told him to look away but the rest of him told ethics to take a running jump. "Put some clothes on will you? I can't think with all that flesh exposed," said his mouth, siding with those damn interfering ethics.

*

It is 3:20 A.M. when my mobile rings. Queen's 'We are the Champions of the World' fills the miniscule flea pit that is my room. Freddie Mercury might have gone to hell for his sexual affliction but they would never be short of a good tune down there.

A streetlamp flickers orange patterns onto the walls through moth-eaten, tissue-thin curtains. Wailing tomcats and loud disagreements between passing louts have so far deprived me of my sleep. I should shut the window but the air inside is thick with my smoke and less pleasant odours. I answer the phone.

"It's Black," says the urgent voice.

It is Alan Black, the junkie. In another life he had been a high flyer in the world of finance. Now he only flies after he feeds his habit. Worn out by the age of thirty-five, he's spent the last four years selling information for cash or drugs to whomever would pay for it. He is an information prostitute. I have a 'no junkie' policy but Black is good and he controls his habit better than most. Besides, I need results fast.

"What have you got for me?" I ask, lighting another cigarette.

"I've got a name and I know who her pimp is."

"Don't fuck with me, Black."

"I'm not, this is gold. I promise you." Black sounds excited.

Either he's high or he's beaten the rush on this one. I'm not convinced. "She's no whore. I've seen this girl."

"Word is she's on the market for export. She's valuable stock. We import all the East European trash and export the quality stuff to the Middle East. The market's worth billions."

After a month amongst the criminal fraternity there are few surprises left and yet this revelation disgusts me. The girl's life means nothing to me but she seems too good to die in the sex trade.

"You're sure it's her?"

"I bumped into an ex-employee of the pimp. He runs an upmarket escort agency. He'd tossed her onto the streets penniless. She's past her prime and is almost giving her services away. I showed her the photographs and promised her fifty when I got paid. You should have seen the look on her face when she saw your girl, it was priceless. I'm telling you this is gold, my friend."

No junkie is any friend of mine and I bet that his source would never get to see that fifty. A junkie's promise was as reliable as a Roman Catholic priest's vow of chastity. "I'll give you five hundred for it," I offer.

"I want two large. No one else can give you this. Turn it down and the trail goes cold. It's gold I tell you."

"What's her name?"

"Savannah Jones."

Savannah Jones, Savannah Jones. It sounds exotic and common, all in one. We eventually agree on twelve hundred and I'm happy. We arrange to *meet at nine o'clock inside a cafe just off Piccadilly, not far from where Aphrodite's Angels is located. I throw the phone on the bed and start to sing.*

"We are the champions, my friend."

The wall to my left vibrates as my neighbour beats against it. A muffled and angry voice filters through, threatening bloody violence. I raise my voice.

"And we'll keep on fighting till the end."

Heavy footsteps thud, a door opens and slams. More footsteps before the banging reappears at my flimsy door.

"If you don't shut the fuck up I'm going to break this door down and pull your tongue out your arse."

I haven't heard that one before.

"No time for losers," I sing right on cue. Rather well too.

The door knob turns and a tall black man bursts in. The man stands bare footed in just a pair of jeans. He is big and muscular and wants me to see this. The fact that the door is unlocked is a puzzle to him. This is a man who is not prepared for violence.

"I've no problem with blacks," I say, pointing to the threadbare armchair. "Take a seat."

"What?" says the man, looking around from wall to wall before turning back to me. His gaze meets my eyes and he looks away. He has already lost.

In his late twenties, the man is a good ten years younger than me. In terms of size and build the intruder holds all the cards. He's probably armed - a blade of some sort. Why doesn't he attack me? What is he waiting for? I love playing with people's minds.

"Are you gay?" I ask, as politely as I can.

"Fuck you," the man replies, feeling behind him. He's snarling but he's nervous. A bead of sweat appears on his brow before running and settling in an eyebrow. Perfect. My heartbeat remains slow and constant. I am in charge.

"So nigger, why don't you pull that blade and fuck me up?" I say.

The hand goes to the back pocket. Now my pulse quickens. I take a step forwards. "Go on," I urge, knowing there is a reason I should stop but I'm too far gone to care.

In a flash the knife is out and thrust at my stomach. I step to my right and grab the armed hand as I twist, turning the arm so the elbow faces the floor. My right knee shoots upwards at breakneck speed and makes contact with the outer elbow. Bones snap, crack and splinter in one melded crunching sound as the arm breaks downwards against the joint. The knife falls to the ground.

The man holds his elbow and stares at his horrific injury. He screams. I pick up the blade and swing it upwards in one motion aiming the point underneath the intruder's ribs. I don't know how but I stop myself before the six inch blade touches skin. I throw the knife at the doorframe. It sticks in deep. I grab my pillow from the bed and cover the screams but allow him to breathe.

Ten minutes later I usher the sobbing man out of the building in a makeshift sling. I flag him down a taxi. I give the driver twenty pounds to take him to the nearest hospital. I flash my neighbour a warning look. He knows not to return for two days.

In my room I walk in a small circle. Am I out of control? I hadn't murdered anyone when I'd promised myself a treat to make up for the missed call. I did stop, right? I imagine the sound of the snapping joint and my heart pumps faster. I hear Sasha's soft voice. My hand drops to my crotch and I touch myself.

"Sasha," I say, closing my eyes. I fall onto the bed.

Fifteen minutes later I am asleep, dreaming of my day of vengeance.

16: Sunday 25th September, 09:00

On Sunday morning in the king-sized bed in one of the junior suites at the Ritz, Savannah Jones awoke with her arm draped over John Smith and her stomach pressed against his back. She disengaged herself, taking great care not to awaken him. She couldn't recall ever having slept so well.

"What time is it?" he asked, as she rolled away.

She jumped. "Don't do that. How long have you been awake?"

"Only about ten minutes. I didn't move because I didn't want to wake you up." John reached over and grabbed his new Rolex. "The time is exactly nine oh one," he announced.

Savannah had bigger worries than the time. "Oh," she managed. How long had she been spooning up to him? Whatever did he think of her? Last night she had offered him sex in return for a favour. Very un-prostitute like, not! Now he had woken up with her attached to him. Get cooler Savannah, she told herself.

"I'm used to sleeping alone," she said. "Sorry if it bothered you."

"Hardly noticed it," John said.

What was that supposed to mean? Was he used to waking up with lots of different women? It didn't seem that way when he had found her in his bed yesterday. Talk about a scene. Then once he knew she was on a rate, didn't his face change. Whatever could have been between them had been destroyed long before she had offered herself in return for the agents' help with Christos. She realised that, even if they got through today and whatever lay beyond, they were never going to be an item.

Savannah's musings were curtailed by a knock at the door. Rather than venture downstairs and eat breakfast with the rich and influential, they had elected to have breakfast in the suite where they could talk about her predicament in private. She had quite fancied a delve into how the rich and successful behaved at breakfast but she doubted if circumstances would have permitted her to appreciate the exercise.

John made no move to answer the door and so she pulled off the covers slid out and did it herself. In the fluffy white dressing gown provided to all guests and worn by both bedfellows, in the agreed pursuit of avoiding further embarrassment, she released the chain from the door.

"Wait a sec," John said.

"What is it?"

"How do we know it's breakfast?"

Savannah sent John an 'are you nuts' look. "Because we ordered it for nine o'clock," she said in answer to his daft question. She gripped the door handle.

"Just humour me and check."

Savannah withdrew her hand and shook her head. She knew that he was right but nobody would be crazy enough to attack them inside the world's most prestigious hotel - would they? She leaned over to the door keeping her feet well back in case whoever stood on the other side attempted to break the door down. It all seemed so bizarre.

"Who is it?" she asked.

"Room service, Madam. Breakfast for two."

Savannah looked back at John who shrugged. What else could she ask? She opened the heavy door slowly, remaining behind it all the time. If they had a gun they could shoot at John first. A smartly dressed man in a dark Ritz uniform entered with a trolley loaded with wonderful smells. There were two tall glasses of freshly squeezed orange juice; two covered plates containing scrambled eggs with grilled bacon, sausage, mushrooms and tomatoes; a pot of steaming-hot tea; two Danish pastries; two enormous muffins and finally, two golden croissants.

If the elderly gent, who kindly unloaded the trolley of its treats and laid them all lovingly out at the dining table for two, was going to murder them, she hoped they could eat first.

"I'm very sorry, Madam," the uniformed man said.

"You are?" Savannah replied, frowning.

The waiter cleared his throat behind his hand before continuing. "As you are cash customers, I'm afraid that management have instructed me to collect payment for breakfast upon delivery."

Savannah and John looked at each other. Savannah remembered that all of their cash was in John's big waxed jacket. She ran to the wardrobe and returned with a fifty pound note which she offered to the waiting employee. He didn't take the note. His training clearly forbade him to show surprise, discomfort or any other emotion that the situation might have been causing him. He was very good at his job.

"Sorry, Madam, but two English Breakfasts at thirty-six pounds each makes a total of seventy-two pounds."

"I'm sorry," she said returning to her hanging coat. "I thought I'd picked up a five hundred pound note."

What had she just said? She knew there was no such note, right? She looked at John whose mouth had disappeared behind his hand but she could see the laughter in his eyes. Bastard. This time she took small and slow steps on her way back with two fifty pound notes in her hand. She looked into the old man's eyes. There wasn't a hint of emotion in there. She handed him the cash.

"Keep the change," she said.

This time a thin-lipped broad smile stretched across his face giving him the look of a man ten years younger, although, what age that placed him at, she wasn't at all sure. She was a dither with acute embarrassment which the heat from her cheeks confirmed.

"Thank you very much indeed, Madam," he said, backing away. "Thank you very much indeed."

When the door closed behind the waiter John removed his hand from his face to reveal cheeks full of air. Savannah delivered her fiercest stare.

"Don't say a bloody word," she said.

*

A chilly wind greeted John and Savannah as they turned off Piccadilly and into the side street where Aphrodite's Angels was situated. The sun appeared intermittently between fast-moving, cotton wool clouds. As expected the street was quiet, offering little to attract the masses at this time of day.

John's new and improved Rolex Daytona told him it was 9:15 A.M. He unscrewed the smaller button above the winder on the watch. Unlike his original this did not enable the stop/start function but sent a signal to agents Johnson and Wilson. Hopefully, if the need arose to set off the transmission, the pair of agents would make good their promise of rapid assistance. With the button already unscrewed he could now activate the watch without making it too obvious. They stopped one door down from their destination and peered into the window of the independent travel agents.

Savannah wore John's black coat over her new black dress. John wore the jacket, shirt and trousers from Harrods. He could have done with an extra layer to protect him from the cold but his anorak didn't suit the image he was looking to portray. Savannah fiddled with her earlobes in which she had inserted simple gold stud earrings bought on route. Her fidgeting was clearly down to nerves and John could hardly blame her. He put his need to urinate down to the cold but he knew he was kidding himself.

"Remember what I said and we'll be fine," John said, gently taking her hand from her ear.

"They itch. They're probably not even real gold for ten quid."

John spoke slowly and clearly. "Keep calm, Savannah. It's just nerves. You'll be perfect. It will all be over before you know it."

Savannah's reaction was far from calm. "That's easy for you to say. If this goes wrong, I could be in Saudi Arabia tomorrow." She pleaded with her eyes which conveyed emotion more readily and powerfully than any other part of her face. "Couldn't we just run with the money that we've got? Wouldn't that solve all of our problems?"

"And go where?"

"I don't know."

"How long do you think the money would last?"

"I don't know."

"Come on, Savannah. You've been a victim all your life. This is your chance to take a chance on me. I'm scared too, believe me, but stick to the script and we'll get through it together."

She grabbed his hand and held it with both of hers. Her grip was tight and her eyes still begged him to take care of her. "You promise," she said.

"Trust me," he replied. He had said the same words many times to his parents and probably to others. For the first time in his life he meant them.

The shop front of Aphrodite's Angels consisted of two large glass panes, from floor to ceiling, and a pair of electric sliding doors with long vertical brushed-aluminium handles at their centre. The glass alone looked thick enough to stop bullets but in addition there were steel security shutters and an alarm system for after hours' protection. Did the escort business have after hours? Wasn't it a twenty-four-seven kind of industry?

Each spotlessly bright pane had a larger-than-life, large-breasted silhouette of a model in hot pink below 'Aphrodite's Angels' which was written with an exotic font in the same brash colour. Savannah slid her arm through John's as they entered the escort agency. It wasn't how John had planned it but it didn't look out of place. He gritted his teeth, hoping that her action was down to nerves and she would keep to the script from now on.

As the doors swished together behind them, Savannah nudged John at once to signal that it was Christos's wife behind the large contemporary desk. The plump woman with long straight dyed-black hair looked up when they entered. John reckoned she was in her mid-thirties. A quizzical look appeared on her face but she said nothing and soon returned her attention to the glossy magazine she was holding.

A plasterboard-walled office to the right of Christos's wife took up one-quarter of the available space. The remaining floor area formed an 'L' shape around the office where the more secretive business was undoubtedly processed. The floor was covered in a cream carpet so thick it significantly gave when John walked on it, like old wooden flooring but without the spring. The walls were painted in a soft pink and carried large framed photos of the prize girls on offer. A black leather sofa leaned against the right-hand wall a few feet away from the office. The office door was to the right of Christos's wife. John wondered if his plan had backfired and Christos was waiting inside.

Wandering around the floor area, they stopped occasionally to look at the hanging photographs. The women were obviously made up to the nines and airbrushed before being given their space on the wall. Such creatures were not natural beauties but the result of breast implants, beauty products and Photoshop effects.

John softly tugged Savannah in the direction of the desk where they occupied the two soft-cushioned black chairs. He felt her tremble through the big coat. He hated himself for putting her through this but the fear suited her role. John spoke in a thick Russian accent, stolen and spliced from many an old Cold War movie.

"You are Helen, no?"

Helen was taken by surprise. She put the magazine in a drawer and sat up straight.

"And you are?"

John held out his hand.

"I am Dmitri Varushkin from Moscow. It is pleasure for me and for you too, yes?"

It took four or five stuttered movements for the chubby hand to grip John's. The woman forced a smile.

"How ... can ... I help you?"

"Straight to point, I like this." John turned to Savannah. "You should be more like this."

John whipped his head back round to the woman behind the desk.

"As you don't like to beat up the bush I will say now what I say." John pulled out a roll of fifty pound notes in the sum of one thousand pounds and planted it on the edge of the desk. He flicked the roll with his finger into the middle of the desk.

"It is like agreement. I pay one thousand British pounds and the girl is mine, okay?"

Christos's wife shot a glance at Savannah and noticed her for the first time since they had entered.

"I think Christos has plans for this one," she said, as she reached for the phone.

John shot forward scaring the woman into dropping the phone. "So girl is lying?" he asked, fury in his words.

He turned to Savannah, his lip curled in a sneer.

"In my country we cut out tongues of liars and make liar eat tongue. It is good job you need tongue to give pleasure to man."

John dry spat at Savannah who looked truly scared. Good girl Savannah. John tapped the desk and stared into the fat woman's blinking eyes. She looked completely out of her depth. He knew how she felt.

"You have money, now we go. All is good, yes?"

"I have to call Christos."

"He is close? I have business."

The woman's bottom lip trembled as she spoke. "I think he is collecting money nearby. I'll call him if you like?"

John banged his fist down hard on the desk and the woman shot back two feet on her wheeled office chair. "Yes, we make drink together to celebrate business."

Both hands of Christos's wife shook as she struggled for her words.

"I will call him from the office."

Not a chance. Forewarned would most definitely be forearmed. She must not leave their sight. John leaned over the desk as far as he could stretch without his bottom leaving the seat. He pursed his lips and narrowed his eyes in an attempt at conveying utter meanness.

"Use this phone," he spat, tensing his face and neck muscles.

"I need the toilet," she whimpered.

"You are trying to renege from deal. In Russia we cut off ears of those who do renege."

"You ... need to talk with my ... husband. I will call from here, but please ... let me go to the toilet."

Gone was the rosy face and disinterested expression from earlier. Christos's wife was teetering on the brink. But John knew that now was no time for backing down. If this was going to work he had to be worse than the enemy and be willing to go way beyond his comfort level. It was the only way to be sure. He picked up the handset of the phone and threw it down on the desk at the woman.

"Call husband here. Piss in bin," he said.

As a trembling fat arm retrieved the handset from the desk, John felt a sharp elbow in his ribs. He barely resisted the need to exclaim. Bloody Savannah. Didn't she remember what was at stake here? He couldn't look at her and risk discovery. One wrong look and their scam was blown out of the water.

Christos's wife dialled her husband.

"There is a man here to see you," she said.

John reached over and punched the hands free option on the base of the phone. Christos's wife flinched and put down the handset.

"Chistos, your good wife she tell me you have plans for girl I have paid debt for?"

"What? Who is this?"

John sat back looking confident and in charge, at least that was the intent. His insides moved around of their own accord and his heart raced. This part was make or break. He imagined how the words sounded before he let them escape from his lips.

"My name is Dmitri Varushkin from Moscow. I pay girl's debt. You agree, yes."

"What girl?"

"Savannah Jones."

The air went silent and thick with anticipation.

"I can be there in fifteen minutes," Christos said, eventually.

"Too slow. I pay one thousand. The girl is mine, do you agree?"

"No."

"You say she is liar?"

"What?"

"Girl tell me you agree, if she pay one thousand she is free."

"She is lying."

"I think you lie, Chistos."

"It's Christos and the girl is a lying bitch but she's mine. I have a buyer and I've taken a deposit for her. I can't let you have her.

"Girl tell me when I have cigarette to eye that you agree one thousand. Waitress also confirm what she say is true."

"What waitress?"

"Waitress at my Pizza Hut."

The air turned quiet again. It was John's turn to elbow Savannah. Savannah immediately began to shriek.

"Christos, don't let him take me. He's an animal. I'll go with the Arabs. I'll do anything but please don't let him take me." Collapsing on the desk, Savannah broke into sobs just as they had planned.

John looked at Savannah and shook his head. "Look she is much trouble," John said, looking directly at Christos's wife. "I will swap her for your fat wife and ten thousand British pounds. I think your wife like the rough stuff, yes?"

Mrs Christos gasped and the line went silent once more. John shot a glance behind him to see if somehow Christos had contacted someone to go to the agency and check on his wife. He knew it couldn't be Christos himself because Savannah had called him earlier to make an appointment in Shepherd's Bush. However it didn't stop Christos contacting his employed thugs to take care of things. His heart thumped quicker and harder as the silence lengthened. The game was up, surely?

"Take the girl and keep the money. She's yours," Christos said.

"Are you sure? I don't mind to take your wife."

"I'm sure. Please don't hurt Helen."

"Okay I am happy. My new bitch will learn to be less trouble in time."

"Noooooooooooo," wailed Savannah.

"Please take her and go," said Christos.

"Chistos, you don't want to have drink and make party? You play with my bitch and I'll play with yours?"

Savannah stomped hard on John's foot. This time a small moan escaped him. His big toe throbbed. He hoped it wasn't broken. Of course this time she was right, they needed to wrap this up. She could have just tapped him though.

"Perhaps another time. Like I say, I have business," he added, reaching over the desk and disconnecting the call, all the time commanding his facial muscles to ignore the pain in his toe.

He grabbed Savannah roughly by her arm and lifted her from the chair as he rose.

"Go make piss now," he said to Christos's wife, whose colour was returning to her cheeks. She looked physically exhausted from her experience, slumped in her chair like she had run a marathon. One more nail was required. "Tell husband if he renege, I will suffocate him with own penis."

She nodded frantically. "I will Dmitri, I will."

"I like way how you say my name, Mrs Chistos."

John picked up the money and with his arm around Savannah's shoulders, bundled her towards the doors. Each time John's injured toe met the floor the pain flared like a miniature explosion forcing him to take most of his weight on the other foot.

An approaching customer, wearing a smart, velour, ink blue Parker jacket with the hood up, moved to his left so that the joined couple could pass through the electrically operated doors unhindered. The man's eyes lingered on John, thin lips offering an oddly crooked smile and for a second John wondered if he knew him. The shadow from the hood prevented John from getting a good look at the man's eyes so he couldn't be sure.

"Later," the man said, as he turned and passed through the open doors.

What an odd thing to say, thought John. Perhaps he did know him.

17: Sunday 25th September, 10:50

I pass Savannah Jones and her companion as I enter Aphrodite's Angels. The man has a limp and an arrogant look about him. He is not the pimp Black described to me. I have told Black to follow the girl and to keep me informed. A large woman sits at a large desk, applying makeup as she looks into the mirror of her compact. She is fighting a losing battle. She is unaware of my arrival. A horse could approach silently on this carpet.

"Where is Christos?" I ask.

The black-haired woman jumps in her chair, dropping her compact. She stares at me in terror. The fat on her arms trembles with fear. Her mouth is open but she is silent. I have not started to interrogate her. She has been worked over already. The young man with Jones is not to be underestimated.

"Who was that leaving?" I demand.

"My ... my husband will be here any minute," the woman says, looking past me at the outside street. She is not in a good way. There is no value in distressing her further. I say nothing and wait. It is Christos I want to speak with.

Ten minutes pass before Christos runs in. He is solidly built and dressed only in black, an attempt at macho no doubt. His hair is oily and he is unshaven. I immediately dislike him. He rushes behind the desk to the fat woman, ignoring me completely. He leans over and puts his arms around her.

"I'm here," he soothes.

She looks up at him, tears rolling down her cheeks. "He said he would suffocate ..." She takes a tissue from a desk drawer and blows her nose loudly. " ... you with ... your own penis."

I smile. "Who was the man that left with Jones," I ask.

The couple turn to face me like they had forgotten I was there. Christos snarls.

"Who the fuck are you?"

I raise my hand. "Calm down. I have a feeling that we can help each other out."

"Like I said, who the fuck are you?" repeats Christos.

"I'm somebody who can help you get the girl back."

"From the Russian mob? I don't think so." Christos strokes his wife's head as she dabs her eyes.

I pull my stiletto knife from its ankle holster. Christos and the fat lady jerk backwards. I throw the blade at a framed photograph of a big-breasted girl with platinum blonde hair on the wall above the sofa. The glass explodes, covering the sofa and carpet. The blade twangs as it reverberates between the eyes of the airbrushed escort. Impressive. I have their attention and I have my patsy.

"Tell me about this Russian," I say.

My mobile rings before Christos can speak. I am bored with Queen now. I must remember to change the ringtone. It is Black with interesting news.

*

Back at the Ritz, John and Savannah were sitting on the bed, buzzing like two highly charged particles. They had raided the miniatures from the mini bar and were having an impromptu party on the bed.

Savannah attempted a Russian accent. "Chistos, you don't want to have drink and make party?" She had to admit it was nowhere near as good as John's. "What were you thinking?"

"I don't know," John said. "I got carried away I guess. My adrenalin was pumping and my heart was beating like I'd sprinted a mile. It was a real rush. That elbow and foot stomping really hurt by the way."

"You were out of control. I mean purposely getting his name wrong. You are a dangerous man to know."

"Heh, we did it, right? At least I didn't try to pay him off with five hundred pound notes."

Savannah laughed louder and longer than she could remember. Their lives were still in danger yet she had never felt so awake, so alive or so grateful. When a shortage of air to the lungs brought her fit of mirth to an abrupt halt, she looked at John as she breathed in.

"Thank you, John Smith," she said. "If that really is your name." She fell backwards on the bed in an even bigger fit of giggles. After only one miniature brandy, she was as high as a kite. The brandy had smoothed down the edges and the exhilaration, born of relief, had flooded out like water from a busted damn.

John put down his drink and lay next to Savannah. She could feel his eyes on her as she stared at the high ceiling.

"I mean it, Smith," she said. "I don't know how to thank you."

"It's not all over yet. We still have the mad bomber to worry about."

"I know but I feel different. You know what you said before we went into the escort agency?"

"I told you yesterday, I can barely remember my name."

"Don't kid around, Smith. You know what you said about me having been a victim all my life?"

"Yes, I remember."

"Well, you're right and now I don't feel like that person anymore."

"That's great." John poked a finger in Savannah's side. "That's for the elbow. I'll get you back later for breaking my foot."

Savannah jumped up and leapt on John's stomach, straddling him and sending the air rushing from his lungs.

"Ooomph! That hurt. Get off me you lunatic."

She looked at his face. His eyes were blue-grey and mischievous, shining with life and vitality, nothing like the eyes that had judged her yesterday morning. Sure he was handsome, but he was also twelve years her senior. Was that perverse? He looked much younger - did that make a difference. Graham had been twenty-seven and looked older than the man beneath her.

"Get off me," grumbled John, making suspiciously little effort to remove her from his person. "Have you got lead in those lanky legs of yours?"

She didn't reply. She was lost in his eyes and everything he had done for her. If she tried to kiss him, would he reject her? Was not throwing her off him a sign that he would like her to kiss him? Shouldn't he make the first move?

She had never trusted or wanted somebody so much than at that moment but it was too important. Yesterday she had been a prostitute. Sure, not a very well paid one, her whole career grossing fifty pounds, thirty of which she gave to that dirt bag Christos. But she couldn't forget the look John had given her yesterday when he realised she was in his bed for money. Could he ever get past that? Could any man? They were proud and strange beasts.

Being sat upon by a silent person was obviously not the correct protocol. "What's up?" John asked.

"Just thinking," she replied.

"About what?"

About kissing him, about whether he found her attractive, about whether he ever could, about how he's the bravest, most selfless man she'd ever met. Not much really.

"Nothing," she said.

He gazed up at her. Perhaps her display of uncertainty was putting him off.

"Your eyes are amazing," he said. "I never saw such bright, shiny eyes in all my life."

That was it - confirmation to proceed. No attempt to shake her off and a compliment about her eyes - it was enough. She leaned forward taking her weight on her arms which she placed either side of John's shoulders. As her face drew closer to his, she hesitated, suddenly nervous and unsure of the advance she was clearly making and the message it gave out.

Her face hovered motionless above John's. His breath was warm and smelt of whisky. Christ, she had to do something now. Warmth in her cheeks, not of the brandy-induced variety, told her that if she didn't go one way or the other soon, her embarrassment would be well and truly on display. John lay still like a lamb to the slaughter - surely another sign? In one slow, smooth and deliberate motion, she planted her lips onto his and rested them there. Her hair fell down around his face like an intimate tent. As his lips pressed back, she was filled with a mixture of happiness, relief and lust. Her heart drummed in her chest every bit as hard and fast as it had in Aphrodite's Angels when she had heard Christos's voice on the loudspeaker.

Their first kiss was soft, tentative and long. When John's mouth opened, Savannah's followed suit and she welcomed his tongue inside. She teased him with her own tongue which darted eagerly around his in a fast, then more measured and sensual motion. Each time her tongue increased its urgency, John's lips would press harder and his breathing became faster.

John raised his head from the bed as his passion seemed to escalate. Savannah sensed that both of their pleasures would be heightened if John was able to move freely. Lifting her left leg over his stomach, he scrambled to his knees and grabbed her by her waist. The straps of her dress fell over her shoulders as John pulled them to each side. She thanked a higher power for the gift of new, sexy underwear from Harrods.

Taking hold of her shoulders, John pulled her towards him and kissed her neck from front to back sending a series of shivers through her that made her squirm with delight. His lips moved to her ear and he breathed heavily. The anticipation of having her ear lobe nibbled by John was unbearable and the shivers continued from the soft touch of his breath on her neck. Most men, and there hadn't been many, ignored her ears, preferring to head straight for the more obvious erogenous zones.

John, thankfully, wasn't most men and was homing in on her second most sensitive area without a single clue. Savannah moaned softly, out of relief as much as pleasure. She had finally come across a man who would treat her right, in and out of the bedroom. But John's teeth never reached her ear and the words he whispered delivered neither pleasure nor relief.

"I'm not paying for this, am I?"

Savannah pulled away, pulled her arm to one side and swung it with every ounce of energy her anger could muster. The flat of her hand hit his right cheek with a resounding slap, such was its force and accuracy. The cheek glowed even before John covered it with his own hand, rubbing, soothing. She felt her own face flush and her anger heighten.

"I thought that you were different. How could I have been so bloody stupid? You're a pig, just like the rest of them."

John stared back, rubbing his cheek, eyes wide and jaw dropped.

"You fucking bastard, you goddamn prick, you mean fucking cunt of a man." Savannah's hands grabbed her hair and pulled. "Is that what you want? Is that how dirty filthy whores talk to their men? Does that get your dick hard?"

John's jaw fell open further.

"Well say something you ignorant son of a bitch. Tell this cheap slut exactly what you think of her now."

Savannah reached over to her right and grabbed one of the huge pillows. As she pulled it to her, John flinched, apparently expecting her to attack him with the feather-filled weapon. The anger was petering out and the hurt was taking over. The hurt churned up her insides until she felt like she would explode. She badly wanted to scream but she wouldn't give him the satisfaction.

God damn him! Others had frightened her, bullied her, cheated her and even died on her. But John Smith had done worse, far worse. He had made her feel completely worthless. Savannah took her pillow, locked herself in the bathroom and cried.

*

As the bathroom door slammed behind Savannah, John finally regained control over his slack jaw, closing it as he continued to rub his smarting cheek. It hadn't been an easy decision to purposely end the excitement and he had to face it, it was the excitement that had worried him the most. He was certain that the sex would have been over very quickly and that would have been the end of it. She wouldn't have been angry and never would have hit him. She would have looked at him with those bloody gorgeous eyes full of sadness for him, because he was a sexual failure, and for her, because he had promised so much, not in words but by his actions. The hero who couldn't satisfy the damsel he saved from distress.

He could have said that he hadn't been with a woman in over a year and that all their near encounters had raised the sexual tension so high he didn't know how to cope with it. Or he could have said that the last woman he had been with was only the second of his life. Both were true, after all. Didn't modern women want the truth? No. Women wanted what they had always wanted from their heroes. They wanted confidence and satisfaction and with John she would have received neither.

John lay back on the bed and considered his next move. He had destroyed everything that could have been and might have been with Savannah. For somebody who couldn't have cared less two days ago, John couldn't have imagined feeling more miserable and dejected. To top it all, her outburst, which some might have thought crass or crude, only made him care about her more. He fully understood why she had reacted with such venom. Those piercing eyes of hers which couldn't lie were unable to disguise the pain he had caused. He made up his mind to split the remaining money with Savannah and to part company at the next opportunity.

*

With a fistful of cash in one hand and the other about to knock on the bathroom door, John was interrupted by a knock at the main door and the shout of 'room service'. What had Savannah done? Spent all their cash on unnecessary food to teach him a lesson? Thousands could easily be paid out on the luxuries available in the hotel. Perhaps she had ordered some medication for a headache? He tapped lightly on the door between them.

"Savannah, did you order room service?"

"Go away," she said, sniffing and then blowing her nose.

"Look, I'm sorry for what I said. I had my reasons and I understand that we aren't meant to be, but there really is someone at the door and I'm not answering unless you tell me that you ordered something."

A few more sniffs. "No, I didn't order anything."

John tried to keep his voice calm for fear that it might carry out into the corridor. "Come on out, I think we're in trouble. We need to get the hell out of here." He tapped again. "Savannah, I'm not kidding."

John heard a crash as the door burst open. He peered round to see the door straining against the brass security chain. He banged harder on the door. "Savannah, they're breaking the door down. Come on."

The lock clicked and Savannah opened the door an inch.

"Are you kidding?"

Another crash echoed out as their hotel door slammed against the inside wall with great force. It was too late. Whoever had been at the door was now inside their suite. John pushed his way into the bathroom sending Savannah backwards.

"What do you think you're doing?" Savannah said, using her hand against the far wall to stop herself.

John locked the door again and cast his eyes around the gleaming room for signs of anything else to bolster the door.

"Pass me the toothbrushes," he said.

The bathroom door vibrated. Someone was thumping at the other side. "Open up, Savannah Jones, this is the police. We know you're in there." The voice carried venom.

John wedged the toothbrushes so they stuck in the gaps below and above the door. It didn't look like they would make much difference. Savannah tapped John on the shoulder with something hard. John turned his head to see a white phone by his ear.

"Call reception," he said, "and tell them we're under attack."

"Is Varushkin in there with you?" asked the voice.

It was Christos's men. They must have followed them back from the escort agency. But why wouldn't they have dealt with them outside the hotel? Surely this was insanity. The real police could arrive at any second.

"Reception says they are the police," Savannah informed John.

John pulled Savannah to him and whispered in her ear. "They don't know that I'm in here so keep them talking while I think."

She nodded, seeming steadier than she had been in Aphrodite's Angels.

"I've done nothing wrong so why should I come out?" she said, shrugging her shoulders at John. He nodded. "What am I charged with?"

While Savannah played for time, John tried to get an outside line on the bathroom phone. No luck. The hotel had presumably disabled the service at the request of the fake police officer. A thought occurred to John and he whispered in Savannah's ear again. She mouthed silent agreement.

"Who's the other officer with you?" she asked.

"I beg your pardon?" returned the voice.

"You said 'We know you're in there.' So who's the other part of the we?"

"It's just a figure of speech." A pause then, "We always say we. If you don't open up, I'm afraid I'll have to break the door down."

"Don't you mean we?" she said.

Then Savannah jumped up like she had seen the ghost of a despised relative. She grabbed John's wrist and tugged him towards her almost tripping him up in the process. She tapped his new watch and John, picking up on her manic gestures, immediately pressed the button to alert Johnson and Wilson.

John's stumble had been heard through the door. "Is there someone in there with you, Miss Jones? If Dmitri Varushkin is in there also, then we have some questions for him too. I'm not sure you realise what serious trouble you are both in."

What if Johnson and Wilson were out of range? Even if they were in range, what if they were half an hour away?

"Time's up, Miss Jones," said the voice.

The door shook as a foot began to methodically kick it midway up its height. The two toothbrushes wedged at either end fell away in seconds. John picked up a toothbrush, wedged it back in the bottom gap and pulled it up until it snapped. He looked at the result in his hand - useless. He chucked the half length of toothbrush in the bath and gathered the second unbroken one from the floor. This time he wedged the end into one of the sink's hot taps, leaving his fingers close to the end so that the pressure remained close to the inserted end when he levered the toothbrush upwards. It snapped perfectly leaving a sharp plastic tapered end. It was no knife but it was a weapon of sorts. Another kick landed and the lock rattled meekly, indicating its intention to give up on the next blow.

"Don't kill them," ordered the voice.

So there were two of them. Was one of these men the rain-coated man from the station? If so how did he know about Varushkin? John signalled to Savannah to stand to the right of the door and open it on his signal. He wondered if she'd understood his frantic gesticulations as he took position on the left. A loud crack accompanied the sound of smashing glass and a bullet blew a four inch hole in the bathroom door, sending splinters of wood into the air between them. A tile behind disintegrated as the bullet passed through it, adding ceramic powder and tiny pieces of tile to the airborne mass.

Christ, now they were shooting too. John looked at the wall where the bullet had hit. There was a huge hole and no sign of a bullet. What were they using, an elephant gun? They were dead for sure. John looked at Savannah, feeling an urgent need to apologise to her but she was busy. What was she doing? She was opening the door!

"No," he yelled.

But it was too late. She pulled the door wide open at the instant Christos's foot appeared, followed by his leg and his body. The look on Christos's face would have been comical if their situation had not been so dire. Without the resistance of the door to absorb the energy from his kick, Christos was travelling uncontrollably forward and downwards with his mouth open in a mixture of anger and surprise. Christos's trunk reached an angle of forty-five degrees to the floor at the exact moment that his left knee hit the ground. John, timing his swing to perfection, plunged the broken end of the toothbrush deep into the side of the man's neck.

John was transfixed by the sight of the writhing, black-clad figure on the floor as he coughed out blood and pulled frantically at the well-embedded toothbrush. Savannah began to scream when a further crack rang out to the sound of smashing glass and a second bullet blew another tile on the back wall to smithereens.

Savannah sensibly leapt into the bath and made herself into a tight ball. John could not reach the bath without crossing the doorway and so lay flat on the ground on his side of the door, inches away from the bubbling-mouthed pimp who still tugged away at the green plastic handle in his neck. He heard movement in their suite followed by another gunshot and another, exploding glass and ... a wall in their suite taking two bullets?

Another flurry of running feet, another gunshot, another explosion of glass and a thud of a striking bullet even further away from the bathroom followed. Whoever was shooting was not aiming at them but at the man who had impersonated a police officer and sent Christos after them. Johnson and Wilson!

John stood up and brushed himself down or rather dusted, as his smart attire was covered in a very fine powder. Christos finally clawed the offending object from his neck, sending a thick jet of blood five feet across the bathroom where it splattered against the white tiled wall. John heard Savannah's bare feet squeak against the bath's surface as she pushed herself upright.

"Don't look Savannah," he said, placing himself between her and the moaning Christos. The jets of blood, which gushed in time with each heartbeat, quickly lost their zeal and diminished to a dribble. With great urgency, Savannah leapt out of the bath and knelt beside Christos's head. She slid her hand underneath his flabby cheek which rested in a bright red pool of his blood and turned his head so that she could look into his eyes. John could see that the light in him was fading rapidly.

"You piece of shit," she exclaimed. "We made a deal."

John had seen more emotions in Savannah's dark eyes than he had seen in the rest of the world's eyes put together but this look frightened him the most of all. Even after the dying man's eyes dulled over and the Grim Reaper collected his soul, Savannah continued to meet his empty gaze. Her lips were pursed tight, eyes narrowed, breath like a snorting dragon, her beauty gone, seemingly sucked temporarily into a place so dark it might well have tainted her soul.

John placed his hand on her shoulder. "Savannah." He shook her gently but she didn't respond. "Savannah," he repeated, shaking her a little harder.

She turned to him, dropping the dead man's head back into the pool of blood. Her eyes were directly on him but didn't see him. She stood and walked out of the bathroom with a face as drained of blood as the body on the floor. He followed her past the bullet-damaged door into the suite. The two other bullets had torn similarly sized holes in the seating area, one five feet from the bathroom and the other close to the main door which was now wide open.

Jagged pieces of glass lay on the floor by the windows opposite the bathroom and beyond, and plaster dust filled the air. A few pieces of furniture were out of place where their other attacker had used them for cover as he made his getaway.

Savannah sat down on the bed and instantly stood up again as if the bed was electrified. She relocated to a chair in the seating area. John assumed her change of mind was due to the memory of their jettisoned love making, although her eyes were still distant and giving nothing away. The image of her face at the moment he had sabotaged their intimacy was far clearer and more painful to him than the memory of the danger they had survived only moments ago.

A knock at the door caused John to duck down instinctively. The memory of the exploding walls and gushing blood might not be so engrained on his memory as the anguish on Savannah's face but the incident had affected him. He straightened his legs the second he saw the two dark-coated agents watching him from the doorway.

Both men resembled undertakers rather than city bankers arriving for an important meeting. Wilson, the shorter man by nearly a foot, carried what appeared to be a case for a large musical instrument at his side. John suspected that the hard black case contained the large-bored weapon they had used to scare off the intruder.

Johnson inspected the nearby bullet hole with his fingers before turning his attention to Savannah who stared beyond a wall, mouth loosely open, arms limp by her sides.

"I think we need to reappraise our relationship," Johnson said.

18: Sunday 25th September, 12:30

Outside is overcast with dark and threatening clouds. My room is gloomier and appears smaller than ever. I don't bother turning on the light. The room suits the dark. It hides the stains on the sheets and carpet, the dust on scratched surfaces and flaking yellow paint on the walls. I sip my takeaway coffee from 'The Pit' and grimace as I swallow. It tastes like Olga has pissed in it. I put down the polystyrene cup on the bedside table and sit on the bed. I light a Marlboro Red and take a deep drag to take the taste of the coffee away. It doesn't help.

It was clear that Earthguard had expected me to show up at the Ritz. It had been a trap, plain and simple. Unless...? Could they have been after Varushkin? Or was Varushkin working with Earthguard? Why hadn't the place been swarming with police and agents? One shooter was never going to guarantee my death or capture. It had been close though - too close. There are too many unanswered questions. I am certain of two things: the two Earthguard agents are operating alone and they aren't looking to take me alive. If the agents are isolated then my chances are still good. Everything is not yet lost.

I must have the weapon by the end of tomorrow if my plan is to succeed. I cannot allow uncertainties to get in my way. I will be on a plane to Australia by Tuesday afternoon with my beloved Sasha. I will not fail.

The Russian presents me with a new challenge. According to Christos, Varushkin is a rival pimp. There are very few people who could kill so efficiently while gunfire whistled past their ears. And none of them were pimps. He smells of Russian Special Forces to me. I never saw the blow or even Varushkin but I did see a floored Christos tugging at the toothbrush lodged deep in his neck. Those guys love their 'use whatever is at hand to kill' shit. Perhaps Varushkin is after the gun too? I have an idea. Maybe Varushkin is the answer.

The more I think about Anorak man, the more I think he is linked to the girl. His disappearance bothers me. He is a loose end. One minute he's in the thick of it and the next he's gone. I remember the expression but not the face as he ran from one car to the next. He was looking for the girl, I'm sure of it. The bond between him and Jones is strong. Perhaps I can use this?

I light up another cigarette while I make a few calls and get the search for Varushkin started. Instinctively, I reach for my coffee and take a big gulp. The cooling liquid tastes worse than before. I spit the mouthful onto the well-worn carpet. It is definitely piss. That bloody cow, Olga.

*

John, Savannah, Johnson and Wilson were on the fourth floor of a seven floor office building directly above Boots The Chemist and directly opposite the shot-out windows of their old suite at the Ritz.

According to Wilson they had cleared out the company that occupied the space the minute they left John and Savannah alone last night. John silently considered the power and influence necessary to make such a large-scale upheaval possible, especially in the middle of the night during a weekend. Whatever Earthguard was, it carried some serious clout.

The agents had taken residence in the corner office which had given them the best line of sight into the junior suite and had kept tabs on them ever since. Activating the watch had made no difference. Two single mattresses and a few half empty takeaway cartons littered the mottled-grey, carpet-tiled floor. A telescope on a tripod pointed across the road. John pressed his eye to the telescope. Despite the curtains being closed he could make out several red blobs of colour moving behind the curtains. Each blob had a number in a circle that followed it around.

"Is this infrared?" John asked. "And what's with the numbers?"

Johnson explained. "It's an advanced form of infrared. It can go much deeper than the standard variety. The numbers are the approximate weights of anything warm-blooded it picks up. It's how I knew I wouldn't shoot you or Savannah."

"Impressive," John said, moving the telescope across the whole area of the suite. "Quite a few people in there cleaning up your mess."

"You made quite a mess of your own," Johnson retaliated. "By the way how are you doing with that?"

"With what?"

"Having killed a man."

John took his eye from the telescope and considered the question for a few moments. "It's difficult to say," he began. "I keep expecting it to hit me like delayed shock or something but according to Savannah, Christos was about as low as you could get, and to be honest, I don't think I'll ever feel bad about it."

Johnson took a step back. "I'm impressed," he said. "Not many take it like that. You're hardcore agent material."

"Don't get me wrong," added John. "I was a bit shaken up after I watched him die, especially with all the blood spurting all over the wall and the gurgling and everything."

"Yeah, that can shake a guy up."

John hung his head and looked at the floor. "I was more worried about Savannah."

"The bedroom incident, huh?"

"No, I mean... What do you mean? I meant keeping her safe."

He swivelled in an about-face manoeuvre to hide his embarrassment and to see if Savannah was in hearing distance. Fortunately, she and Wilson were en route to the kitchen in the main office, presumably to rustle up some hot drinks.

Typical of most executive offices, the corner office's top half was constructed solely of glass so watching the workforce was easy and privacy could be achieved with the aid of blinds. John could see Savannah talking to Wilson as they walked, and he wondered if he was dropping the same bombshell on her. Her eyes were hidden by the angle of her head but her visible cheek appeared to have regained a little colour.

"Jesus, you were watching that?" he said, without conviction. After all, there had been nothing to see.

"Just two coloured blobs with numbers on. Could have been cells under a microscope if we hadn't known. The sound on the other hand…"

John looked down at the offending item on his wrist. "The watch," he said.

"You got it."

John hadn't thought he could feel any worse about his treatment of Savannah, but the fact that the agents had witnessed his crass behaviour only added to his feelings of guilt. He exhaled long and hard before sitting down behind the large space-age desk in an executive chair that could fit two people. The head of this firm was either super large or looked super tiny in the high-backed cream leather chair.

Using his feet, John spun himself round and round until his vision became blurry and his head weightless. Any feeling was preferable to the one that gnawed at his conscience from within.

Johnson stepped over, stopped the chair rotating with his hand and leaned over John. "Look John, we're working here and we don't have time to worry about people's feelings. This isn't the movies where they turn up the receiver's volume because they want to jack off or turn it off out of respect for privacy. We kept our eyes and ears open every second because that's our job. Do you understand?"

John shrugged his shoulders, "It's okay, I get it. It's just that I've pissed her off big time and I don't know why I did it."

"Because you're just a scared kid."

John shook his head. "I'm thirty-two, I wish people would realise that."

"I'm not talking about your age. In terms of life, you've never lived, done anything serious or been anywhere that wasn't a vacation. You've virtually no experience of the world and its pleasures, and you think Savannah will see right through you. You might be one brave son of a bitch but you've got zero self-confidence."

Strangely, John found no offence in Johnson's words. "I would have … how do you Americans put it … sucked?"

"So what, we've all sucked at one time or another. She'd get over it and she'd still be there in the morning. You bailed her ass out of trouble more than once and until you screwed up, you're the only guy she's met who's treated her right. These facts alone reward you with a few 'Get out of screwing up free' cards, although what you said last night used up at least two of those."

"So what do you suggest, Dr. Johnson?"

The agent let go of John's chair, stood upright, and moved to the window. "What do I know?" he said, tapping the glass as he stared at the traffic below. "I've yet to have a successful relationship of my own." He turned his head back to John. "Just don't waste your next 'Screw up' card. It might be your last."

John sat forward in the chair, resting his elbows on his knees and placing his fists under his chin. Listening to relationship advice from a man who killed people for a living somehow seemed like the most normal thing that had happened today. The tall agent wasn't telling John anything that he didn't already know, but it did feel good to share his troubles.

A worrying thought crossed John's mind. "You're not taping this are you?"

Johnson's head jerked back almost imperceptibly and he let out a short puff of breath from his nose. It was too quiet to call it a snort but it was the closest to laughter John imagined the agent got.

"No. We don't go in for photos or videos or recording or evidence of any kind, unless we need to set someone up, of course. We are the elite of the security agencies, global and without direct supervision. Keeping evidence and invisibility don't go hand in hand."

It sounded like the role was a little too self-policed for John's liking. "Sounds like a licence to do whatever you want," he said.

"We do have to report in to a controller and he has the ability to track our location at any time, but other than that we work unhindered. The selection system has proved very successful in avoiding the recruitment of those that would use the power for their own benefit."

"That sounds like a line," John thought aloud. When was Johnson going to get out of his face? Having him so close was quite disconcerting. He felt like he was on trial.

Johnson turned his eyes upward to the ceiling. He seemed to be contemplating John's throw-away remark. "Yeah, I think it may well be," he said eventually. "Anyway, enough about Earthguard, it's time to powwow with the other two."

*

Savannah handed Wilson a mug of steaming coffee. "Two sugars, right?"

"It smells great," Wilson said, accepting the mug by the handle and reading the large red words 'My Dad's A Spy' on the side. "Good choice," he declared, smiling. He took a sip, pleased to note that the aroma preceding the taste had lived up to expectations. He twisted his head, leaving his eyes on Savannah. "That's the best cup of coffee I think I've ever had."

Savannah blushed ever so slightly. "Nothing to do with me. It's freshly ground with fresh cream too."

Savannah collected her herbal tea from the counter and joined Wilson at the seating area in a fifteen feet square communal room adjoining the kitchen. Aside from six small circular tables, one at which they sat, there was a dartboard and a cupboard full of magazines and newspapers.

"So why did you leave the room?" Wilson asked, keen to start a conversation.

"What do you mean?"

"You came out of that office like you were on fire. So who is it, Johnson or Smith?"

"Huh?"

"Which one makes you uncomfortable?"

She spoke without hesitation. "Smith."

"Because he turned you down?"

Savannah jerked in her chair spilling tea onto her big coat. Staring at the running liquid, her cheeks flushed crimson red. She jumped up and ran into the kitchen. Wilson wondered if she'd reappear. He heard the sound of paper kitchen towel being pulled from a dispenser and a moment later Savannah returned, dabbing at the coat as she sat back down. He sighed with relief. Perhaps he'd been a little too direct.

"I'm sorry," he said, raising his hand. "It's this job. Sometimes I forget how real people communicate."

Savannah looked up at him as she put down the damp kitchen towel in front of her. "I should have guessed you'd be listening in when you left our room without putting up much of a fight. It's my own fault. I tend to fall for bastards."

"Maybe it's for the best. He's hardly relationship material."

"What do you mean?"

"He has a menial job which pays peanuts."

"He has? He seems very intelligent."

Wilson elected not to mention the maths degree from Oxford University, instead just shrugging his shoulders and taking a sip of the wonderful coffee. Savannah watched him as he put his cup down.

"So what about you?" she asked.

The cup wobbled in his hand. When was the last time anybody had wanted to know about him? "What about me?"

"You didn't hang around in the office either."

He didn't understand it but the girl in front of him relaxed him. There was no accusation in the remark and her big brown eyes exuded a kindness he hadn't noticed before. He spoke without considering his words. "You nearly had sex with a bastard, I just work with one."

"Oh," she said, looking unsure what to say next, eyes on the kitchen towel.

"My wife died eight days ago," he said, gazing at a dark green wall. "Cancer."

Savannah sat up and leaned forwards. "My Mum too. Three years ago."

"Really?"

"Yes. I'm sorry for your loss. How come you're working?"

"It seemed preferable to spending all day feeling sorry for myself."

"Are you religious?"

"No. Why?"

"After Mum died I went to church every day for weeks and it really helped."

"Why did you stop?"

"My Dad died and I was thrown out of my home, so I had other things on my mind. Once this is over, I might start again."

"I'm not sure that God would be interested in helping me. I've sent too many souls to meet his rival."

"If they were all like Christos then I'm sure he wouldn't mind too much."

Wilson had always scoffed at those who relied upon religion for their salvation. Yet Savannah was such an obviously good person that hearing it from her mouth made it hard to disagree. Julie's doctor had hinted that he might find some comfort there. No, it was ridiculous. Wasn't it?

"I'm not so sure. I could do with someone to talk to. It feels good to talk to you. Johnson doesn't want to know."

"Some boss. Haven't you got any family?"

"A daughter, her name is Kate. We don't see eye to eye."

"How old is she?"

"She's about your age but she's pierced and tattooed and constantly under the influence of drugs and alcohol."

"I know that some churches provide family counselling. Perhaps that might help."

"I think her skin would burn if she went inside."

"You never know what might happen if you stay positive and give it a go."

The thought of dragging Kate to church almost made Wilson laugh out loud. It was a crazy image for sure. It would require physical restraints to get her inside a church. But until this moment he'd have rather left the country than consider meeting up with Kate. She'd made her feelings towards him plain and unambiguous. He'd left the army and his family to play Supercop and just because he paid for her flat didn't give him the right to have anything to do with her. Maybe with her mother's passing she would be more amenable to reconciliation.

"You know Savannah. I might just give it a go."

For the next few minutes they chatted away like they'd known each other for years and Wilson talked more and felt better than he could remember in a long while.

*

It was chilly in the main office. Johnson reckoned that the evicted employees had turned off the heating before leaving. Who could blame them? Savannah nodded towards John but did not meet his eyes. They took their seats around a small circular table like four friends about to play cards. John sat opposite Savannah. She stared at the centre of the table.

As the senior agent, Johnson chaired and opened the discussions.

"Firstly, as promised before you guys went rogue on us, we will tell you as much as we can about Mark Bradshaw and his invention which is at the core of our problems."

Johnson went on to explain how they had recruited Mark after he had completed his Natural Sciences Tripos at Cambridge University, his fourth year option being Experimental and Theoretical Physics. As Mark's parents had died in a motorway car accident a year before graduation and he was excelling in the field of lasers, he had inadvertently ticked two very large boxes on Earthguard's recruitment radar. John shook his head as he listened. It wasn't the Mark he had known.

Around ten years ago they had been looking to develop a field weapon that allowed agents to avoid reloading issues. Apparently, a high percentage of deaths in the field resulted from this problem. While Mark was in the last year, Earthguard asked him if he thought lasers could be the way forward. At first Mark was adamant that it couldn't be done because lasers required huge amounts of power and power supplies meant either cables or huge batteries.

"So that was why he went with nuclear power?" John asked.

"Exactly," Johnson said. "Mark was obsessed with the project and promised that he could deliver a nuclear-powered laser firearm which would never require reloading."

"Wouldn't the agent get radiation poisoning?"

"No. That was the brilliance of Bradshaw. He encased the miniature reactor in a leaden handle and developed a converter so that radiation-free energy could be used to power the onboard laser."

"I know nothing about nuclear power or lasers," John said, glancing at Savannah whose eyes hadn't moved from the table in front of her. She seemed determined to ignore him.

"Me either, but Mark made it happen. He made the gun adjustable so that it could also be used in a non-lethal capacity. Sure, the guns would need careful destruction after their useful life but the positives were beyond imagination."

"So he'd completed the project?" John asked.

"No," continued the agent. "There was one flaw that Mark couldn't iron out."

"Which was?"

"Occasionally, the prototypes, especially the earlier ones, would release their full capacity with one pull of the trigger. We're talking a fifth of the blast size of Hiroshima with the ability to fire it from several miles away. We lost a few good people in the underground tests."

John rested his head on one hand. It was unbelievable. "A terrorist's dream produced by an anti-terrorist organisation."

"The irony is not lost on me," Johnson admitted.

There's so much the general public don't know, thought John. "So because Mark wouldn't give up the gun, he got murdered?"

"Yes and no." Johnson shifted in his seat. "Mark was selling the weapon to pay off his gambling debts."

That was the first thing said about Mark that made sense. "So Mark contacted the killer?"

"No. Somehow paperwork regarding the gun's existence was handed by the Ministry of Defence to a high ranking SAS official. He happened to be on the lookout for a more reliable firearm. This paperwork was discovered by Gregory Fisher who broke into this guy's office at SAS HQ."

"A soldier? How did he know where to look?"

"He wasn't after details of the gun. He was looking for evidence that the MoD had signed off on the abolition of the continuance policy."

"Continuance, what's that?"

"It allowed special forces soldiers to serve up to the age of forty-five, an extra five years above standard army regulations. As Fisher was forty, he was one of the casualties."

"So what does he want with the gun?"

"We don't know for sure. Some form of payback for losing his job, perhaps?"

"So how did he get in touch with Mark?"

"The document must have given him the information required to track Mark down. From what we can work out, Fisher came up with three hundred thousand pounds by selling his home in Hereford. This, we assume was to pay Mark."

"But Mark's apartment alone is worth several million."

"Mortgaged to the hilt."

"Jesus," John sighed, still beleaguered by how little he had known Mark. "So why did he kill Mark?"

"We think Mark's conscience got the better of him. We never thought that Mark would actually sell the gun. He was only under additional security as a precautionary measure."

"You mean he changed his mind?"

"As far as we can make out. We were on our way to check on him when he was killed." Johnson threw Wilson a knowing look. Wilson's gaze was firmly on Savannah. Johnson continued regardless. "Thankfully we arrived long before the regular police or you might now be behind bars."

"At least I'd be safe." A comfy cell didn't sound so bad. "What about Parkes, the concierge? Was he in on it?"

"Not intentionally. He was paid five hundred pounds by Fisher to ensure that nobody disturbed him. He's being held by the police for aiding and abetting a murder. It won't stick but it'll teach him a valuable lesson."

John hoped they gave Parkes a rough time. "How come you didn't pick up Fisher before it got this far?"

With his eyes fixed on his partner, whose attention still lingered on Savannah, he deflected the question. "Wilson, why don't you take this one?"

Wilson turned and answered calmly. "We had no idea who we were looking for until the DNA match from the cigarette butts he left at the station. It was the first time he'd left any DNA behind. We suspect that he doesn't know that his gene code is on record. The SAS don't officially admit to keeping such information."

"So the SAS owned up to the killer being one of theirs?"

"They alerted us two hours ago and filled us in on the stolen paperwork. Our edge is he doesn't know his DNA is giving him away." Wilson turned back to Savannah but she was in her own world.

"So you can pick him up easily?"

"I wish." Johnson's gaze hung on Wilson, who appeared to have lost interest in the conversation. Johnson cleared his throat. "When we were supposed to be observing Bradshaw, we left our posts. I've convinced HQ that it was because Bradshaw blew our cover, which we suspect may be true. But it doesn't change the fact that we weren't where we were supposed to be."

John couldn't believe what he was hearing. "That's why you weren't there to save Mark, because you left your posts? Is that what you're saying?"

Johnson didn't even blink at the outburst, instead averting his gaze from his partner and leaning forward to meet John's stare head on. The man loved a confrontation. "Yeah, that's what I'm saying. But before you have a hissy fit think about this. Mark was planning to sell the weapon and once this was confirmed my orders were to take him out."

John held his ground. "But he changed his mind, you said."

"We're only surmising. Maybe he got killed because he upped the price. We know nothing for sure. Besides, our techies reckon that Mark had gone as far as he was going to get with the gun. His head was no longer in the game. His time at Earthguard was fast running out."

"You would have killed him anyway?"

"No. What do you take us for? If he'd come clean about his problems on his own, there would have been help provided. I'm just saying that if we'd witnessed the meeting with Fisher, chances are we'd have been ordered to take them both out. Either way your friend would most likely be dead."

John ran this around his head for a while and decided that Johnson was telling the truth. Why else admit to the screw up? "So where do we go from here?"

"Our controller is trying to set up a meet with Fisher's commanding officer. Hopefully, this will happen soon and throw up some better leads. I have an idea to run past my partner which will lure Fisher out and point the blame at the SAS."

"You would do that?"

"Our controller isn't stupid. He knows there's something I'm not telling him. He told me that the only words he was interested in were 'complete deniability'. My job and my partner's depend on it. The SAS trained this lunatic. It only seems fair that they take the blame. Now let's take five."

Johnson signalled to Wilson to follow him to the corner office. Wilson smiled at Savannah and complied. John guessed that Johnson was about to tear his partner down a strip. John welcomed the break as a chance to mend bridges with Savannah but she headed for the toilets without a word, leaving John to his own thoughts.

19: Sunday 25th September, 13:45

Exiting the lady's toilets, Savannah Jones had made up her mind to bolt.

She was a fighter, she had always been a fighter, would always be a fighter. She had realised this at the moment her mind recovered from the temporary shutdown it had experienced in the bathroom.

The stupor had begun, not with the gunshots whistling past her ears and threatening instant death, but with the realisation that she was glad Christos was dead. No, that wasn't true. It was far more than that. For a second she had wanted to scream out with glee, sling on her shoes and to stomp a narrow heel through his unseeing eyeball, covering it with ruptured eye entrails and skewered brain matter. For someone who had never wished anyone dead, not even in jest, this revelation had tipped her over the edge.

When the agents had offered to 'take care' of Christos in return for her assistance, her brighter mood felt justified. She had passed on the responsibility and would never have been witness to the outcome of what 'taking care' might have meant. Even so, she had realised that there was a part of her surfacing that she neither liked nor knew existed.

Her mother had always told her, 'there are no good or bad people, only shades of grey and mixtures of fortune'. Savannah had always taken this to mean that even the kindest of people could do the evilest of things if put in a set of particular circumstances. Maybe it was true, she really didn't know anymore. She did suspect that her recent exposure to violence was at the root of her lack of empathy at the death of Christos the Greek. If she could remove herself from this influence, she would return to the person that her mother had strived so tenaciously to raise.

The toilets were behind Savannah, opposite the lifts, which with the stairwell, made up the centre of the building. A fire door stood between her and the stairwell and then, before she knew it, the door was behind her and her right foot was on the first stair downwards. A shiver passed through her and she froze. Was she leaving because of her mother and the moral dilemma or was it because of the danger to her life? Or was it because of Smith?

Truthfully, she told herself and so therefore it must have been true: John Smith was not really her type. So what was her type? She had never been a good judge of partner material. All she knew was that she had made poor choices and that she knew enough about Smith to understand he was a continuation of this trend. Why couldn't she get him out of her head?

Savannah's left foot eased down onto the second stair to freedom, her hand gripping the cold metal railing like a separate entity which refused to follow her feet. A plethora of jumbled thoughts exploded in her head rooting her to the spot.

Was freedom just a staircase away?

Out there was a maniac who had already attempted to spread her limbs and organs around the inside of a luxury Mercedes. The danger to her person existed whether she fled or stayed. What if her mother had been wrong? Why shouldn't she take comfort in the bloody death of a man who was literally willing to sell her backside for profit?

Why hadn't Smith wanted her? Maybe he was gay? No she had felt the passion in his kiss and through his jeans. Yet, he had deliberately upset her, hadn't he? Did he already have a girlfriend or was he actively pursuing someone he had feelings for? John Smith, John Smith, John Smith... Why did it keep coming back to John Smith?

Whatever his reason for snubbing her advances, she couldn't fault his chivalry. What had her mother raised anyway? A victim? A coward? An idiot? Her mother's teachings heralded from the Valleys in Wales, where small, close-knit communities rallied round one another. This was modern times in the big city and victims, cowards and idiots were the fodder for London's criminal community. Savannah was no longer the victim, would no longer be prey to the scum that sought to crush her spirit. She shared her mother's spirit and that was gift enough.

John Smith, damn him, had taught her to stand up for what she wanted, not just wanted but deserved, and so what if he didn't want her? Her chances were better with him. The decision had nothing to do with feelings, she told herself truthfully.

Savannah Jones turned and headed back to the main office.

*

Johnson and Wilson faced the outside window to ensure they were not being watched from the main office. There were two men on a pulley-operated platform replacing the shot-out windows of the Ritz. All destruction required repair. It's what made the world go round.

"What the fuck's the matter with you, Wilson?" The force of Johnson's breath misted the window in front of him. He rarely swore and he was surprised when he heard the bitterness in his question.

There was the same calm in Wilson's voice as when he had addressed the meeting. "I don't know what you mean, Herb."

The tall agent resisted the temptation to turn and face Wilson, fearing that he might draw his gun and shoot his partner on the spot. Now was not the time. He couldn't remember a time when he had felt so on edge. He clenched his teeth so hard he imagined they might shatter.

"You've been staring at the girl like she's family, and you're acting like your head's in the clouds."

"I thought I explained the DNA situation quite succinctly."

Clenching his fists, Johnson counted out five massive breaths, breathing in through his nose and releasing the air slowly from his mouth. Finally he relaxed his fists. He was okay. He could handle this.

"I have a plan, Wilson, and I need your assistance to make it work. Can you do that?"

"As long as Savannah's life isn't put at risk."

It was going to be dangerous and he could not promise anything. Although...? "You can protect her personally. That way you can be sure."

"Let me know what you need," he said, in the infuriating, nondescript British accent of his. It hadn't annoyed him in five years but at that moment it seemed like grounds enough for murder. But he needed his partner's assistance first.

He saw Wilson's reflection in the glass out of the corner of his eye. The big lug was almost grinning at the prospect. What the hell had those two been talking about? It wasn't recovering the gun, that was for sure.

"Johnson," Wilson started. "Do you believe in God?"

Johnson's fists tightened once more. He began to hum Ave Maria to himself.

*

John drummed his fingers on the meeting table where he had been left alone. He watched the agents staring out of the window in the corner office. It looked like they were watching traffic. He wondered if their heart rates ever increased, contradicting their outward personas. How much death did a person need to witness, or inflict for that matter, to form a husk so impervious to emotion? He was one to talk. Today he had killed a man, and all he could think about was whether Savannah would ever forgive him for snubbing her. How mixed up was that?

John heard the main office door open and turned to see Savannah marching towards the meeting table. He sat upright. They were alone. Say something John...

"I'm sorry," he said, as she sat down directly opposite him. She looked a picture of health but her eyes were hard and guarded as if they were part of a wall built up to protect her. She dug her hand into one of John's coat pockets and pulled out a handful of notes and pushed them across the table towards him.

"Forget about it," she said. "This money belongs to you. I'll let you have the coat back when all this is over."

John searched her eyes for traces of feelings but there was nothing, even the energy seemed purposely subdued. He pushed the mixture of various denominations and crispness back at Savannah.

"Some of this is yours. We recovered a large chunk from Amy what's-her-face and that belongs to you." It seemed that Savannah was hammering home the change in relationship. It was like he had thought. He had blown any chance of romantic reconciliation.

Using both hands, Savannah thrust the cash back to John once again. "Most of the money came from the sale of your watch. There's less than two thousand left. Please take it."

John held up his left arm. "I've got an even better watch now." He neglected to mention that it had been used to listen in on their every move, even their failed intimacy. He counted up the notes. There was just less than seventeen hundred pounds as they hadn't the nerve to ask the hotel for a refund of their upfront room fee when they had collected Savannah's passport.

John split the money into two equal piles. "Let's just share it," he said, picking up the right hand pile and placing it in the centre of the table. Savannah made no move to take it.

Johnson and Wilson appeared as if from nowhere. "Playing poker, are we?"

"More like cryptic bullshit," said Savannah, picking up her pile and stuffing it back into the black Barbour coat.

John sighed. It was clear that she would never trust him again.

"Shall we get down to business?" suggested Johnson as the two agents took their seats. "Wilson here has some information regarding your new identities."

John could feel his world tilting further towards the vertical. It would not be long before his feet could not grip the ground beneath him. "New identities?" I thought that the object was to let Fisher find us and then you take him down, whack him or whatever term you secret agent types use. Shouldn't we be ourselves, wearing microphones under ten inch bullet proof vests or something?"

Johnson looked unusually tense. Facially he was the same but his neck and shoulders seemed slightly scrunched up.

"What?" he said.

"Too easy," Savannah jumped in, perking up noticeably at the suggestion. "If we're out in the open, then it looks like a setup, right?"

She'd certainly picked up. A snort of coke in the toilets, maybe?

"Clever girl," Wilson said, bordering on the cheerful. "You two are the bait that will bring in Fisher. No pun intended," he added. A joke from Wilson - John's world tilted a little further. "I have a private detective friend who has just retired. He has a small office in Twickenham. You will take over the agency. John will be the proprietor and Savannah his employee."

Wilson too? What had Johnson been saying? It can't have been a dressing down, that's for sure.

Savannah was almost trembling with excitement, unable to stay still in her seat, eyes eager and back to full disclosure mode. Her mood swings were impossible to predict. Maybe she was schizophrenic. John didn't know whether to be happy or scared. He watched in wonder, head in his hands as questions leapt from her lips.

"So how will he find us? Will you be waiting with your high-powered rifle to blow his brains out when we give you a signal? What sort of signal will it be? Should I flick my hair back? No, I might do that accidentally. What if I open a particular drawer of my desk? I will have a desk, won't I?"

Savannah was all but bouncing in her chair. John would not have been surprised, given the enthusiasm with which she threw out the questions, if she had asked for a gun.

The shorter agent's mouth wavered on a smile as he threw a red European passport spinning across the table at John.

"From now on you are Ethan Justice, private detective."

John picked up the passport and flicked straight to the photograph page. It was him all right, complete with compulsory miserable passport face. Where had they got the picture? He could not remember it being taken. The name, how long would he be stuck with that?

"Where's mine?" complained Savannah, pouting.

"We had this blank in stock but there was no time to establish a new identity for you," Johnson said. "Besides, you have your passport and John didn't. We didn't want to break into Adelaine house."

Savannah folded her arms and looked around the room. The disappointment had sapped her nervous energy which John reckoned was a good thing. She was up and down like a yoyo and she had thought he was crazy?

"You know where my parents live?" John asked, glad that his family had not been dragged into his mess. His Mum would have needed therapy for months.

"There's not a thing we don't know about you two," confirmed Johnson.

"But Ethan Justice for Christ's sake."

Johnson did not appreciate John's complaint. "It's the last of our batch. There were no choices. We'll make sure we order some more before you stab anyone else with a toothbrush." The agent paused for a breath. "Just make sure you practise the signature when you get a minute."

"Sounds like a perfect name for a private detective," Wilson said.

"In Toyland maybe," John snapped. "Johnson, can I speak to you in private, please?"

Johnson looked to his left at Wilson. Wilson nodded.

"Sure, we'll go into the corner office," Johnson offered.

Both men got up, leaving a sulking Savannah and a smirking Wilson behind.

*

John closed the door of the corner office behind him and immediately laid into the unsuspecting agent who was peering through the telescope. "I have two questions."

"Go on."

"Firstly, if Earthguard has the gun, then there's no chance Fisher can get to it."

"That's not a question."

"The question is why do we all have to risk our lives to catch one man?"

"Because we have to clean up the mess or I lose my job. The gun and Fisher must be disposed of."

"That's your mess. Why do we have to clean it up? What if I just walk out the front door?" Another question leapt into John's head. John tapped the agent's shoulder and Johnson turned round. "You mean the gun isn't destroyed yet?"

"That's three more questions," the agent said, putting his hand on John's shoulder and pulling him closer. "You have to help clean up because I say so and you can't walk out because you wouldn't make it to the front door."

John grabbed the agent's hand and pulled it from his shoulder. "I thought as much. And the gun?"

"Do you know how to safely dispose of a live nuclear reactor? The gun is like a used battery, you can't chuck it in a dustbin or a bonfire. It's in a safe place only Wilson and I know about. Now is that it?"

John refused to let the tall man intimidate him. If he was going to risk his life then he wanted answers to his questions. "No. What the hell is up with Wilson?"

Johnson returned his eye to the telescope. "What do you mean?"

John marched over to where Johnson stood.

The agent's eye stayed put. "The two of you have the most unreadable, expressionless, corpse-like faces I've ever seen. Wilson is suddenly telling jokes and I could swear that he was smiling in there. Something's up and I want to know what it is."

"I reckon he's got a soft spot for your Savannah."

"You mean he's got the hots for her?"

Johnson took his eye from the telescope and turned to John but looked past him at his partner in the main office.

"Wilson, that old son of a bitch, I don't think so. He's been through a lot lately. I think he just needs someone to talk to."

"But can you trust him?"

"Let me worry about Wilson. You should worry about Miss Jones. If it wasn't for her pupils looking normal, you'd think she'd shot something in her veins during her visit to the bathroom."

So Johnson had suspected drugs too.

"She is kind of spaced out at the moment," agreed John, noticing for the first time there were no pictures or mementoes on the walls or desk of the corner office. All removed as per protocol, he assumed. He looked over to the other office where Savannah and Wilson were deep in conversation. What he'd give to be a fly on that wall?

"You're the detective, Mr Justice," Johnson said. "You keep an eye on her and make it work. When I'm not around, keep an eye on both of them. You and I might be the only sane ones left."

"Great," mumbled John, feeling anything but sane. "Ethan Justice... You've got to be joking."

"Do I look like the joking kind?"

John looked back at the face that observed him. It was a countenance with complete detachment. There was life in the eyes but no movement, depth or emotion. This was not the face of the man who had offered him half-decent relationship advice. Not an occasional facial muscle twitch or telling flicker that would be present in ... well ... everyone else, was to be seen.

Johnson could like, hate or be indifferent towards him and John would never know. If the need or justification arose, this man could risk his life to save John or equally put a bullet in John's brain. In either scenario the agent's expression would be identical, like he was watering the plants on a lazy Sunday morning. The thought was deeply disconcerting. Did he look like the joking kind?

"No. You don't," John said. "Not at all."

20: Sunday 25th September, 17:05

Finally, the sun is shining but I'm stuck in this God damn hotel room. The wind has dropped. My radiator has turned itself on. I could be in a hut in the Sahara desert. Things are not going my way. It is fast becoming evening and in two hours' time the light will disappear along with my chances of picking up the trail of Jones or Varushkin.

My phone rings as if to challenge my negativity. 'Simply the Best' by Tina Turner echoes around the room. I am already bored with the new ringtone. It is my paid informant from the Ritz. He had refused to give his name in case I reported him. I had been in no position to argue.

"Talk to me," I say.

"Two massive blokes were at reception when Jones checked out."

"Was she alone?"

"How do I know you're with the police?" he asks.

"Because if you don't start talking, I'm going to nick you."

"She was with some young bloke."

"Did he have a limp or speak with a Russian accent?"

"No. He spoke well. No accent. Wealthy student I'd guess."

"Where did they go?"

"I don't know."

"Is that all you got?"

"I'm risking my neck to give you this for a measly fifty. Do you know...?"

I hang up the call. Her companion must be Mr Anorak. I can't just sit here and wait for the phone to ring. Everyone on the streets is looking for Jones and Varushkin and so far I've got nothing. Varushkin has a pronounced limp. How hard can it be to find a Russian with a limp for God's sake? They must have gone to ground. I put out my cigarette. The ashtray is overflowing. I clench my fists into balls. I grab the phone and call Sasha. She picks up after three rings.

"Hello."

"Sasha, it's me."

"I'm at work. I told you not to call me until after seven."

I squeeze my fists harder. Does she really work on Sundays? The question remains unasked. I don't need negativity right now. I need comfort. "Things aren't going too well. I just wanted to talk."

"Call me back after seven." She lowers her voice. "There are people here."

Her whispers stroke my ear and stir my lust. I can't help myself.

"Can you put your hand in your skirt without being seen?"

The call ends.

I stand up and throw the phone onto the bed. I take two steps towards the bathroom wall. I pull my right fist back behind my head. I scream as I let my punch go with every ounce of pent up frustration in my body and mind. My knuckles crunch through two layers of plasterboard and a two by four inch piece of timber. Pieces of plasterboard explode into the air before falling to the floor, leaving a cloud of dust in their wake. I suck up the pain and hold it in. My mind clears. I will not be stopped.

*

The Earthguard agents had relocated John and Savannah to a small safe house in Hammersmith, close to the tube line. They were to stay there until Monday morning, at which time they would take up their new identities at Justice Investigations. Every five minutes or so the two up two down, cramped residence would shake on its very foundations as a train rattled by. All the terraced houses on the run-down street must have been built with rubber bricks, thought Savannah.

In the lounge the agents were preparing to leave. Johnson threw an envelope onto the green two-seater sofa which, other than a small rectangular dining table with two chairs and an old portable television set on a wooden stool, was the only furniture in the room.

"If you want to paw each other I suggest you do it silently or press the top button twice, and twice again when you've finished. We'll be busy and so won't be listening most of the time. If there's an emergency unscrew and hold down the bottom button for five seconds."

"Where will you be?" Savannah asked. She did not want to lose their protection and more importantly she did not want to be left alone with Smith. It was easy to ignore him with the agents around but, once departed, she did not relish the stilted conversations to come. Why hadn't she been given a new identity? It was like all the focus was on Smith.

With Christos out of the picture, it was no longer her battle. The way things were with Smith had scratched the lustre from her involvement. She wanted to help and part of her relished the anticipation of tomorrow and the danger it would bring, but right now she wished she could take a bath and sleep until the morning light.

"I got a call from SAS headquarters. We're going over there to question the commanding officer of Fisher's squadron and any other soldiers who might be able to help. In the morning I have arranged to meet with experts who will destroy the gun as I watch." Johnson turned to face the front door and was about to take a step.

"You won't be nearby when we act as bait in Twickenham?"

"No, but Wilson will be taking good care of you from the second office."

She noticed that Wilson, who was standing close to her right side, had remained rooted to the spot. Clearly he was not so eager to leave. She also observed for the first time that the beefy agent was a few inches shorter than her.

"Where do you go to destroy something like that?"

This time Johnson swivelled to face Savannah. The words were monotone and carried no aggression. "What is it with you two and questions? If I don't tell you, then you can't tell anybody else. No matter how small a risk *that* might be, it's a risk we can't afford to take."

Despite the emotionless delivery, the words themselves suggested annoyance and Savannah reeled like she had been pushed in the chest. Wilson placed his hand on her shoulder.

"Don't worry yourself, nobody will find you here. Just remember no phone calls, no going out and you'll be back to your own life before you know it. There won't be a weapon to fight over once it's destroyed and if

Fisher's as desperate as his actions so far indicate, then we'll pick him up by the end of tomorrow."

"So how will you lure him in?"

Johnson looked at Wilson. "We really should go now."

"Just a second," Wilson said, his arm now around Savannah's shoulders. She didn't mind, it seemed kind of sweet, but John was giving her the strangest of looks. "As far as we know he is trying to get to us through you."

"And John?"

"Well there's no reason for us to suspect that he even knows who John is. He's never met him and to our knowledge has only seen him from a distance in dark conditions. You, he knows by name."

Of course, even though John and Fisher had locked horns twice they had never had a good look at each other. On the other hand, Fisher had become fully acquainted with her ex-pimp.

"Christos," she said.

"Exactly. We'll put the word out that you have been seen frequenting Justice Investigations in Twickenham. From what we can tell, Fisher has spent the last few weeks building up a network of contacts throughout the city who feed him information for sizeable cash pay-outs. If we play it right, it won't take long before he sniffs you out."

"Ugghhhh, that sounds disgusting."

"I'll be waiting in the back office so don't you worry. I promise that nothing will happen to you."

"Or John?" she asked, looking at John who was attempting to catch Johnson's attention and failing. The tall man's eyes were regarding Wilson thoughtfully, presumably willing him to shut up, hurry up or both.

Wilson shrugged. "Or John."

"Come on, Wilson. Let's move it," Johnson said, opening the front door.

Wilson removed his arm from Savannah's shoulders and gave her a comforting nod. She felt a little better as he joined Johnson, but, as the door closed behind them, the thought of being alone with John loomed ominously and she felt her stomach drop.

*

After two hours of silence, sitting side by side on the well-worn sofa, John could take no more. It was clear to him that Savannah had pressed up against the armrest to maximise the distance between them. He felt like a kid on his very first date, and it was driving him crazy. He pressed the top button of the Rolex Daytona twice in rapid succession. This conversation was not for anyone else's consumption.

"I thought I'd be rubbish in bed," he announced.

She turned and looked at John, suspicion etched on her face. "What are you talking about?" she snapped.

John shuffled up to her until their legs were almost touching and leaned towards her, looking into her beautiful eyes. "That's what this is all about, isn't it? The cold shoulder treatment?"

Savannah pressed further against the armrest and into the corner of the sofa. "I have no idea what you're talking about," she said.

"Liar," John said. Savannah looked straight ahead and wouldn't meet his gaze. "Listen, Savannah, I've only been with two women in my life and I'm thirty-two years old. I didn't want to disappoint you."

Her eyes moved to meet John's but her head barely turned. "And that's a good reason to treat me like a whore?"

"It was the only thing I could think of to make you stop in time."

Her head turned and she sat forward. They were face to face. "In time for what?"

"In time to stop me from making a complete fool of myself."

Savannah wasn't getting it, her movements were agitated like she couldn't fathom his words and it was infuriating her. "You were with these two women sexually?"

John shivered and cringed. This was getting pretty personal now and he knew he could not retreat or insult his way out of it again. They had a whole night to get through and he wanted closure on his mammoth faux pas - one way or another.

Keep the answers short and don't offer more information than asked for, he told himself. "Yes," he said in answer to her question.

"And you put it in the right place?"

Jesus Christ. His heart hammered in his chest and he couldn't swallow despite the feeling that he desperately needed to. "Yes, as far as I know. With one girl..." God this was so difficult. Mark had been the only person he had ever talked to about this stuff.

"Yes? With one girl...?"

Spit it out man, he chastised himself. "It was only once and with the second, who was over a year ago, it was a few times but always in the dark."

"And these were prostitutes?"

Good God no, he thought. Mustn't say that though - anything to do with prostitutes was a no-go area. Back to short answers. "No," he said. Damn his heart, it would not settle down, would not give him a break.

"Okay, so we've established that you're not a virgin and that you know where to put it," she said, her gaze intensifying.

John wanted to get up but felt physically restrained as if bound by invisible ligatures. To not face the music would be a step backwards, and he had back peddled enough lately to last a lifetime. He placed both his hands, palms down, on his legs and they immediately began to sweat. He had no idea where to move them or what to say next. He kept them on his legs and said nothing. Savannah was toying with him, teaching him a lesson he knew he deserved. It was uncomfortable for him. She undoubtedly sensed his unease and was not going to let him off lightly.

She twisted the knife a little further. "But you have a phobia of prostitutes?"

"No. I couldn't care less what you did before. I really like you and I screwed up. I'm really sorry. Please can we wipe the slate clean?"

"I still don't understand why you wanted to stop?"

"It seemed like you thought I was some kind of hero or something and I didn't think I would match those expectations if I had allowed it to go any further."

"So you wanted me?"

"Oh God, yes." John hadn't meant for that to come out quite so honestly.

"And you know that I wanted you?"

Where was she going with this? "I thought so," he said cautiously.

"So why didn't you just take a chance?"

"Because I thought I'd lose you. That you'd laugh at me, that the hero would be a let-down. All of those things. You'd already got my interest when you offered yourself to me in exchange for getting Johnson and Wilson to sort out your Christos problem. I was sorely tempted then but did the right thing because it would have been taking advantage of you. When we were finally about to actually ... get together, I could tell in my bones ..." John felt the warmth from his cheeks as he approached his confession, "... and other parts, that it would be a short-lived experience."

They sat looking at each other in silence. The truth was out, and while John felt better about that, he couldn't tell what was going through Savannah's mind as she continued to stare at him. John's heart had slowed down, but his stomach still acted like he was falling down a chasm and was forever trying to catch up with the rest of him. Was he imagining it or were Savannah's eyes wider and a little brighter?

"I guess I did come on a bit strong," she said, tapping her fingers on her thighs and looking around the room. "You really wanted me, huh?"

"Of course I did. Have you not seen yourself? You're beautiful."

"So you just like my body?"

"That's not what I meant and you know it." John took one of her hands in both of his, "You just want me to suffer a bit more for what I did, and I guess I deserve that and everything you called me in the hotel."

"I've never sworn like that before."

"Forget about it. I earned it."

John wasn't sure what he was doing but it felt right to him, and he wanted to share his feelings with another woman for the first time in his life. "I'm amazed at what you've been through and that you still managed to stay a sane person. What you went through with your Mum dying, your Dad drinking and gambling away your inheritance and that arsehole boyfriend cleaning you out, would be enough to make anyone give up."

"I nearly did give up yesterday."

"I'm not finished."

"Sorry."

"The truth is that you never gave up." John kissed her hand, hoping the gesture wasn't too pathetic. "You're intelligent, resourceful and I could stare at your eyes forever. I've never felt about anyone the way I feel about you and I have no idea if we could be good together or not but if we live through tomorrow and they catch this bastard, then I think we should give it a try."

Savannah's face beamed and John swore he saw a little flush in her cheeks. "Does that mean we have to wait before we kiss?" she said.

John's heart picked up pace again and his stomach somersaulted several times. "No," he said, leaning forward and meeting her lips as they approached his. Their lips parted and tongues urgently searched each other's mouths. Breathing became rapid and John's mouth seemed to suddenly go dry. No other girl had ever affected him this way. There was no time for water. There were no brakes this time, he was freefalling out of control to a place he had never been, and he was loving every wonderful second.

*

The first time had lasted ... well not very long, but the second and the third and the fourth times had been out of this world. Even now certain intimate muscles twitched with the residual memory of heightened pleasure. His moves, which began tentatively, grew with confidence after the enjoyable, but short lived and frantic, first sexual encounter. After that, John was unbelievably keen to explore every part of her body, leaving virtually no part untouched.

She had figured that he might take a little persuasion to let loose his inhibitions, and she wondered exactly what had kept him from neglecting his sexual wellbeing for so long. A part of her was glad and a little smug at the fact that she had brought out the animal in him that no other woman had yet experienced. If it hadn't been for the duration of their first time she might have suspected that the whole inexperience story was a ploy of some sort, but, given that she had thrown herself at him three times already, she couldn't think, for the life of her, what that ploy could be.

Men and their insecurities Savannah mused. Although she had to admit, only to herself, that a tiny seed of doubt had considered what she would do and say if the experience had turned out to be a disaster. John could have always said 'I told you so' and she would have been forced to face bitter disappointment with words of solace and encouragement. It didn't matter. It had been everything she had hoped and more. She had a hero for a man and if they lived through the week it might turn into ... who knew?

In the small bedroom upstairs, Savannah lay with her head on John's chest.

"Yes," she said, blowing on his chest as her finger circled his nipple. She liked that what little chest hair he had was soft, not thick and wiry.

"Yes to what?" John asked, stroking Savannah's hair.

"I'll go out with you."

John laughed. "I thought that was implied or is it inferred? I can never remember."

Savannah giggled, catching herself unawares. Was that her? Of course it was, silly. When was the last time she had giggled? She couldn't honestly remember if she ever had, not like that. Even to her own ears, the sound had been girly, playful and most of all just plain happy. She didn't know what would become of them, whether they would make it through the dangers that lay ahead. If they died tomorrow it would be on a high, and given that she couldn't recall another feeling even close to the utter contentment that hummed inside her now, somehow that wasn't so bad.

*

Tina Turner wakes me. I grab my phone from beside the bed. My knuckles still throb from my wall punching. It is the counterfeiter known only as Saturn.

"Your passport and papers are ready," he says.

I blink my eyelids to bring the room into focus. "When can I get them?"

"They are behind your hotel reception desk."

Of course, he wouldn't take on my work without knowing where I was staying. They say he is the best and so far I'm impressed. Now I can book the plane tickets. There is nothing like good news to awaken the mind.

"Good," I say.

"Are we agreed that our transaction is at a close?"

What an odd man. "Yes," I agree.

"Then I bid you great success."

I don't know how to reply and so I end the call. The news of a trip will excite Sasha. She has hardly travelled and will be keen to keep me happy when I spring the good news on her. No more council house for her. I check the time. It is just before 8:30 P.M. I have slept for over three hours. The time is perfect to call my sister. This call will be the best yet. Tina Turner shrieks out again. Why did I choose such a grating tune? Black speaks. His voice is slow and slurred.

"My friend. I have more gold."

"Are you drugged up?"

"I have more gold," he repeats.

I want nothing to do with him in this state but time is dwindling. "Pull yourself together."

"I'm okay. I'm okay. I'm okay... The girl will be at an office in Twickenham tomorrow morning."

I catch my breath. This is what I've been waiting for. "And," I say.

"Two... two thousand."

I'll have left the country in two days' time. I can promise anything. "Okay. Where?"

"Opposite the rail station. Justice Investigations."

I am back in the game. The gun will soon be mine.

"When can ... I collect..." Black jibbers.

I end the call.

Everything is now in my grasp. Nothing can stand in my way. Revenge, love and a new life are within touching distance. I steady my breathing before calling Sasha. I make myself comfortable on the bed and unzip my trousers.

She knows it's me. "Yes?"

"I have good news."

"You're not going to call anymore?"

She is often sarcastic and I don't take offence. "We're going on a trip." The call goes quiet. "I said we're going on a trip." I can hear her breathing. I wish I could feel her breath in my ear.

"You agreed that we didn't have to see each other... That we'd keep it to the phone calls."

"Yes, but this is a new life in Australia. I have a new passport. No one will know we're related. We can live as a couple." I can picture her elated face even though I haven't seen it in over twenty-five years.

"You'll hurt me just like Dad used to."

It is a slap in the face. "I'm not Dad. He did things to me too. Don't you remember?"

"You've become just like him. Ever since we've been in touch again, you've got worse."

"I thought you loved me."

"You're my brother. Of course I love you. But not like that. It's not right."

"We used to... When Dad made us."

"Yes," she screamed. "Because he made us."

She needs time to digest the news. The excitement is too much for her. "I've been getting counselling. My therapist says it's not my fault and I'm going to get better."

"Are you still seeing him?"

"It's a her."

"Her then?"

"Yes," I lie. I just need to get her to Australia and then everything will work itself out. She just needs a little push.

"And you won't touch me?"

"No."

"Not ever?"

"I promise. Think of a beautiful house with a swimming pool. It will be fantastic." I picture the bedroom. She is wearing white stockings and nothing else. She's been bad.

The line goes quiet again. "Sasha?"

"Prove it," she says.

"What?"

"Hang up now without making me say stuff to you."

"But?"

"Hang up now and I'll go with you if you promise to continue therapy."

The bigger picture. Think of the bigger picture. "I'll need your passport details to book the tickets."

"I'll text them when you hang up."

My mind spins. I stand up and lean against the wall for support. The change of position does not dampen my desire. I want her filthy whispers in my ear. I can't end the call.

"Do it Gregory or I'm staying."

I place my thumb on the red 'end call' button but I can't press it. My whole body tenses like a statue. I must end the call. Why is it so hard? Finally my left hand presses my right thumb and the call ends. I did it. Five minutes later the phone vibrates and I have Sasha's passport details.

I think of our new life together and what we will do once she comes round to my way of thinking. When I orgasm, it is the best ever. It is a climax of victory.

21: Sunday 25th September, 21:25

The SAS's Eurocopter Dauphin was indeed 'dolphin' like in shape, except in place of the dorsal fin sat a bulbous hump from which the four main blades sprouted. The agents had not spoken a word during the fifty minute journey from RAF Northolt. It was just as well the helicopter had cut more than two hours off the time it would have taken to drive.

Wilson had been glad of the peace that their silence provided, taking the opportunity to stare into the darkness of night and trickle charge his failing batteries. This assignment had been the toughest he could remember in seventeen years with Earthguard. He was no longer the energetic and hardened soul who joined the anti-terrorist organisation at the age of thirty. But then he was hardly the man of even four months ago. It was a good change.

He glanced over to his partner and boss who keenly eyed the pilot's use of the vast array of controls. The man virtually hummed with energy. Never before had their thirteen year age gap seemed as obvious as it did at that moment.

Wilson had clearly lost Johnson's trust. But it didn't matter anymore. After this assignment, if they still had jobs, Wilson would request a new partner. After that he would request a leave of absence and spend every day of it with his daughter, Kate. She was stubborn but he could be worse. He would refuse to meet her rent payments any longer unless she went to church every day with him. Kate would have no choice and from there it would be a small step to enter into the church's family counselling program.

It comforted him to think that Julie was in a peaceful place. She had been a good woman and deserved better from him. He could make it up to her by rescuing their daughter and sharing Julie's faith that he and Kate had ridiculed. He didn't know why it all made such sense suddenly, but he knew it was all thanks to Savannah. By trying to help him without an ulterior motive, she had shown him the light. Kate was going to have a fit, but they'd get through it together.

Wilson looked down to see the lights of the helipad on the south side of RHQ Credenhill SAS barracks as they neared their landing. The surrounding unspoilt countryside was bathed in the light of an almost full moon and seemed an unlikely setting for the small band of specialist armed forces. There had been a time when he was younger, in his late teens, when such a vista would have lifted his spirits and revitalised his resolve, but not anymore, and certainly not tonight. There was too much to get through before he could appreciate the future beyond this assignment. He had hope now, but there was a way to go before hope translated into reality.

The rest of the looming site consisted of nine large, uniform, rectangular barracks adjacent to the helipad, mostly unoccupied empty fields in the centre of the site and some twenty odd further buildings to the North which included the 'H' shaped head office where they would carry out their interviews.

This was the agent's first visit to the home of the 22nd Regiment since it moved from Hereford in May 1999. As they disembarked from the sleek-lined helicopter, Wilson was once again amazed by the lack of substantial noise from the engine and blades. This smooth and stealthy bird, capable of speeds of almost 200 miles per hour, would have looked more at home on top of a corporate skyscraper than here at the headquarters of the most elite regiment of soldiers in the world. Like the peaceful countryside harboured men trained in the art of killing, so the friendly dolphin shape hid its deadly capabilities.

A cold wind had picked up and the air was damp with imminent rain. Savannah might laugh at their antiquated-style coats, but they kept the cold at bay. What he'd have given to have been blessed with a daughter like her. But girls like Savannah were one in a million and came with losers for fathers. Nature was messed up.

A staff car met the agents on the helipad, and they were greeted with great formality and zero courtesy. Their visit was not a welcome one. Even less was known publically about Earthguard than the SAS, and when orders were issued from the very top of government to provide full disclosure to international outsiders, it didn't go down well at Credenhill. Wilson had seen it all before. Every security agency and special fighting unit in the world believed that they had earned special treatment. It went with the territory.

Four minutes and three, ninety degree turns later, Johnson and Wilson were inside the expansive head office building. Their escort departed with a salute, leaving them with the squadron leader outside his office door. Major Harris greeted the agents with a single nod, about faced and re-entered his office. The uniformed man was a couple of inches shorter than Johnson and had most of the typical army-engrained traits: slim but solid, stiff as a board, unnaturally upright, permanently aggressive expression and not at all pleased to see them.

"I'd say welcome to you both but you'd know I was lying," Major Harris said, sitting behind his black metal desk which was clear but for a flat computer screen and wireless keyboard. A framed picture of a younger Harris meeting The Queen and Prince Phillip hung behind the officer, telling Wilson that it was for the benefit of visitors rather than his own enjoyment. Wilson looked behind to see what, if anything, the Major stared at for inspiration when he wasn't planning rescue missions or assaults deep into enemy territory. The wall was bare, which probably said more about the man than any piece of art or photograph could.

Strangely, the Major's stiffness appeared to ease somewhat as he sat back in his chair, as though he felt more in control behind the desk. Maybe he had a gun pointed at them from under the desk? Nothing in this job surprised Wilson anymore. The open hostility was not new ground for the agents. As protocol dictated, Johnson spoke first, toning down his crass American accent for once.

"We appreciate your discomfort at our invasion into your privacy, Major. We will endeavour to make this whole process as quick and as unobtrusive as possible."

The Major rubbed his chin, his small predator-like eyes analysing Johnson from head to toe. He made no offer of a place for the agents to sit.

"You're Johnson, the American, aren't you?" It was rhetorical and Johnson, as was typical, showed no reaction.

Johnson indicated to his partner with his right hand. "This is Agent Max Wilson. He will be interviewing you while I start on the list of those that worked or socialised most closely with our man. How many are we looking at?"

Wilson was shocked. He couldn't believe that Johnson would let him interview the Major. It was completely outside of protocol. Johnson must be feeling the pressure. This was a blatant disregard for Earthguard procedure. Did he still trust him? What was his agenda?

"I was led to believe that you, as senior agent, would be interviewing me," Major Harris said, leaning forward in his chair, stiffness returning to his body.

"And why was that?"

"Because I talked to your controller less than three hours ago."

Johnson's face hid the surprise well, but his words were less successful. "You spoke with our Controller?"

"Yes, that surprises you, doesn't it?" Harris said, sitting back again. "Would it also surprise you that I know him by name?"

It did surprise Johnson, which was a rare event indeed. It wasn't his face, which was as inscrutable as ever, but the lack of his partner's immediate response that told Wilson he was just as taken aback as he was. Neither partner had access to the identity of their controller, knowing him only by a number. In fact, given that their only voice contact was electronically disguised, they couldn't be certain that it was a man at all.

"If you have spoken to our controller, then I'm sure he has informed you that how I operate is dependent upon how I see the circumstances. It is clear to me, Major Harris, that you have an issue with my heritage, and therefore I believe that matters would be expedited if you were interviewed by a fellow countryman."

There was no argument over protocol or procedure. This was little more than a pissing contest. Playing the racist card was genius but so unlike Johnson. Earlier he'd been treating John Smith like a son in need of fatherly direction and now this. What was he playing at? Perhaps this assignment had been getting to Johnson too. He just didn't show any physical signs.

"If you have access to our controller, we can leave the room while you talk to him," continued Johnson. "I'm sure that he'll confirm that what I say is true."

Johnson was calling the Major's bluff.

The Major grumbled something into his hand.

"I'm sorry, Major. I didn't quite catch that," Johnson said, taking a step forward, giving his stream of piss a couple of extra feet.

The Major sat upright, banged his fists down hard on the desk, which undulated under the force, and snarled with his best battle face. It was a look that would have buckled a civilian's knees.

"You Yanks think you can take over anything. Well, let me tell you this. If you put one foot out of line or upset one of my men during your stay, I will personally shoot you in the head, put you over my shoulder, throw you back in the chopper, fly over the Bristol Channel and dump you."

Johnson remained calm. "Let's hope it doesn't come to that," he said. "If we start now, we can get this wrapped up before morning. May we proceed?"

Major Harris waved his hand in agreement, wiping spittle from the corners of his mouth with a white handkerchief. He might as well have waved it in the air, thought Wilson.

*

Johnson departed to a nearby meeting room with a list of five names and an internal phone number to get things started. Harris let Wilson know what he really thought of his boss.

"Thinks he's tough does he? Bloody Yanks, they're all talk and no action or all action and no brains."

The Major was starting to grow on Wilson. He told it like it was or at least how he saw it. Too many people in positions of authority communicated between the lines these days, allowing ambiguity to cloud a straightforward message. It was a survival mechanism which permitted deniability after the message was badly received. With Major Harris, you couldn't squeeze an ant's privates between the lines of his communication. It was refreshing.

Wilson was getting fed up of standing. He looked around the office for signs of available chairs. There was only one grey plastic chair in the sizeable office. It wouldn't have surprised the agent if Harris had removed the comfortable chairs before they arrived.

He gestured to the lonely seat in the corner of the room. "May I?" he said.

"Yes, pull it up." He pointed to a row of coat hooks to the left of the door. "You can hang your coat up there."

"I'm good, thanks."

"Suit yourself."

Wilson picked up the chair by its back and carried it to the desk. As he positioned the chair to face the Major, a gust of wind rattled against the window to the right of the Major's desk sending leaves and rain against the pane. Wilson looked out of the window into the adjoining car park where the only activity was the howling of wind as it propelled leaves from place to place and bent tree branches into near submission.

"Some night," Wilson commented, sitting down and pulling a pen and pad from inside his pocket. "Are we going to be able to fly out of here later?"

"The Eurocopter Dauphin flies in just about anything." The Major raised his eyebrows as Wilson jotted the date at the top of his pad. "I thought you Earthguard lot didn't believe in evidence?"

"I haven't slept in two days and my mind is shot. I'll take my chances." Wilson wriggled in his chair but failed to find a comfortable position. "So what can you tell me about Fisher?"

The Major's hand returned to his chin, which he massaged between thumb and forefinger as he regarded the agent through narrowed eyes. "Personally, very little. I know that he didn't fit in well at first, and he's one of the toughest soldiers we've ever put together, but that's about it."

"Any disciplinary issues?"

"Nothing official, but a lunatic in the general population can appear completely sane here. We take a man's destructive nature and give it direction. From what I hear, Fisher arrived with a mean streak longer than the Amazon."

"Anything documented?"

"No. You might get more from the other guys. Discipline tends to be instant here. Problem candidates are weeded out at the training stage and RTU'd. That's returned to unit to you civilians."

"I remember," Wilson said, immediately regretting the comment and moving on quickly. "Any problems with the other soldiers?"

Major Harris stroked his imaginary beard with real purpose as he scrutinised the Earthguard agent. Wilson realised that he'd messed up and the squadron leader was not about to let him off the hook.

"You failed the training?"

"No, I meant that I remembered the term RTU from when I visited the old barracks at Hereford, before you moved here. One of the guys from 'B' squadron was communicating with a known terrorist."

"Either you tell me, or I ask your pillock of a partner."

Wilson was back pedalling fast. "It won't do you any good," he said. "We each know nothing of the other's past employment. There is nothing he can tell you."

"I can check our records."

"Records of past employment are expunged. Our names are changed, our histories deleted and it's like we don't exist."

Harris tapped the forefingers of both hands onto the metal surface of his desk as he pondered his next question carefully. "So you won't admit to having taken our training program?"

Wilson didn't move a muscle. This conversation was going nowhere and Johnson would not be best pleased if he left the Major's office empty handed. He couldn't risk Johnson making him the scapegoat in order to keep his own position. If only he didn't feel so damn tired.

Even though he hadn't admitted to anything, he knew if Harris mentioned the conversation to Johnson or their controller he would be put out to pasture with immediate effect. It was one thing to divulge history to Johnson, but to give details to another organisation would not be tolerated. Wilson was wealthy, the pay had always been excellent and the retirement package plentiful. Why not? He was on his way to being a new man. It was a calculated risk, and the way his mind and body begged for rest or even the luxury of a comfortable chair, retirement didn't seem like such a scary thought. Perhaps he could use the situation to his advantage.

"This goes no further than this office, agreed?"

The Major broke out in a big smile and threw himself back in his chair. "I knew it. You've got that look about you." He sat back up, elbows on the desk, hands clasped together. "Good God man, you were one of us. They could put my balls in a vice, and I wouldn't say a single word."

The thought wasn't a pretty one, but the straight-talking Major knew how to embellish a promise, and Wilson believed him. "Joined at twenty-one, and like most, I came from the Paras. Left at thirty when Earthguard made me an offer I couldn't refuse. Not much else to say."

"If Earthguard head-hunted you, then I guess it's safe to say that you saw some serious action. Am I right?"

It all seemed like a lifetime ago. "To be honest, not much until Desert Storm in ninety-one. Seemed I had a talent for thinking on my feet, and after I got back they contacted me and asked me to join. Earthguard was barely a year old at the time and I wasn't fully sure of their purpose or reach. Over time I realised that it wasn't that different to being in the SAS, except that my actions would be solely for the benefit of the UK. Fortunately for me, they kept in touch and after two years ... like I said..."

"They made you an offer you couldn't refuse," Harris finished.

"Exactly."

"Somehow I get the impression that you're being modest, Soldier. But I won't press you any further, and you have my word that this won't go any further."

From that moment on the Major was cheerfully answering every question that Wilson threw at him, occasionally interjecting his own memory of battles won, lives saved and near-death experiences. At one point the Major pulled out a bottle of single malt Scotch whisky and two plastic beakers which Wilson politely declined, not out of protocol but for the effect it would have on his already-exhausted mind.

"So the only problem occurred when the rumour of cutbacks became widespread?"

The Major shook his head, looking down at his hands. The wind howled outside as if to introduce the telling of a spooky story. "Fisher apparently had his whole life worked out. He was going to stay in the squadron until he was forty-five and then emigrate with his sister, Sasha, to Australia."

Wilson stopped scribbling in his note pad and looked up. "Sister? We never saw anything on file about a sister."

"It's not a nice family history. Both mother and father were registered drug addicts, living in a council flat in Norwich. Fisher's father beat his mother and sexually abused both him and his sister."

"How old were they?"

"It's not certain when it started, but his sister is two years older than him and was sixteen when she became pregnant."

"By the father?"

Yes. Eventually she was removed by the local authority after it was proved that her pregnancy was incestuous. Sasha Fisher was given a new identity and relocated to York after the foetus was aborted. By all accounts, the abuse of Gregory Fisher continued until he was sixteen when one drug-addled evening his father beat his mother to death with his bare hands and then stuck his head in a gas oven."

Domestic violence was no different to terrorism. It boiled down to anger and disappointment in yourself, or more usually, others. Both ended in needless destruction of lives and, left to fester in a warped mind, often resulted in the loss of innocent lives. Wilson was well aware that his view was simplistic and that there were so many other factors to consider, but in his profession there was no time for convoluted discussion - you killed someone or you didn't - there was no time for a chat.

While he worked solely in the terrorism business, he despised the perpetrators of violence against women and children every bit as much. Fisher's life had been tainted by his childhood, yet he had still carved out an envious career in the SAS, got his life together and put the past behind him. He couldn't be disappointed in himself, so who was he mad at?

"So the list you gave to Johnson, there's no one else."

"Not to my knowledge."

"What did he do with his spare time, go and visit his sister?"

"No idea. He was a very private person by all accounts. I've spoken to a couple of the men on the list, and all I discovered was that he wasn't one for a night out with the lads, and wherever he went, he never talked about it."

"Can you tell me about the incident?"

"You mean the stolen papers?"

"Yes, do you know what they were?"

"No, well above my pay grade, so I'm told. I know Fisher was looking for confirmation of the cutbacks and whether he would be affected. The Major General has an office here, and as most of his work is done in Whitehall, there was no reason to suspect that anything of great importance was held in there."

"But there was?"

"I'm told that highly classified papers were taken. The MG didn't notice until after Fisher had been released back into Civvie Street."

"When were the papers taken?" Wilson asked.

"We don't know exactly. All we know is that when the MG visited two weeks ago, the shit hit the fan. The documents were placed in the cabinet seven weeks ago and Fisher was discharged five weeks ago, giving him a two week window of opportunity."

"Johnson said you told him over the phone it was a DNA match?"

"Yes, our investigators found a single hair and matched it to our personal DNA database."

"The one the men don't know about?"

"Exactly. Doesn't your agency do the same?"

"That one's above *my* pay grade, but it wouldn't surprise me." The thought of Earthguard filing away his DNA records didn't bother Wilson. "Did you try and track him down?"

"We notified the police that we were looking for him, and we checked out the address we had for him. Turned out that he'd sold his house in Hereford and was nowhere to be found."

"Did you try his sister?"

"I contacted her, but she said that she hadn't seen him in six months, and the last time she had spoken with him was while he was still enrolled with us."

"Did you believe her?"

"I had no reason not to, but I'm no investigator. It might be worthwhile you paying her a visit. I'll have someone make you a copy of our file which will give you her details along with other addresses and numbers that were checked out."

"I appreciate it," said Wilson, meaning it. He knew that this was most definitely not standard procedure. "Tell me, Major Harris. Have you any idea what this guy is up to?"

The Major rubbed his chin against the back of his hand, keeping his eyes on Wilson as he pondered the question. "If I had to guess, then I'd say he wants payback for losing his living five years early. How he plans to do that, I have no idea."

"I thought you'd say that. Do you sympathise?"

"Off the record?"

"I don't keep records and this goes no further."

"The idiots at Whitehall deserve a good kick up the arse. They take some of our most experienced men and throw them on the scrap heap without a single thought how that might damage our ability to deal with the growing number of terrorist threats. It's insanity."

"Please answer the question."

"Provided he directs his anger at them, and not here, then good luck to him."

"Even if he takes innocent lives?"

The Major shot forward stretching his body across his desk. Instinctively, Wilson's hand reached inside his jacket for his gun. "Jesus, Wilson. What the hell has Fisher got hold of that makes him so dangerous?"

Wilson returned his hand to the pad on his knee, heart pumping fast but expression unchanged. "Nothing yet. Is there anywhere I can make a private call?"

*

The air was turbulent and buffeted the Eurocopter Dauphin from all sides. Sheets of water crashed into the windows like waves against a boat, and it seemed at times like they were not airborne but afloat on a choppy sea. Johnson kept his eyes on the pilot. Only a sign of nervousness on his part was the signal to begin explaining matters to God. He wouldn't make a deal that he couldn't keep in exchange for survival, but he might let God know why he had done the things he had done. It would be a last ditch attempt to sway the decision as to where he would spend the rest of eternity. Johnson was not a believer, but he knew how to hedge his bets - he wasn't stupid.

Johnson put on the supplied headphones to dull the storm's noise and focussed his thoughts on the recent interviews. It was better than trying to talk to Wilson who would have got nothing out of the major.

In the fifty minutes it had taken Wilson to interview the Major, Johnson had laid into five of Fisher's closest cohorts. They were tough, battle-hard cookies all right, but their minds were no match for his. One every ten minutes - he was pretty impressed with himself. The cold hard truth was that nobody here knew Fisher that well and, other than his love of his sister and the hate he harboured for the bureaucrats who axed him, he had learnt nothing.

Nobody seemed to bother Fisher, and Fisher didn't bother anybody else. True, these were fiercely loyal men who closed ranks when one of their own was threatened, but it was clear in each interview that they didn't see Fisher as part of their club. He was too introverted, too different. He was trusted when out in the field where he excelled at explosives and hand to hand combat. But he was quiet and odd, and no matter where you worked, in an office or in the middle of Afghanistan, odd did not include you in the ring of loyalty.

As they opened the helicopter doors moments after touching down at RAF Northolt, the cold air greeted Johnson. It was uncannily nippy for late September, but at least the rain had passed and the wind had lost its ferocity. He paced away from the downward air of the blades and waited for Wilson to catch up. The older man didn't look so good.

"Some flight eh?" Johnson said, turning up his thick coat's collar.

Wilson didn't say a word, his face pale and drawn.

"We've been up in worse, Max. Is it something the Major said?"

Wilson walked past his boss with a file under his arm, heading towards the rental car they had arrived in. The VIP car park, used mostly by high-flying military types, was right next to the airfield. The pea green Ford Mondeo sat alone in the unlit area, its colour revealing itself beneath the moonlight. It was no Mercedes, but it was virtually new, and it would do until their new one arrived. John Smith was sharp. He had known Wilson for a couple of days and spotted that the man was steadily unravelling. Johnson caught up with his partner at the Mondeo.

"If you're gonna puke then make sure it's on the outside of the car where no one will notice."

The rare joke from the tall agent didn't have the desired effect. Johnson thumbed the key which released the door locks and lit up the interior. "Get in. We'll talk about it on the way to the hotel. We've got a busy day ahead, and we need to grab a few hours sleep."

Without further discussion, both men got in the vehicle. Johnson started the engine and turned to his partner.

"Something I should know?"

Wilson snapped his seatbelt into position, faced Johnson and shrugged his shoulders. "Fisher's pissed off at losing his job. If he goes after Whitehall, what do we care?"

"Can you hear yourself?"

His partner shrugged again. "What?"

"It's our job to protect people from terrorists. Do you think letting some disgruntled soldier steal a nuclear-powered weapon and exact revenge is doing our job?"

"Maybe there are higher powers at work?"

Johnson reversed the Mondeo, wheels screeching, mirroring the stress his face refused to accommodate. He wasn't sure how much more of Wilson he could take.

"Your job is to protect Smith and Jones and take down Fisher. If you're not up to it, then tell me now and I'll find someone else in the private sector to protect your precious Savannah."

"I'm good," Wilson said.

"I thought so." Johnson shook his head. He doubted very much that Wilson was good. He wondered if their controller would sanction Wilson's demise or whether he'd have to carry out his first unauthorised kill.

*

Back at the prestigious hotel, Wilson sat on his bed and opened the folder on Fisher. Put it away, he told himself. Lie down and go to sleep. But a stronger voice was guiding him. He shuffled through papers until he found what he was looking for. There was still time to change his mind. He held the page and stared at it, caught between conflicting loyalties for the first time in his career.

There was no such thing as coincidence. There was no change there. He had always believed that. Too many signs were rearing their heads today for it to mean anything but a divine hand at work. He understood and wished he could have believed when Julie was alive. He had a chance to make a difference by doing the work of God. Picking up the hotel phone, he obtained an outside line and dialled. A tired voice answered on the seventh ring.

"Yes?"

Last chance Wilson, last chance. He cleared his throat.

"Sasha Fisher?"

"Yes."

"I have a message for your brother. Get a pen."

22: Monday 26th September, 08:45

Twickenham was a hive of activity fifteen minutes before most people started their working day. The pavements were bustling with pedestrians and the roads crammed with slow-moving buses and cars. It turned out that Justice Investigations was above a coffee house on the busy London Road, opposite Twickenham Railway Station.

Horns sounded so frequently that the sounds overlapped each other as motorists took their frustrations out on vehicles in front that they couldn't even see. The tension generated by the need to be somewhere was clear on virtually every face John observed. Many pressed phones to their ears or spoke into Bluetooth devices wrapped around their ears as they attempted to sip boiling hot coffee from takeaway cups. Even Wilson looked tired and ruffled today.

Upstairs in the small, brightly lit office, John and Savannah made themselves at home. Two desks were pushed together in the centre of the room, directly between the door to the back office and the entrance. Savannah would have her back to the window and face John. A rectangular table with three chairs was beside the main door. Wilson assured them, not convincingly, that he could be out in a second, and he would be perfectly positioned to take Fisher down. Wilson could hear and see the stairwell and the main office by way of hidden microphones and cameras in the ceilings.

John found himself watching Savannah in her supplied office clothing of knee-length black skirt and white buttoned blouse which Johnson had brought to the safe house earlier. It seemed a little stereotypical but apparently it was the best Earthguard could do on such short notice - more like he'd had to go and buy it himself.

John wore a smart charcoal grey suit, light blue shirt and yellow tie. Savannah said that he looked important and sexy. John blushed. Occasionally he would catch her looking back at him, and her whole face would light up, and he would question the reality of the night they had shared. It was surely an omen of the disaster to follow. Today, one or both of them would die a most grisly death, and last night was God's way of softening the blow, a last mortal treat sort of thing. Nothing good lasted, not that he had much by way of comparison to this sort of good.

Wilson wandered about like a bear with a sore head, occasionally glancing at Savannah and muttering to himself. The agent approached John with a scowl that etched lines deep into his forehead like the cracks of a crumbling conscience. "Smith, stop staring at Savannah and get ready. If Fisher shows we need to be ready."

Not even on first name terms anymore? The agent looked every bit as stressed as the hundreds of frantic commuters outside. Either Wilson reckoned that they were in grave danger or maybe Johnson had been wrong and his interest in Savannah was not as innocent as the tall man had suggested.

John sat down at his desk and went through his drawers as he'd been instructed.

"What are we supposed to do other than sit at our desks and look busy?" asked Savannah, staring wide eyed in apparent disbelief at the agent's attitude. Her hands were on her hips and John knew that aggressive stance well from their discussions at the Ritz. Boy, but what gorgeous hips they were. Every part of her, which had already looked perfect before, was amplified tenfold by feelings he could only guess at being part infatuation and part lust. He was tempted to consider love, but he was too much of a cynic and death was too close round the corner for him to allow it room in his thoughts. Maybe if they were together next week? Wilson approached his girlfriend. His GIRLFRIEND!

"I'm sorry, Savannah," Wilson said, throwing a case file onto John's desk. "I'm tired and I'll be glad when this is all over. Don't worry yourself unduly. Fisher won't turn up."

John guessed that the agent sounded sincere, but he was definitely spooked about something and getting tetchier by the minute. Wilson wasn't finished.

"This is a single office with only one entrance and one window. A sniper has clear sight from the roof across the street and will fire if I give the order. This won't happen because I'll have already taken care of Fisher from here."

"But why aren't you expecting him to come?" John pressed, pleased to be distracting Wilson's gaze from its constant focus on Savannah. "I thought you and Johnson put the word out that Savannah had been seen here?"

"Just a hunch, Smith. Now mind your own business and get on with your work. I'm not to be disturbed until I'm sure Fisher isn't turning up. Got it?" With his outburst over, Wilson marched into the back office and slammed the door behind him so hard the partition wall shook.

John didn't reply. He'd have felt better if Johnson was here.

Savannah sat at her desk and looked up at the ceiling before grabbing a pen and note pad. She scribbled and tore out a page, showing it to John while taking care to tilt it enough to be hidden from the camera above. It read, 'What's up with Grumpy?'.

John pulled out an identical pad from his fake in-tray and wrote back. It read, 'I think he loves you'.

Savannah chuckled and began to write a new note.

A booming voice came from behind the door of the back office. "It's not a game."

John and Savannah eyed each other like naughty school children. John considered talking to Wilson but decided against it. Perhaps he was right - maybe they should be taking it more seriously. Savannah screwed up her face at the camera, pulled out the started page from her pad, crumpled it and tossed it in the bin beneath her desk. They sat in silence for an hour and a bit before things became incredibly strange.

*

In the back office, Wilson nibbled on his fingernails until he reached skin. Had he misinterpreted God's signals? He was hardly an expert in such matters. If Smith wasn't around, he could have talked to Savannah. What she saw in the layabout, he had no idea. By now Fisher should have found where he'd hidden the gun and be on his quest for justice. Wilson could do no more. It was out of his hands.

What if Fisher directed his anger against innocent people? It would be his fault and he would be damned to hell for eternity. No. It was wrong to doubt his new found faith. Everything would be fine and Savannah would be kept away from harm thanks to him. How could Johnson have tried to put an innocent girl in danger for the sole purpose of protecting his treasured job?

Soon Johnson would arrive at where they had buried the gun, only to find it missing. Despite the tiredness from three days without more than a catnap, the thought brought a smile to his lips. The last three days had brought many revelations, not least the downright selfish nature of his partner. How he hadn't picked up on it before was a mystery. He wouldn't take a bullet for anyone again. As far as he was concerned, he only answered to one man from now on, and he could take care of himself.

Once Johnson called to confirm the theft of the gun, he would effectively end his own career. Wilson would call it in and Johnson would be history, blamed for whatever retribution on the government Fisher carried out. Johnson should have never allowed Wilson back on the job. There was no evidence to suggest that Wilson had stepped outside of protocol at any time. It was all in Johnson's head and the senior agent had messed up royally. He picked up his phone from the table where the surveillance equipment sat and dialled the Earthguard laboratory. A voice simulator answered.

"Code please."

Wilson entered the code for the laboratory.

"Simpson here," a male voice replied. "How can I help you, Agent Johnson?"

Wilson smiled. How easy it had been to switch phones with Johnson. Picking pockets was part of their training and when Johnson had put on the headphones during the turbulent flight from SAS headquarters, Wilson had seized his opportunity. As soon as he had made the switch, he was certain he had felt the hand of God on his shoulder. Wilson pressed in the code to disguise his voice. On this setting, he would sound like the computer that had answered the call, and there would be no chance of the call being located.

"Simpson, I've got the gun here in front of me. What settings result in the most powerful explosion?"

"Why are you using voice disguise, Agent Johnson?"

"Just a precaution." He shouldn't say too much. Bradshaw's young assistant was sharp. "Tell me the settings."

"The chances of that one exploding are over a hundred to one. Aren't you supposed to be taking it for disposal?"

That wasn't what he wanted to hear. Fisher had to be after the gun's explosive qualities. It sounded like Bradshaw had lied about the ease with which this might be triggered. "I thought the fault wasn't fixed?"

"The odds are still unacceptable which is why we have instructions to dismantle the remaining prototype and send the power pack to be destroyed."

"You have another prototype in the lab?"

"Version 6 of the first one. Bradshaw wanted to keep it for sentimental reasons."

"Isn't that dangerous?"

"Only if you clip on the nuclear power pack, turn both dials to full and pull the trigger."

"That's it?"

"Well, don't point it at the ground or they'll bury your remains in a matchbox." Simpson laughed at his own morbid joke for a moment. "I'm just kidding. Not that you'd want to fire the original prototype without checking your life insurance, but the general rule with these babies is not to fire on full power unless your target's over a mile away."

Wilson had to have the original prototype. "Interesting stuff," he began. "We'll have to have a chat about it some time. Anyway, the reason I'm calling is that the controller has asked me to check and see what prototypes are left and take them to be disposed of with this one here."

"But he knows we just have the one. Why would he ask you to check? I should call him."

"That's why he asked me to take care of it. You're not in his best books. He blames you for letting Bradshaw take this one out. I wouldn't bother him if I were you."

The call went quiet. Wilson rested the phone on his shoulder and put his hands together in prayer. Then, "When can I expect you?"

"I'll send Wilson, he's closer. I think he can be with you in fifteen. Okay?"

"Okay," Simpson said. "Tell your controller I was helpful, will you?"

"Sure thing," Wilson said, ending the call and making for the window. He had to get to Kingston upon Thames before Johnson found the gun missing. It was doubtful, given his partner's keenness to mop up messes without involving their controller, but if Johnson called HQ when he discovered the gun was gone, Wilson would be walking into certain disaster.

*

John winked at Savannah for at least the tenth time when the sound of the buzzer on Savannah's desk sucked the romance from the air. Fisher was here. Savannah stared at John and took three deep breaths before pressing the intercom button.

"Justice Investigations, do you have an appointment?" John could detect the slightest tremor in her voice which hopefully the intercom would disguise.

"My name is Fletcher. I would like to hire your firm's services."

Savannah released the door lock remotely and the door swung inwards.

Fisher wore blue jeans, a red sweatshirt under an unbuttoned black Donkey type jacket, and newish black Adidas trainers. He was a good inch taller than John, at about six feet two, with a slim but solid build. He had short, light brown stubble for hair, grey eyes and a fairly everyman face which wouldn't have stood out but for the paleness of his skin. It wasn't that the man was an albino but he looked like the skin under a newly removed sticking plaster. It wasn't a healthy look.

But for his body type and height, the man was nothing like the scarred figure John had spotted at Waterloo station. Fisher's eyebrows shot up in surprise, and his mouth broke into a crooked smile. John's eyebrows shot up even higher. He had seen the smile before. It was the man from outside Aphrodite's Angels.

"Varushkin," Fisher exclaimed.

John braced himself, expecting Wilson to burst through the door or a shot to smash through the window spraying glass and parts of Fisher around the room. Fisher approached the desks slowly, warily looking from side to side. No Wilson, no glass, no brains. John glanced at Savannah who stood up. Fisher turned his attention to her.

"Sit down Jones," he said, barely moving his lips. "Varushkin and I have business to discuss."

Savannah looked at John and John nodded. What was Wilson up to? John resurrected Varushkin's speech patterns in his head.

"Yes, time to make business," John said, hoping his accent would hold fast under greater stress than before. "The girl can go into back office, yes."

Fisher waved his hand in disinterested agreement. Savannah didn't need asking twice and quickly jumped up and headed to where Wilson would remove her from harm's way. As she turned the handle, John tensed uncontrollably as he prepared to take any necessary action, but when the door opened, it was apparent that unless Wilson was behind the door, he was no longer in the back office. Once Savannah was behind the closed door, John looked back to Fisher.

"Are you nervous Varushkin? What were you expecting behind the door?"

John needed to think fast. This wasn't supposed to go down like this. He remembered his premonition of disaster. If they were to survive, he had to dig deep into previously unreachable depths of confidence. He laughed out loud, a deep throaty laugh which might befit the toughest of Russians.

Fisher's mouth turned down, and his eyes narrowed suspiciously. "What's so funny?" he said.

John rocked back on his chair.

"I think you are with Earthguard and have agent in back ready to take me in, but I recognise you now."

"You do? You know who I am?"

"Sure, you are Fisher, no?"

The surprise on Fisher's face was as obvious as if he'd been attacked physically. His eyes darted about the room as if he'd been trapped and needed an instant escape route. Seemingly satisfied, he rubbed his head with his knuckles. John stayed still, his forced smile starting to ache deep in his jaw bone. He had no idea what to expect. Finally Fisher sighed and patted John on the shoulder.

"I knew you were no pimp," he said. "But how do you know who I am?"

"I know many people," John said. "I hear you are good at the combat and the explosions."

"Who told you about me?"

John swung his legs up onto the desk. Where the hell was Wilson? He hoped to God that if Wilson had climbed out of a window that Savannah had the sense to do the same.

"Earthguard of course, who else?"

"You're with Earthguard?"

"I'm with whoever can get weapon. Can you get weapon?"

A flash of anger crossed Fisher's eyes. "Don't mess with me, Varushkin. If you've talked to Earthguard, then you know they have the weapon."

John felt the familiar speeding of his heart, and he fought to keep his breathing even. This man would kill him in an instant if he messed up. This was the man who had killed his best friend and attempted to blow up Savannah. Fear and hatred fuelled his resolve. "No amount of money was enough. They are, how do you say, incruptable."

"Incorruptible."

"Yes, incruptable," John repeated, praying that his over the top accent was not becoming too theatrical. "You think you can get weapon?"

Fisher walked to Savannah's desk and sat opposite John. He pulled out a red pack of Marlboro cigarettes and expertly tapped one from the packet. As he lit the cigarette, he continued to suck down smoke for the deepest of breaths. He picked up a file and flicked through it. When he spoke, his words were accompanied by clouds of smoke. "So what's this place? Is it for real?"

"Sure. You not answer my question. You think you can get weapon?"

Fisher tossed the file back onto the desk. "I did, but I thought that the girl was the key." He pushed himself backwards and forwards on the five-wheeled chair by pushing and pulling the front of the desk while the cigarette hung from his lips. "I saw a young man at Waterloo station. I think he can help. At first I thought he was homeless, but I think he was looking for Jones. He wore ripped blue jeans and an old blue anorak. Have you bumped into him?"

"No," John said, a little too fast. Fisher didn't seem to notice as he blew a long stream of smoke towards the ceiling. John suspected that Fisher was in need of a solution and that he needed to help push him in the right direction, whatever that might be.

"Girl is with me," John said, feigning his own deep thought by pulling on his nose. "I think maybe she could persuade short one to make deal. Tall one is too like rock. No break easy. Wilson, I think, has feelings for girl."

A twinkle of interest glistened in Fisher's eyes. "You think we could still use her?"

"Perhaps. But she is gone now."

Fisher emptied a metal paper clip holder and extinguished his cigarette. "She's in the other office," he said.

She'd better not be, he thought. "I doubt it," he said.

Fisher jumped to his feet and rushed to the door. John followed him, a huge lump stuck in his throat. What if she was still in there? A gust of air from the open window greeted both men. Wilson's surveillance equipment was sitting on the table in the centre of the tiny office. John looked under the table to see the plugs had been removed from the electrical sockets and breathed a quiet sigh of relief - well done Savannah. But that wasn't his main concern. John swallowed the lump in his throat. Please don't let her have fallen.

John went to the window and peered down at the flat roof which was on an equal level with the floor where they stood. A metal fire escape ladder at the far end of the flat roof provided access to ground level. Savannah was fine. John turned to Fisher, but Fisher spoke first.

"What happened to your limp?"

"What?"

"When I saw you leaving the agency, you had a limp."

John almost sighed with relief. For once a lie was not required. "Girl, she kick me. She has big spirit."

"So where is she?"

"Like I think, she is gone, but I know where she go," he said, walking with Fisher side by side back towards the main office. Fisher observed the equipment on the desk, but without a live screen showing several viewpoints of the main office, there was nothing suspicious about surveillance gear in a private detective's offices.

"Where is she?" Fisher asked again, raising his plastic lighter up to another cigarette.

Using all of his strength, John slapped Fisher's back, catching him off guard and sending him stumbling forward, his cigarette and lighter tumbling onto the carpet. "First you tell me what you need weapon for, then we make deal, then we meet girl. This is how we do business in Moscow."

Fisher righted himself and turned back to John, shrugging off the blow as if it was nothing. But there was no mistaking the confused expression in the weary eyes. It was a 'do you know what I can do to you with my bare hands, so why are you messing with me?' look. John returned with an equal measure of mock bewilderment which wasn't too hard because his current behaviour bewildered the hell out of him. Who in their right mind manhandled a killer?

Fisher's eyes flashed between anger and uncertainty, and John's survival mechanism hovered on the verge of flight. The only thing stopping him from running was the certainty of a bullet in his back before he reached the main door. He had no choice but to continue his tough guy act and pray that his bladder would hold out.

Fisher continued to glare at John who, unable to stand the tension for a second longer, broke into his most insane-looking grin - again not much of a stretch given his predicament. His smile was not returned, but it did result in a wary nod from the pale-faced man. Fisher picked up the dropped items and resumed the process of lighting his cigarette. John's ploy had succeeded, and it was clear he had unnerved Fisher into a begrudging respect for Varushkin.

John's insides more closely resembled those of a nervous ballerina before a first live performance than the edginess of a merciless Russian killer. He held his grin of madness until he turned towards the door and marched back into the front office. The short walk allowed him a few moments when only his back was on show to Fisher, and he used the time to catch his breath which he realised he must have been holding for some time.

"Come," John said. "Let us make deal."

Fisher followed John back to the desks, both men sitting down and facing each other.

"So tell me plan with gun?" John said.

"I want to sell it to the highest bidder."

John shook his head. "I don't think so."

"Is that what Earthguard told you?"

John stared directly into Fisher's eyes. "No. But people like me buy weapons. Soldiers like you use them. So why you want weapon?"

"What's it to you?"

"I think you have mission. I see it in eyes. If we get gun, maybe you can do mission and then I take gun? I can pay big, yes?"

A look of disgust spread across Fisher's face, his pale nose twitching as if he'd breathed in a nasty smell. "I have no need of more money."

John laughed. "Better for me then. When you need gun to do mission?"

"Tomorrow."

"And how long it will take?"

"You can have the weapon back tomorrow evening, but the power will be depleted."

"Depleted. What is this word?"

"The nuclear fuel will need replacing."

"You plan to use full power of weapon?" John nearly lost his accent, his voice rising an octave with the surprise. Shit, shit, shit. Had he blown his cover?

"What do you care what I do with it?"

John had got away with it, but he needed to hold it together. "We already have nuclear weapons. We want gun for technology."

"You know it can initiate a small nuclear explosion from four miles away?"

What would the Russians, his newly adopted people, want it for? "Of course, but it is not major concern to us. In Russia we need nuclear power, and this could solve energy crisis. It make us world power again."

"And there was me thinking you wanted to kill people with it."

"Just because I have killed many people, it not mean I am bad person. My country, it dies, and it needs the technology to save it."

Fisher pulled the chair tight to the desk, leaned forwards and regarded John carefully. John did his utmost to maintain a sincere expression, but, having never previously tried under such dire circumstances, he had no idea of what Fisher was seeing.

"Are you for real?" Fisher said, motionless.

This was it. The game was up. Why had he ever thought he could pull this off? John prepared his legs for action and looked at the main door to the office. He considered the best escape route - back room window or main door?

"You need to be somewhere?"

John spun his head back around, taking his gaze past Fisher, through the gaping back office door where the open window beckoned. Window or door, he asked himself again? He had the sinking feeling that if he bolted, Fisher would still hunt down Savannah as a means of getting to Wilson.

Fisher was still talking although John's mind wasn't fully listening, assuming it was all a precursor to a gun being drawn. "It's refreshing to meet someone as adept in killing as yourself who does it for the right reasons."

"Huh?" John said, his attention returning to Fisher.

As the smile appeared on Fisher's face, John could see the scar, to the left of centre on his bottom lip which caused the smile to deform as it grew. The wages of war, he supposed. The kink vanished as Fisher spoke. "I'm impressed. I had imagined killing you once we had tracked down the gun, but I see no reason that we can't work together."

Calmness ran through John's being like a huge injection of Valium, and the relief was so welcome he was tempted to reach out and shake Fisher's hand. Words of gratitude hung on his lips, and only a handful of subconscious brain cells prevented the sudden loss of fear for his life from wreaking havoc with his adopted accent.

"Da... Da... Da... " he repeated, bringing his hand to his mouth to stifle a yawn brought about by the sudden reduction in adrenaline. He might just live - for a little longer.

"Are you okay, Varushkin?"

John pulled his hand away from his mouth, his eyes focussed on his knees. He was a long way from safety yet.

"I'm sorry, Mr Fisher. I get emotional when talk about Mother Russia." John looked up at Fisher. "Tell me what you do with gun and then we find girl."

"Like you, Varushkin, I am acting in the interests of my country. Tomorrow, the Secretary of State for Defence addresses a meeting on the future of the SAS in Whitehall's offices."

John had a bad feeling. "Yes?"

"I will use the gun to destroy him and the others who have chosen to save money at the expense of our country's war against terror."

John clenched his teeth to prevent his jaw from dropping. "I believe Whitehall offices are many. You know which to destroy?"

Fisher's smile widened, exaggerating his lip injury and giving his face a ghoulish demeanour. He took a deep drag on his cigarette before stubbing it out on the desk in one motion, like a dive-bombing aeroplane. "Not one, Varushkin. All of them," he said.

23: Monday 26th September, 10:25

Savannah slumped in the far corner of the downstairs coffee house facing the window.

It was still a little early for the mid-morning caffeine seekers, and a couple of elderly, respectable-looking ladies were the only other customers. By positioning herself with her bottom just past the edge of her cushioned chair, she could rest her elbows on the seat to prevent her slipping further down. This awkward pose permitted her sight over the top of the chairs on the opposite side of the table. From there she could see if anyone exited via the adjoining stairs from the office above.

"Can I take your order Miss?" said a smartly dressed young woman with a whiter than white apron. Her straw-coloured hair was cut short and neat, adding to her aura of efficiency. She showed no sign that Savannah's awkward pose, halfway down a chair, was anything but ordinary.

"I'm trying to avoid an ex-boyfriend," she said, not particularly caring whether the waitress believed her or not.

"We get that all the time," said the woman. "I find that an Americano goes down well in these situations."

"Okay," she said, annoyed at the distraction from her vigil. The woman winked in what might have been an attempt at female solidarity before walking back towards the nearby kitchen, leaving Savannah to ponder her options.

Her first instinct was to try and contact Johnson until she realised that she had no way of getting in touch with the Earthguard agent. Added to this was the uncertainty as to Johnson's agenda. There was every reason to assume that Wilson's partner was not on their side. She wondered if John had reactivated the watch this morning. Wilson had not mentioned that he should but then Wilson may well not be taking orders from Johnson anymore.

The only person she trusted one hundred per cent was John, and he might be in immediate danger if not already dead. Could John be believable as Varushkin for any length of time? To Christos, a muscle-bound idiot over a phone, John's Russian accent was believable, but face to face with a more intelligent psychopath, she feared the worst.

Two minutes later, with numb buttocks and aching back, she could no longer bear the thought of John coping alone. Standing and stretching, she pulled out a five pound note and walked up to the counter. The short haired waitress was chatting with the two ladies about the possibility of them sharing one of the fresh cream cakes and pastries displayed beneath the cooled glass counter.

Savannah strained her ears for sounds that might suggest a struggle above her, but the absence of any noise did little to allay her fears. Finally, the cake sale fell through, and the friends elected to settle their bill. Swapping her attention repeatedly between the window and the waitress, wishing the elderly women, who both insisted on paying half each, would hurry up with their spindly fingers and fiddly coins, Savannah could no longer wait. She fished out a fifty pound note from her skirt pocket and threw it at the waitress.

"I'll get those and the coffee I never had. Give the ladies a cake each on me. I'm going upstairs, so if I don't come out in the next hour, call the police."

The two old ladies remarked on what a kind young thing she was as the waitress tucked the cash into her own pocket. She nodded and looked at her watch. "One hour," she said.

Savannah ran to the door, up the stairs and back into the lion's den.

*

Pedestrians veered off at either side as Wilson carved his way through the morning hustle and bustle of Twickenham's streets as he made his way to the car. Johnson had left Wilson the phlegm-coloured Mondeo and hired himself another vehicle. No doubt it would be a petrol-guzzling, turbo-charged German sports car of some description.

Down the narrow side street where the Mondeo had been illegally parked, a plump man in his thirties was resting a ticket against the bonnet as he filled in the details. Wilson was thirty feet away when the red-faced man placed the ticket under a windscreen wiper blade.

A bright yellow wheel clamp, or as Johnson called them, a Denver boot, was attached to the front passenger side wheel. This was quite a regular occurrence for an Earthguard agent given the number of times they needed to park illegally. It wasn't possible to protect the country from terrorists if you spent hours looking for a parking space. Usually, they paid the fine on the spot and everything was taken care of. Today was anything but usual.

Wilson reached inside his coat and pulled out his Glock-17, pointing it at the head of the man as he walked towards him.

"You've got fifteen seconds to remove that clamp."

The chubby clamping attendant didn't look up. "Look, Mister, I don't make the rules and I don't take any shit. You think they let jerks that can't handle themselves do this job?"

"Ten seconds," said Wilson, now only ten feet away and approaching fast, gun outstretched, aim following the fat man's head.

The man looked up lazily like he had seen it all before and then realised instantly that he hadn't. The nonchalant sneer vaporised, and his hands shot into the air, his considerable belly freeing his shirt from his trousers, exposing his undulating sun-shy flesh. "Don't shoot me. I'm sorry for dissing you. I get so much shit in this job, but it ain't worth dying for."

Wilson shook his head. He pressed the barrel of his handgun deep into the protruding flesh of the man's stomach. "Look at you. You're a disgrace. Get the clamp off now and I might just let you live."

"Yes, Sir," said the man, digging out the tools from his bag to remove the heavy metal obstruction.

That was the great thing about guns: they brought back good manners to those who most needed them. Wilson scanned the street for any unwanted attention as he put away the gun under his coat. Its job was done, and the man scrabbling around with the tools at his feet was shaking enough without the constant threat of death hanging over him.

Wilson leaned over as the man's fumbling continued. "Just take it easy. You're not going to get hurt."

A few grunts later, a sweat-dripping red face looked up at Wilson. "It's off, Sir."

"Good. Now give me your mobile phone."

The man rummaged in his jacket pocket, pulled out a top of the range iPhone and offered it to Wilson.

Wilson took the phone, dropped it on the tarmac and ground his heel into it until it became a mess of broken glass and electronics.

"Got any others? A work phone or radio?"

"No, Sir."

Wilson double checked the street for movement. "Good. Stay on the ground, and count to five hundred before you get up."

"Okay."

"Okay what?" Wilson recognised the voice as his own but the words and tone reminded him of his dead father. He couldn't help himself and looked over his shoulder to be sure. It was his tired mind playing tricks on him. He had to calm down.

"Okay, Sir?" the fat man offered.

The clamper's mouth was downturned in a miserable and defeated expression, his body trembling as if the cold had cut through him. A pang of guilt hit Wilson hard. He had no right to vent his anger on this man. How had everything become so messed up?

"Do you know why I did this?"

The man on the floor looked up at him like a frightened child who would say anything to be left in peace. "You need your car?" he finally suggested.

"Because I work for the Lord."

"Sir?"

What was he doing explaining his actions to a stranger? Wilson felt the familiar vibration of his phone against his chest. It would be Johnson. He would know the phones had been switched and the gun was missing. He let it ring. It was time to trust to higher powers again.

"Five hundred and not a second earlier. Got it? And say your prayers every night."

"Yes, Sir," the man said.

*

Johnson slotted the phone back into the dashboard of his rental car. How come he had his partner's phone? Where was his? Wilson's phone had signalled that the phone's tracking system was off so it could be anywhere.

Another screw up he'd have to explain away to his controller. They were stacking up thick and fast.

The BMW was an improvement on the Mondeo, but it was only a three series and lacked the legroom and panache of the far superior Mercedes. Still it wasn't pea green, or a Ford, and that was a bonus. He was parked seven miles east of Oxford, just off the M40 motorway. His thoughts turned to the grave matters at hand. Where was the gun, and what was his partner playing at?

Over the years the agency work had provided him with many dilemmas, but he had to admit that the appropriate resolution to his current conundrum escaped him. Facts were facts, and however he looked at them, the gun was gone and Wilson was off the radar, probably with his phone.

The gun thief, who might or might not be Wilson, had made no attempt to refill the hole with the soft earth that now surrounded it. Could he and his partner have been followed when they buried the briefcase? There had been no evidence to support this, but surely it was a scenario as likely as his partner returning to retrieve the weapon in the dead of night. He tapped the leather bound steering wheel as he racked his brains for other possibilities.

Eventually, Johnson had to admit the likelihood that his long term partner had gone rogue on him was high. Of all of the four Earthguard agents Johnson had been paired with, he liked Wilson the most. Not only because he had saved his life on more than one occasion, but because he had trusted him completely. Agents were chosen partly based on their inability to be compromised, which virtually ruled out blackmail. It was times like this when additional information on your partner would have paid dividends. Knowing nothing about a man in whom you entrusted your life seemed fairly ridiculous, and yet it had always been this way.

Policy dictated that he should call in his suspicions and let his controller take care of it. Wilson would be dead before the day was out. But Johnson wasn't ready to convict and hang his partner yet.

Johnson glanced at his gold Patek Philippe chronograph. It was ten past eleven. It would take at least an hour and a half to get to Twickenham, and he needed to know what was going on now. If he called the fake detective agency, he might inadvertently put Smith and Jones in danger. If they died, not only would his agent days be over, he'd be behind bars or under six feet of earth. But the overriding truth was that he could not have their deaths on his conscience.

He pressed the top button on his watch three times. He had thought it paranoia when he had slipped the watch beneath the casing of the briefcase but how grateful he was for it at that moment. The watch on his wrist was tracking Smith and the briefcase.

*

John and Fisher remained at the desks in the offices of Ethan Justice awaiting the return of Savannah Jones. John guessed that most of the air in the room had been replaced with tobacco smoke. He had never seen anyone smoke so relentlessly.

"Are you sure she'll come back here?" said Fisher, clearly not happy at having to wait around, flicking through anything he could find to read on Savannah's desk. John reckoned the files must be more convincing than his accent because Fisher, although silent when reading, raised his eyebrows at a few choice places. Better not ask me anything, thought John, who was beginning to suspect that the waiting game might not be the answer he was hoping for. He reminded himself to stay in character.

"We agree, if no phone contact, return here in one hour." John looked at his watch and jerked in his chair as it started to vibrate in short even pulses. Was it Johnson or Wilson, and could he trust either of them?

"What's up?" Fisher asked, noticing John's change in demeanour.

John waved his watch arm in the air. "I have Parkinson's disease. It is no matter." It was the first thing John could think of to say. When he didn't respond immediately to questions, Fisher would mumble to himself as if questioning himself for trusting John.

"You're a bit young for Parkinson's, aren't you?"

"It is early onsit," John said, hoping that Fisher knew little of the disease.

"Onsit?"

"Sorry my English ... not so good today. Onset, I try to say."

Every time John spoke, he sensed that his disguise was getting thinner and thinner. Please let it be paranoia. He had managed to convince Fisher that Savannah would return in one hour, and they had spent the last ten minutes swapping tales of daring raids or, in John's case, bogus stories of the men he had killed in various ways. These blood-riddled accounts of fake assassinations and expert knife manoeuvres seemed to calm Fisher, but they were becoming ever harder to create. Soon he would say something impossible or improbable or just plain unbelievable, and his cover would be in tatters.

John thanked all the wasted hours of watching action films since he was eight. His mother had said his favourite pastime would never be of any use in the real world. Would he ever get the satisfaction of telling her 'I told you so' for the first, and probably only, time in his life? His watch went off again, and his nervous system followed suit, his whole body jerking involuntarily.

"Aren't you taking pills for that? It looks pretty bad," Fisher said, putting out his cigarette and emptying untold smoked butts from the paper clip holder into the circular bin beneath the desk before tapping another from the red and white packet.

"Doctor say pills not so good with alcohol. A Russian without vodka is no Russian at all." John cringed inwardly at his own words. Shut up John before you get yourself killed.

"You're one tough bastard, that's for sure." Fisher thumped the side of his neck with a stabbing motion. "I've never seen a man taken down so effectively with a toothbrush before, and I've seen some things. Do they teach you that in the Special Forces, or is it self-taught?"

"It is gift. I do what is necessary."

"Well, I'm honoured to have you by my side. I feel closer to you right now than I ever felt with my SAS buddies."

John didn't doubt it for a second but was eternally grateful all the same. Fisher was off the deep end and looking to murder hundreds, maybe thousands of innocent people to prove a point and save a few jobs. Ethan Justice was the only person who could save the day. Shit.

"It is good to meet honourable man also for me," he said.

Fisher glanced at his watch, and John took the opportunity to press down twice on the top button of his own fancy timepiece, trusting to chance that Johnson's or Wilson's voice wouldn't start crackling out of it.

"Where is Jones?" said Fisher. "It's been over an hour."

John didn't know what to say. He could suggest searching for her, but where would he take Fisher, and once he realised John was bluffing, it would be easy for him to dispose of him and start searching for Savannah for real. He couldn't allow that to happen. The buzzer on Savannah's desk made both men jump. Fisher pulled out a gun from behind his back, and John's heart leapt into his throat once more.

Fisher stood up. "Take out your gun," he whispered, cigarette still in his mouth, as he silently made his way to the door.

"I'm good," said John.

Fisher smiled his crooked smile and mouthed, "Tough bastard."

John's head reeled as though the overflow of adrenaline to his heart had diverted to his brain so that it could operate at super speed. Incoherent thoughts bounced like lighting inside his head, neurons sparked at immeasurable speeds. But without the certainty of facts, heightened awareness was useless. He was out of ideas and more importantly out of his depth. The only single thought his brain could hold on to was the burning hope that it wasn't Savannah at the door.

Fisher pulled the slide back on the semi-automatic pistol and motioned to John to activate the remote door entry system. John hesitated. It was one of those decisions he could never take back and would be the difference between life and death for him and others. He swallowed as he pressed the door release button on the intercom system. Fisher aimed at the doorway from the left where the door would keep him hidden from the visitor. Why hadn't they asked who it was over the intercom? Pull your finger out, John.

Savannah Jones strode in like she hadn't a care in the world.

"Heh, Vushky baby," she said. "What's next?"

"You're late," Fisher said, returning the gun behind his back, under his jacket.

"I may well be ..." she said, turning but not registering any surprise at Fisher's presence behind the door, "... but I know where the super gun is so you boys better play nice with me."

24: Monday 26th September, 11:35

After picking up the original prototype from the lab in Kingston, Wilson had driven to Teddington on a hunch. Or was it a hint from the heavens? Either way, his plan had hit a bump in the road. At the garden centre in Teddington, Wilson had recovered the briefcase containing the latest prototype from where he had hidden it during the night. Fisher had not collected the gun.

Nobody batted an eyelid as he shifted four heavy bags of fertilizer to reveal the case underneath. Both identical briefcases now resided in the back of the Mondeo. He guessed that only one of two things could have happened. Either Fisher suspected a set up or Fisher's sister had not passed on the coded message. All SAS troops knew the code, and if he had received the message, deciphering the code would have been straightforward. How was he going to get in contact now?

The road back to Twickenham was busy, and Wilson tuned the radio into a religious channel. There were some fairly mixed-up callers on the show, but most of them were just after attention and were not real believers like him. He was amazed at just how calm he felt despite the problems he was experiencing. Julie had been right all along. God came along when you least expected him. As he hummed along to a well-known hymn whose words escaped him, he was struck by a thought. What if Fisher had turned up at the office in Twickenham?

He grabbed Johnson's phone from his pocket and called Justice Investigations.

*

Whenever remotely possible, Johnson weaved the silver BMW in and out of every available space of the M40. Angry motorists flashed, hooted, shook fists and some even opened windows and shouted obscenities which were lost in the air behind him. He pictured an unknown but severely bad-tempered controller at his termination debriefing. First things first, though.

With his partner's watch and mobile phone off the Earthguard grid, Johnson had no way of locating Wilson. His last known location was Kingston upon Thames, but if he was hiding, there were plenty of ways he could have disguised his position. The positioning systems of the phones and watches were for an agent's safety but easily adapted to deception purposes. If Wilson had made contact with Fisher, then the weapon may soon be in the hands of a man capable of anything.

Surely Wilson would not allow the death of innocents? Johnson had to assume the worst and go after the weapon. All he knew for certain was that John Smith and the gun were both in Twickenham, not more than half a mile apart. Wilson and Fisher could be with them, or not. He had no way of knowing for sure. The weapon, with its potential for death and destruction, must be his first port of call. Everything revolved around Bradshaw's invention, and he doubted that its death toll was even close to being over.

Johnson's mobile rang and instantly switched to Bluetooth, which was just as well because at over a hundred and forty miles an hour, he needed both hands on the steering wheel. It had to be Wilson. Finally, some sense to all of this.

"Wilson?" said the loud speaker.

Johnson recognised the uptight tones of Major Harris.

"Harris, what's up?"

"Johnson? I was calling the number your partner left me?"

"He's off the grid. You got something?"

There was a lengthy silence. There was no love lost between the two men, but Johnson could not afford to antagonise the Major.

"Look, Major, I know we didn't really hit it off last night. I can be a huge pain in the ass, but we've got problems, and I don't know for sure what's going on." Johnson swerved onto the hard shoulder to undertake traffic in the fast lane. A lorry driver sounded his horn and stuck up two fingers at

Johnson. "If you know anything that can help me, I'll happily kiss your ass the next time we meet."

Another silence followed.

"Major?"

The loudspeaker burst back into life. "One of my men came to see me after talking to Jenkins, the third person you interviewed."

"Yeah, Thomas Jenkins, I remember him. So who's the guy?"

"It's not who he is but what happened to him in Hereford when he saw Fisher."

"Go on."

"The soldier saw him coming out of a psychologist's practice, and when he teased Fisher about being a mental case, Fisher damn near killed him."

"You got the number of this place?"

"I looked it up and wrote it down. I thought you'd be interested."

Johnson entered the number into his mobile, all the time darting in and out of traffic like he was sitting at the wheel of a racing car simulator. There was no telling what either madman had planned for the weapon. Whatever the target, their chances of remaining at large were getting shorter by the minute, and mad or not, they had to realise that fact. He pressed down a little further on the accelerator. The number of lives he could end in a motorway pile up fell far short of the numbers a small nuclear explosion in a built up area like Twickenham could end. He brushed the side of a Mitsubishi pickup. Of course, the chances of preventing the explosion were far better if he stayed alive.

"I'll look forward to puckering up my arse," said the Major.

Johnson disconnected and called the psychologist's number, metal scraping against metal as the car brushed against the barrier of the central reservation. Keep it together, Johnson.

As Johnson left the M40 to join up with the M25 the call was answered.

"Hello, Doctor Meredith's secretary."

Johnson ran a red light on the busy roundabout and missed colliding with joining traffic by the finest of margins. Further horns and abusive gestures ensued.

"Shit, that was close." The line went dead. "Son of a bitch." He pushed the button to redial as he forced the BMW in front of a slow moving lorry. Another booming horn sounded the driver's displeasure.

"Hello, Doctor Meredith's secretary."

"Doctor Meredith, please," said Johnson. "It's a matter of life and death."

"I'm sorry, Sir, but Doctor Meredith is with a patient," said the secretary.

"Look, I'm having a bad day, and if one of Meredith's patients ends up killing thousands of you Brits, then I'll make sure everybody knows that you wouldn't help."

The secretary cleared her throat. "Just putting you through."

What was wrong with connecting? Why did the Brits have to say things in such a nonsensical way? A soft female voice with a New England accent came over the speaker.

"Doctor Meredith speaking."

Johnson was taken aback. Fisher's mind doctor was a fellow American. The accent was strong: Boston he reckoned. Maybe now he'd get some answers. "Hi, Doctor, I'm driving down the M25 at ... let me see ... one hundred and forty-six miles per hour, so if I swear or go quiet, please don't hang up."

"Slow down. Do you need an appointment? If you're considering suicide I can come to you. You can always kill yourself later. One less New Yorker won't cause many tears, but there's no need to take others with you."

Johnson liked her immediately. "No suicide, and I don't need a shrink, but I do need to know about one of your patients. I could give you a number to ring for authorisation but by then it would be too late."

"You must know then that I can't let you have that information and the reasons why."

"Sure, but thousands of lives may be at risk."

"May?" Meredith said. "I can't make a decision based on 'may'."

"Gregory Fisher *may* have acquired a nuclear weapon and *may* blow up thousands of innocent people. I really need your help, Doctor."

The sound of fingers rapidly hitting computer keys was almost masked by the screaming four litre, eight cylinder engine as Johnson shot down the hard shoulder leaving the dawdling traffic bemused and behind him. The M3 Coupe was growing on him.

"Doctor?"

"Call me Susan. I'm just going through his file. How many words do you want this in?"

"As few as possible."

Johnson heard police sirens behind him and looked in the mirror to see an unmarked maroon Vauxhall Omega. He put his foot down to the floor and accelerated further away, amazed that the M3 still had torque to spare.

"He's capable of great violence, and he loves his sister."

It was a concise summary, but it didn't help in the least.

"I know this already. Give me something I can use."

"I mean he *really* loves his sister. He was planning to relocate them both to Australia after he had all the money together. He was going to change their identities and set up as man and wife. In five years he would have the funds to make it all possible. Fisher and his sister were sexually abused by their father when children. This made them closer, and this is what sometimes happens."

"Is the sister complicit in all of this?"

"I doubt it... What is your name anyway?"

"Call me Herb."

"I have no idea, Herb, what all of this is, but I'm quite certain that his sister wants nothing to do with him and has moved home within York to avoid his visits. He forces her to engage in phone sex, which she does, provided he makes no attempt to discover her new location."

"Jesus, that's disgusting."

"He's a product of his father's abuse. The poor man never stood a chance."

"Yeah, well that poor guy may well blast Twickenham to Kingdom come if we don't find a way to stop him. Would he listen to his sister?"

"Maybe, but she's three hours' drive in the opposite direction."

"Do you have her phone number, Susan?"

"Yes, but it might be better if I call her. Tell me what you need."

"Okay, that would be great. Tell her to promise him anything to stop."

"She might not be up to this, Herb."

"I know, but it's worth a shot. If I don't make it in time, it might be all we've got. Call me if there's anything I need to know."

Johnson gave Susan Meredith a number which would divert to his or rather Wilson's mobile.

"Keep me informed please, Susan."

"Will do, Herb. And Herb?"

"Yeah?"

"Mostly Fisher's in control, especially when in a structured environment like the SAS. Out of these types of surroundings, he's..."

"Yes?"

"In terms I won't admit to, this guy is off the wall nuts. He's psychotic, he's clever and he's dangerous. His moral boundary is virtually non-existent."

"Got it. Anything else?"

"How about dinner after this is over? You sound like an interesting man, for a New Yorker that is!"

"Only if I can wear a mask... Protocol you see. We can't be recognised."

"Boy, do you need my help. But whatever starts your engine, Herb. As long as you're not a Yankees fan, I don't care."

The call ended. Johnson smiled as he checked the rear view mirror. The Vauxhall Omega was dropping back, but it wouldn't be long before the helicopters were out and the road blocks began. Still, might get the techies to supe up one of these M3 babies and drop the Mercedes brand when he ordered his new company vehicle - if he still had a job. If he took the back roads, he would waste time but might just avoid detection.

He would take the turnoff onto the A308 which would get him to Twickenham via Hampton. If there wasn't a road block before then, he might just stand a chance. As he veered onto the grass verge to drive around a broken down metallic blue Saab, he wondered what Susan Meredith might look like. She certainly had a beautiful voice - for a New Englander.

*

The phone at Justice Investigations began to ring just as Savannah, John and Fisher were about to leave.

"Leave it," Fisher said. "I want to get the gun now."

"What is rush," John said. "We get today. Is soon enough, no?"

Savannah picked up on John's lead. "It might be Wilson trying to contact me. I should take it."

Fisher walked around Savannah and whispered in John's ear. "Are you sure we can trust the girl?"

John nodded. "Absolutely," he said. "Let girl speak. Few minutes only."

Fisher patted John's shoulder with force. "If you say so, Vushky baby." He laughed and headed into the back office. "I need to make a call myself, but let Jones know that I have my eye on her," he said closing the door to leave just an inch where his eye looked back at John. He obviously didn't trust Varushkin or Savannah fully, but he had cheered up noticeably.

"Don't worry," John called after him. "I'll stay close to her." He wasn't going to let her out of his sight again.

Savannah picked up the phone at her desk and John sidled up next to her. She tilted the receiver towards John so he could listen in.

"Hello, Justice Investigations," Savannah answered.

"Can you talk," said Wilson.

"No, Mr Justice is with a client."

"Is Fisher there?"

"Yes, thank you very much for that," Savannah said as if she were truly grateful.

"Look, Savannah, I have the gun, and I'm going to use it to get you out of this. Tell Fisher that Smith will take the gun to him."

"No, we can't do that."

John nudged Savannah and mouthed silently, "Tell him yes." John wanted to grab the phone and tell Wilson that she would do exactly what he suggested, but it would only alert Fisher to their deceit and that could get them all killed.

The voice on the phone sounded incredulous. "Don't you want to live?"

"Either we are both on the case or both off the case," Savannah said, raising her eyebrows at John.

John shook his head trying hard to keep Savannah directly between himself and the gap in the back office door. She was damn good at making up ambiguous conversation on the spot, but she was putting herself in harm's way again when she had an easy escape route. John was sure that Wilson would not hurt Savannah regardless of what his exact plans were.

"You'd risk your own life for that layabout?" the voice said.

"In a heartbeat. Tell me where and how we can collect our fee," Savannah answered.

"You're making it hard for me to help you."

"Are we both on or off the case?"

"All right, have it your own way, Savannah. I have to make one more stop. Meet me in half an hour at the ticket office at Twickenham Rail Station."

The line went dead. John and Savannah looked at each other as she put down the phone. John was desperate to speak and turned to the crack in the door to see if he could risk it. To his surprise, the door had been fully shut. There could be useful knowledge to be had. John crept over and pressed his ear to the partition wall. Fisher's voice was raised.

"Sasha, I'm not like that anymore. I told you, I've had help. We can make it work."

Savannah made her way to join John and eavesdrop, positioning herself so that they faced each other as they listened in.

*

I circle the table of surveillance equipment as I search for the right words. Life with Sasha is only a day away. I can't blow it now. My heart is racing.

"I've booked our tickets for tomorrow evening, first class all the way."

"First class? Can you afford it?"

She's impressed. "Yes, of course I can. Only the best for my sister."

"Okay, Gregory, let's do it."

I've done it. I've really done it. Once Whitehall is a pile of rubble and dead bodies, I can start my new life. After twenty-five years, I finally get my sister back.

"You're sure? You mean it?"

"Yes."

Images of sunny days, a garden and a pool play in my head. Sasha strolls around the pool in a neon green bikini and calls to me to join her in the cooling water. We swim for a while before taking a shower together. She reaches between my legs. The thought makes me gasp, my heart pumps even harder and my body tingles.

"Tell me what to do with my hand."

"No."

"Come on, my darling Sasha. I'll never really touch you. It's just a game." *I'm playing with fire but I need relief. The feeling is too strong to control. Lust is in charge of me, and I can't stop it. Once she is mine, she will learn to love me as her husband. She will be as eager as I was when we were young and we were forced to perform for our father. "Just talk to me, Sasha. Help me relax."*

"You promise that nobody will get hurt?"

Where the hell did that come from? "What are you talking about?"

"I mean that you'll come straight here, right now, and we'll plan our move together."

Alarm bells ring in my head. "Who have you been talking to?"

"Nobody." Silence. Then, "You want to be inside me?"

The tingle returns, my breath quickens and my penis stirs. Desire tugs at my will like an unquenchable thirst, but a nagging doubt hovers between me and my surrender to the moment. Sasha is too keen. She has never been keen. She has betrayed me. My dream had been so close I could have touched it, and now it is in tatters.

"What's going on?" I demand. "Who's got to you?"

"Please ... please don't kill anyone, Gregory. It's wrong, just like you and I are wrong."

All thoughts of sex evaporate and my heart's pounding is now fuelled solely by anger. My world has been destroyed, and somebody has to pay. A faint and pleading voice passes by my ear as I draw the phone back. I launch the phone against the wall next to the window with such force that it bursts open as if it has exploded from within, showering the room and table with shards of plastic and broken electronic components. Those responsible must die.

*

Savannah and John jumped back from the partition wall, their gazes locked together in astonishment. Another deeper crash sounded which John guessed was the monitoring equipment on the table being swept onto the floor. The psychopath was pissed off.

John grabbed Savannah by the hand and pulled her over to her previous position by the desk and handed her the phone. Savannah's gaping mouth snapped shut the second the adjoining door clicked open and a red faced Fisher burst through. She was smart and quick.

"So you won't be there when we collect it?" Savannah said into the phone. John could hear the dialling tone but Fisher was too far away - he hoped. "We'll meet soon. You can take me for a night out. Okay. Bye now, Sweetie." Savannah finished, returning the handset to its home.

Fisher's face trembled and twitched like the muscles had a life of their own. John sensed real danger. Fisher was fuelled with anger, and like a fizzling firework, he was in danger of going off at any moment.

"Savannah say now we get gun," John said, a lump of trepidation rising in his throat, threatening to sabotage his accent. "It is near to lunch, I am hungry."

"Were you listening to my conversation?" Fisher asked, hand reaching behind him.

John resisted a glance at Savannah. It was clear that Fisher was itching for confrontation. Any knowing looks between them could be fatal. "No. Only heard smashing of things. Good job gun pay for damage."

In the blink of an eye Fisher had pulled out a semi-automatic pistol and pointed it at John. The gun jerked more than shook with the twitching of Fisher's hand, but at this distance, it would still be hard to miss. "Good job or what, Varushkin?" he said, through clenched teeth.

A person this jumpy could accidentally fire the gun. It was a shame that Fisher couldn't internalise his rage and blow his own brains out.

"Calm down. We are comrades. Tell me who make you feel this way. I will kill for you," John said, taking a tentative step forward. What was he doing?

Fisher lowered the gun a few inches. "Stay back, Varushkin, or I'll shatter your kneecaps."

Taking twitches into account, John was likely to be hit anywhere from his waist down, and the thought stopped him dead in his tracks.

"Look boys," piped up Savannah. "Are we done here? Haven't we got a gun to pick up?"

Fisher swung the gun up and round to point at Savannah's head.

"No!" John said, stepping between Fisher and Savannah.

Fisher walked up to John and pressed the end of the gun against his forehead. The small, jumpy movements of the gun made John's head shake in unison.

"What happened to your accent, Varushkin?"

John closed his eyes. The constant stress of possible death was becoming unbearable. He pressed his head back against the gun.

"I live here for long time. My accent gets mixed. We get gun now or you shoot? I prefer to get gun, but I am bored, so either is good."

Fisher exhaled through pursed lips as he pulled the gun away and turned his back on his captives. Savannah came up behind John. He felt her short and rapid breath on the back of his neck. "Take it easy, hero," she whispered.

Fisher spoke with his back to John and Savannah. "I have nothing against you, Varushkin, or you, Jones. I need to get the gun and make those responsible pay for what they did to us."

While curiosity begged a question of John, he figured anything more than straightforward agreement was a risk too far. "We go now," he said, signalling to Savannah to lead the way while he followed closely behind Fisher.

*

I don't trust Jones. She is pretty, more than pretty - young and beautiful, like Sasha after she had blossomed in the sunlight of our parents' deaths. Pretty only means double-crossing to me now.

My body is numb as I follow Varushkin and the girl. Varushkin is obviously my equal or superior in combat. I never thought I'd see the day. He will have to die, as will the girl. I don't thirst to torture these two. I can vent my artistic side on those that deserve it most. First I need the gun.

My mind wanders and loses focus. The sharpness is wavering. I am drifting in a sea of memories. I remember my childhood and my parents. They had been parents by genetics only. If there is a gene providing a duty of care or nurture, then theirs had long since been driven into submission by the constant intake of alcohol and drugs. The social workers had been useless. Sasha, my mother and I wore fresh bruises and cuts every day. 'Not enough evidence' they would repeat over and over. Mould grew in the corners and insects fed on the mould. Different social workers would visit us weekly and express concern but flinch and run the moment our father shouted and raised his fists.

My spineless bitch of a mother had retreated within from the physical and mental torment, taking pain free refuge in her best friend, heroin. I remember our father kicking her on the ground and shouting, "You'll take any man's cock in any hole for a needle, but you won't touch mine with gloves on."

My father had brought about the change to the family dynamic by getting Sasha pregnant. She had been the only good thing in my life, and her forced departure left me as the focus of his beatings and molestations. Not once did I surrender to him, not once. It would have spared me countless punches, bruises and broken bones. I was only fourteen, but I took everything he had. My persistent resistance rewarded me with more anger, harder blows and more sadistic rapes. I absorbed every bit of pain, held it and stored it up until I was ready and it could wait no more.

I'll never forget the look on the bloated drunkard's face as he realised that his sixteen year old son was stronger than him. Every weight lifted in every spare second, until my head throbbed with the effort, had been worth it just to see fear in the bastard's eyes as I forced his trembling head into the gas oven.

My drug retarded mother had looked on in her permanent dreamlike state, like a zombie whose only appetite was for a syringe of heroin rather than flesh. I had smashed her face in with my fists clenched tightly in my father's gardening gloves, the ones he used to protect his own knuckles when raining blows upon me. The irony was heavenly. I had done her the biggest favour imaginable. Blow upon blow rocked her head sideways and backwards until it finally flopped and sagged like a rag doll. She had toppled face first to the lino floor like a felled tree whose connection with the living was severed forever. I had finally broken free.

"We don't like to split families up," Social Services had said in their defence at the inquest of his parents' deaths. Why couldn't they have saved me when they removed Sasha?

It had been a real life tragedy. Forget about ghosts and monsters, they had nothing on good old Mum and Dad.

"Fisher," says Savannah, pulling me back from the kerb. A red Fiat Punto misses my foot by inches.

"Huh?"

Why hadn't she just pushed me in front of the car? Perhaps it would have been for the best. There is nothing but my vengeance to keep me here. It's better than nothing. It is clear that Sasha wants nothing to do with me as a sister let alone anything more. I know that she enjoyed the sex in front of our father. She never speaks of the times we played together when father was out. Or that there had been every possibility that I had made her pregnant. There is no point in telling her this now. It won't get her back.

It isn't my fault I've turned out like my father, Doctor Meredith had said so herself. So whose fault is it? Who had allowed us to drown in our despair until all of our needs, even sexual, were provided solely by each other? Yes, somebody needs to pay more than Whitehall. They can wait. My plans need to change.

25: Monday 26th September, 12:15

A minute green light pulsed beneath the centre of Johnson's watch face, alerting him that a sound transmission was being received from Smith.

Distracted by phone calls and high speed driving, he had no way of knowing how long he had been oblivious to the flashing alert. He twisted the winder back a notch, pairing the Bluetooth device with the cars loudspeaker. At first there was only silence, but upon turning up the speaker, he realised that the noises were similar to the ones that surrounded him. It was the sound of traffic but in a built up area with car horns and revving engines going nowhere fast. He couldn't risk making verbal contact with Smith via the watch. For all he knew Fisher or Wilson or both could be listening in.

He checked the proximity of Smith to the watch he had planted inside the briefcase. They were no more than a quarter of a mile apart, and the distance was reducing. If he didn't get there soon, his death-defying driving would have been in vain. He activated the vibration on Smith's watch once more. If Smith still had the watch, he might just take the hint.

*

John Smith, Savannah Jones and Gregory Fisher approached the row of glass doors which formed the main entrance to Twickenham station. It was cool and breezy. The clouds above were thick, high and white, suggesting little chance of rain or sunshine. With the morning commute to work over, few bodies entered or emerged through the doors. John jerked his arm as the vibrating Rolex once again caught him unawares. Bloody watch was going to give him a coronary.

"What's up?" Savannah asked as they entered the quiet station through the glass doors.

"Doesn't she know?" Fisher said. John almost believed there was genuine sadness in Fisher's tone, but he was past trying to rationalise the minds of others. For whatever reason, good or bad, the ex-soldier was nuts, and John's only concern was to save Savannah and himself.

"Is not her business," John said dismissively, longing for the time when he could explain the remark to Savannah. If they were meeting Wilson, then surely it must be Johnson setting off his watch. If so, Johnson should have worked out that the three of them were together and were on their way to meet Wilson. Maybe the agent was close and trying to signal his arrival? He looked around, keeping his head forward and allowing his eyes to wander, but there was no sign of the tall man in the distinctive dark coat. Then it struck him. Johnson wanted information. John stopped and tapped Fisher on the shoulder.

"Fisher, tell Savannah what you plan for weapon."

Fisher snarled his annoyance. He was not pleased at the halt in their progress. He ignored John's request. "Do we have to catch a train from here?"

"No. The weapon is in the station. Tell Savannah about Whitehall."

"Where in the station?"

"I don't know. I'm following Savannah." John wanted to mention Wilson to let Johnson know that they were meeting his partner, but he thought that Fisher's surprise at the sight of Wilson might be to their advantage. "Where is it Savannah?"

As they passed through the door in single file, Savannah stopped and turned to the two men behind her, a look of annoyance on her face. "Keep up, boys, and all will be revealed." John wished he felt as confident as Savannah acted.

*

The small square lounge was littered with beer cans, crisp packets and old celebrity magazines. Cigarette smoke engulfed the top third of the room. Wilson fanned the air with his hand as he walked in. He placed the two briefcases down by the side of the sofa. The old cathode ray tube television blared out tuneless music at a volume meant only for the hard of hearing.

Wilson moved a box of Frosties to make room to sit on the sofa where the air was more breathable.

"What do you want?" Kate asked, opening a tin of strong Heineken lager and taking two large swigs. "I thought with Mum dead, I'd never have to see you again."

Wilson was calm and impressed with himself. It had been six years since he'd been around his daughter and not wanted to slap her face. It convinced him that everything would work out for the best. He examined Kate as she looked back at him. She was thin and pale with a thick head of bright red hair just short of her shoulders. The face and tongue piercings had always offended him the most, but in reality they were just challenges to be overcome. There was some hard work for both of them ahead.

"I'm a changed man, Kate," he said, shifting a t-shirt beside him to allow his daughter to sit down.

Kate slurped down another few swigs of lager from the tin and burped hard and long.

Wilson swallowed. "Why don't you make us a cup of tea, and we'll have a chat."

"Why don't you just fuck off?" Kate said, walking over to the television, grabbing the remote control and turning the volume up.

The din was unbearable. Wilson jumped up and pulled the plug from the wall socket. The relief was instant. He could do this. He could make this work.

"Please, Kate. Let's talk." He placed his hand on her back and pressed gently, trying to edge her nearer the sofa. She recoiled from his touch.

"Get your fucking hands off me."

"Kate, it's all right. Everything's going to be just fine."

His daughter took a step towards the sofa and turned. Her eyes were bloodshot and her face gaunt.

"No, it's not. Mum's dead, and you didn't even visit her."

"I was in hospital. I was shot."

"So fucking what? You were never there for either of us. The least you could have done was have her moved to a private room. You let her die in an NHS ward. You fucking bastard."

Wilson moved slowly to his daughter, his arms outstretched. She backed away.

"I know that I let your Mum down, and I know I haven't been there for you. All of that has changed now. I've found God."

Kate's retreat abruptly ended. Her mouth opened registering an astonishment he had not witnessed from his daughter in many a year.

"Oh my God," she said, covering her open mouth with a hand.

"Yes, it's true. You and I can be a family again." He moved forward and Kate remained still. She knew he was telling the truth. He raised his arms again and moved in to hold her. As he enclosed her into his grasp, her body began to shake. It was the first sign of real emotion. They were going to be fine. He thanked God, closed his eyes and squeezed lightly with his arms. It was the start of their salvation.

"I'm here, Kate," he said. "We're going to be fine."

Kate's shaking became more pronounced but the expected tears never surfaced. Instead of cries of anguish, the sound of laughter rang in his ears. Not the happy, cheerful sound of merriment but long, loud howls of ridicule with barely a breath in between. She pushed him away, and he saw the look of derision in her red eyes. It was unmistakable.

"You're the devil," he said, dropping his hands to his sides and stepping back. "You can't be saved."

His words drew more belly laughs from his daughter as she struggled to find the air to speak.

"Please no more," she said, supporting herself with one hand against the wall.

Wilson charged forward and slapped her hard against the side of her head sending her halfway across the room. Only the wall stopped her falling to the floor.

Kate's right cheek glowed red from the blow. She steadied herself against the wall. Her eyes flashed with anger as she stared at her father defiantly.

"Welcome back, Dad," she said, through bared teeth.

Wilson was lost for a second. How could he have been so wrong? Why would God have lied to him? And then uncertainty vanished, and he knew exactly what was expected of him. He marched to the sofa and picked up the briefcase containing the latest prototype of the gun. Laying it flat on the sofa, he opened the case and pulled the casing which housed the gun out and onto the sofa.

"What the fuck is that?" his daughter asked, eying the shiny chrome contents of the casing.

Ignoring his daughter, Wilson spotted the watch immediately. He couldn't help but smile before replacing the gun and casing back into the briefcase. Johnson was so predictable. Closing the case with a loud click, he turned to Kate.

"If my partner, Johnson, turns up, I want you to give him this case."

Kate made her way to the sofa, rubbing her cheek as she neared. "Why can't I keep it? That gun looks cool. A lot more fun than those Tasers you get for me."

Wilson handed the case to his daughter.

"If you tamper with the case, it will blow up in your face. I want you to give Johnson a message."

"Why the fuck should I after you hit me?"

Wilson raised his hand and Kate jumped back. Wilson smiled.

"If you don't, I'll have you evicted from this expensive flat, and you can live on the streets where you belong."

"All right. Keep your hair on. I'll fucking do it."

*

Johnson screeched through the traffic lights at the crossroads that lead onto Wellington Road at Hampton Hill. He was less than two miles away from Twickenham and the weapon. He no longer cared that several police cars followed him. He glanced at the watch for a new proximity reading. The briefcase carrying the weapon and Smith were less than a quarter of a mile apart.

An old couple leapt out of his path as he mounted the kerb, his hand pressing down hard on the horn as if it would help them react faster. Other pedestrians further along cleared a path for the oncoming vehicle but not the green rubbish bin which flew into the air and over the bonnet sending tins, bottles and other debris over the windscreen. Johnson stamped his foot on the accelerator, and the V8 engine roared with approval.

*

Belying his physique, Wilson smoothly came up behind Fisher and thrust his Glock pistol into the man's back.

"Hold it right there, gentlemen and lady," Wilson said, turning to a bench on platform four. "Let's take a seat over there shall we? No trains departing from platform four today, so I'm told. We won't be disturbed."

Fisher looked back over his shoulder. "Earthguard, I told you we couldn't trust her, Varushkin. Women are all deceitful bitches."

"Watch your language in front of the lady, Fisher. Let's keep it polite, shall we?"

"Meet the man with the gun," Savannah said, as Wilson relieved Fisher of his Beretta 92. "Or should I now say, two guns and a super weapon?"

Wilson admired the Berretta for a few seconds in the concealed space between himself and Fisher's back before tucking the gun into his trousers beneath his coat and shoving Fisher in the back.

"Move it tough guy," he said, reckoning that while Smith had a bit of the hero in him, Fisher was the only threat to his control of the situation. The group of four, who had been thrown together by Fisher's actions, sat side by side on the bench with Wilson between Savannah and Fisher and Smith on the far right next to Fisher. Nobody said a word until Wilson turned to his right and broke the silence.

"Tell me how you plan to take revenge against the bureaucrats that put you out of work."

Fisher stared back into Wilson's eyes as he reached inside his jacket. Wilson directed the gun, which was now held under his coat, at Fisher.

"Hands away from your pockets."

Fisher ignored Wilson, pulled out a packet of Marlboro Red cigarettes and proceeded to remove and light one.

No smoking signs were everywhere. Fisher could attract unwanted attention. The disobedience could not be tolerated. Wilson stood up and turned round to face Fisher. With his unarmed hand, he pulled the cigarette from Fisher's mouth and demolished it beneath the sole of his shiny black footwear. "Hand them over," he demanded.

Fisher looked up. "I don't think so."

Wilson pulled the Glock from under his coat and pistol whipped Fisher on the side of the head. In a flash, the gun was back under cover. "Give me the cigarettes, or I make a call and your sister dies."

The pale seated figure smiled in a strange misshapen 'v' as he wiped blood from his temple area. It gave Wilson the creeps. Fisher wasn't all there. Wilson edged forward and held out his hand. This time Fisher handed the packet over. Thank God.

"So tell me about your revenge plan."

Smith interrupted. "Are you fucking crazy?" he said, a spray of spittle joining the condensation on his breath. "This guy plans to blow up the whole of Whitehall."

Wilson didn't look at Smith when he spoke. "Keep it down, Smith. You're the only one here expendable at present. Fisher, did you speak to your sister recently?"

Fisher was staring at Smith like he was an age-old enemy he knew existed but had never met before. His feet were twitching as if he was about to launch himself. Wilson grabbed Fisher's left shoulder and spun him round with force.

"Fisher, what's going on with you two?"

"He told me that his name was Varushkin, a Russian Secret Services operative. I'm going to snap his neck."

"The kid's quite a character, I'll give him that," Wilson said, looking at Savannah. She looked pale but otherwise none the worse for wear. "Try John Smith, Junior Clerk at Walker's Imports." She never would have guessed Smith's job was quite that menial.

Smith threw his hands in the air. "I'm thirty-two so will you please stop calling me kid." Smith shrugged apologetically although Fisher was facing Wilson. "In all fairness, I think you made the assumption that I was Varushkin," he said.

Fisher pulled free of Wilson's grip and spun round to face Smith again.

"But I saw you at the agency." He regarded John with narrowed eyes. "You killed Christos with a broken piece of toothbrush."

Smith shrugged again. "It was in self-defence, and I got lucky."

Fisher was in a trance. Then the ex-SAS soldier's face began to twitch like he had been struck with a sudden nervous disorder. His face went crimson, and he grabbed Smith by the front of his shirt, pulling him close with little effort.

"Hey," Smith said, several shirt buttons flying loose as he attempted to pull back.

"You're scruffy anorak man," Fisher said, blinking and twitching as he snarled into Smith's face.

Smith snarled back. "You're psychopath killer man and no bloody fashion icon yourself."

Wilson was impressed. The kid had come a long way in a few days, and he could see why Johnson and Savannah were so enamoured with him. The agent rose from the bench and turned round to face the other three, letting his coat fall open to display Fisher's gun.

"Enough of the chit chat. I'll do the talking. Fisher, when did you last talk to your sister?"

Fisher's eyes still burned holes into Smith. Wilson gave him a hard kick in the shin with his steel toecaps. Fisher's attention was returned.

"Did Sasha ring you during the night?"

"What... No, I spoke with her this morning in Varush ... Smith's office."

"Did she pass on a message to you?"

"No," Fisher said, his jaws clenching and the muscles in his neck tensing. "We just argued." The man was fragile. It was obvious to Wilson that his sister never had any intention of passing on his message giving Fisher the coded gun location.

"I wasn't expecting you in Twickenham this morning. Seems you and your sister have a few issues. Is it true what Smith said about Whitehall?"

"I've other things to do first." There was madness in Fisher's lopsided smile.

"What things?"

Fisher's face drooped, and his smile evaporated. His hands reached for his head as he doubled over. His body started to shake. This wasn't going to be easy.

"I'm going to kill the social workers responsible for making me like my father," he said.

"What are you talking about?"

"I'm a monster like my father. I'm going to kill the people that made me like this, and then I'm going to end my own life."

Wilson looked down at Fisher who now sobbed openly, tears dripping onto the floor between his feet. He caught Smith and Savannah sharing a moment of understanding. It would be one of their last. Only Savannah was going to leave the station alive.

"Pull yourself together, Soldier," boomed Wilson. "Have you forgotten your training?"

Wilson needed to reach the soldier inside the broken shell. Somewhere deep down in the man's core was a battle-hardened warrior who fought the good fight and sought the right cause. He needed to bring that person out.

"Stop snivelling like a little girl, and pull yourself together. You are not your father," Wilson shouted, slapping the side of Fisher's head with enough power to rock the man's head to one side. "Can you hear me, Soldier?"

Savannah and Smith looked at each other again. Wilson sensed the strong bond they had formed. It was a bond that would soon be broken for eternity. He caught her glancing up at him, and he smiled back apologetically. She didn't understand because she didn't realise he was saving her from a huge mistake. Time would heal everything. He was sure of it. The sobs continued from Fisher, and Wilson repeated the blow to the side of his head even harder than before.

"Can you hear me, Soldier?"

Fisher didn't look up, but his sobs petered out, and he said, "I hear you, Sir."

"Good soldier," Wilson said, nodding to Savannah. His control over a man who had caused her fear would make Savannah feel protected by him. This was good.

"Savannah, you can go now. Find a taxi and get out of here."

Savannah's brow furrowed in an expression of pure befuddlement. Wilson half expected her to look behind the bench and across the station before turning back, and say, 'who me?'. What was wrong with her? Surely she wanted to be away from this madness, to be protected, safe? He pushed her for an answer with his eyes.

"I'm staying, thanks," she said, reaching to her left and taking hold of Smith's hand. Smith accepted the hand like the uncaring bastard that he was.

"Don't you understand, Savannah? I'm trying to get you away from this. I'm not like Johnson who risked your life to capture Fisher or this loser who dragged you into all of this in the first place."

Savannah looked at Smith as she spoke, her eyes almost caressing the useless excuse for a human.

"He's been trying get me out of this from the start." She turned her head back to Wilson. "I'm staying."

It was hopeless to argue with her. She was strong, and he admired that in her. If he antagonised her, it would only make her resist more. If she stayed a while longer, he could prove he was protecting her from the likes of Fisher and Smith, and she would remember him with affection. Perhaps even weep at his death?

"Okay, but just stay close to me, okay?"

She looked back at him, but there was no answer clear in her big eyes, just uncertainty which would do for now. Wilson lifted Fisher's head up by his chin and knelt down so that their faces were inches apart.

"Are you ready to do whatever it takes, Soldier?"

Fisher's eyes were still uncertain and distant, but the soldier at the very centre of his being was surfacing. "Yes, Sir," he said. There was little conviction but the hardest part was already over.

Wilson reached under the bench where he had been sitting only minutes before and tugged free the briefcase containing the weapon. Smith gasped and Savannah's mouth opened. She was impressed, Wilson was sure of it. Placing the heavy briefcase flat on the bench between Fisher and Savannah, Wilson popped open the two catches and lifted the top of the case.

A chrome-plated tube gleamed in the glass-filtered light from the overcast sky. There was no slide or hammer, like a normal semi-automatic gun, just a sixteen inch long, fat, cylindrical barrel with a two inch square box underneath, two thirds of the way along, from which the trigger and its circular guard protruded. The grip of the gun, which housed the nuclear material, was in a separate sunken enclosure away from the main body of the gun and had two small dials one directly above the other. The top white dial read 'beam' and the red one below 'level' in small black letters.

All eyes were fixed on the briefcase. Wilson pulled out the two separate pieces and snapped them together making the weapon appear more like a regular handgun, only bigger. Power hummed through his hand and arm. He turned to Smith.

"Stay there, Smith. If you move one inch, I'll take your head off. And no talking." Wilson grabbed Fisher by the arm and dragged him out of earshot. Smith was powerless to do anything, but if he knew his plan, he would be more likely to risk his own life to save others. He wasn't too bright, but he was brave and that could mean trouble. He watched Smith and Savannah out of the corner of his eye while he spoke with Fisher.

"What do you know about the gun?"

Fisher looked at Wilson blankly, and his eyes began to mist.

"I said, what do you know about this gun, Soldier?"

"Not much, Sir," barked Fisher. "Once Bradshaw suspected I may be requiring its long distance explosive capabilities he clammed up, Sir."

"Did you know that the gun you were coveting was unlikely to fire a nuclear explosion?"

"No, Sir."

"Well, thanks to me, you now have one that will. So what was your plan?"

"Like Smith said, I was going to take down Whitehall. I know the wife of a soldier who died in Afghanistan, and she's keener than me to get payback. She works at Millbank Tower about a mile away and was going to get me up on the roof. I thought I'd get a good shot from there. I know there's a meeting tomorrow morning about the future of the SAS and that the bean counters who stole my job will be at the MoD offices."

No wonder this guy never made it past private, thought Wilson. He might be good on the ground, but a planner or leader, he wasn't.

"Are you crazy, man?" Perhaps not the best question under the circumstances. "I'm guessing you'd be aiming for the cabinet office or the Old Admiralty Building where the Ministry of Defence are based, but I doubt you'd have line of sight as far as the MoD building. How were you planning to hit your target?"

"From what Bradshaw told me, I wouldn't need to be that close to do the damage I'm looking for. All I need to do is set the beam on full width and the level to full and there'll be no one left standing in a half mile radius."

"Well he was lying. You might have made a few holes in the walls, but you'd have been picked off by a sniper in minutes. Did he say anything about the range?"

"Apparently it will reduce in power after two miles but fly straight for almost four."

"On full beam and power?"

"He didn't say."

Wilson looked around the station. He was certain that he had time on his side, but he knew that Johnson would fight to his last breath to secure the guns without harm befalling a single person. It was time to brief Fisher on the new plan. His heart raced with excitement as he spoke. God was on his side.

"Listen to me, Soldier. There's been a change of plan," he started, sending puffs of white condensation into the air as his breathing quickened to match his heart's oxygen requirements. "You'll get to make your statement in support of the SAS and take your own life. If you do this, I promise to kill the social workers responsible for what happened to you and your sister."

Fisher gazed up at Wilson, his mouth opening and closing, but no words were formed. He was fully compliant now. He was sure of it.

"Are you with me, Soldier?"

"Yes, Sir. You can rely on me."

Wilson held out the nuclear gun. "Take this and position yourself just inside the main entrance. Keep it hidden at all times, and wait for ten minutes from ..." Wilson looked at his watch, "... now."

Fisher checked his watch. "Yes, Sir. And then what, Sir?"

"Then set both dials to full, point the gun at the ground and pull the trigger. You'll be a hero to your cause and show those bureaucrats what you're made of."

*

I walk to the main entrance. My head hurts. Wilson is incredibly strong and hits like a truck. He thinks I'm compliant, a good little soldier. The gun hums beneath my jacket. I hold all the power. But Wilson is keeping his pug-ugly mug in my direction. The gun is unstable and not usable for escape purposes. Could Wilson have Sasha killed? I can't take any chances. Wilson must die before I make my escape. I must bide my time and wait until he is distracted.

I take my place at the entrance. The world is oblivious to the danger beneath my jacket. I slide my hand inside and turn both dials to low. The odds should be against an explosion at this level. I consider testing the gun on a few passers-by. Wilson is still looking. My face is twitching. Why can't I stop blinking? I am not myself. I need a cigarette.

*

Johnson pulled the BMW up outside Justice Investigations and scanned the surroundings for obvious signs of unusual activity. He had left the police cars far enough behind to give him space to breath. Thankfully, the electronics inside Smith's watch were more sensitive than human ears. Ten minutes, his partner had said, until the mother of all explosions took place. This wouldn't be confined to local or even national headlines. This would be a disaster worthy of global attention. This was the UK's 9/11. In a population as dense as Twickenham's, the death toll could reach thousands.

He checked his watch. There was still a distance of two to three hundred yards between the briefcase and Smith which contradicted the conversation he'd been listening to in the car. He inserted an earpiece and switched his watch's sound output to the mobile device.

"Keep your distance from Smith, Savannah, he's poison," Wilson said, before Johnson's earpiece went disturbingly quiet.

"C'mon," muttered Johnson. "Speak to me, dammit."

It was clear to the Earthguard agent that Wilson was as mentally unstable, if not more so, than Fisher. He realised that he should have called it in when he first had his doubts, but there was no time now. This mess was his to clean up.

Resisting the strong pull of both common sense and protocol, Johnson headed in the direction of the gun's signal, knowing that it might be the biggest mistake he could make. The agent had never been one for hunches, but he had a nagging feeling that the second watch signal, that should have been with the gun, supplied a vital clue to how he needed to handle the situation. Information was everything and distinctly lacking as he ran towards the block of flats behind the station where his watch told him the source of the second signal resided.

With one hand he pressed all of the buttons to request entry while his other hand felt around the door to ascertain its strength. Three kicks at most, he reckoned. A long buzz sounded, and he watched the signal metre on his watch as he climbed the stairs three at a time, a perk of the long legs he had been blessed with. The stairwell was shabby and in need of some decoration, but the condition was generally good with working lights and zero graffiti.

At the fourth floor of the six possible, he found his source. He lightly tapped the tarnished lion's head brass knocker. He wanted someone to be in, someone who could shed some light on his partner's actions. Wilson had gone off the rails fast, and it had all started after the visit to the SAS headquarters. Major Harris had tipped him over the edge, probably without even realising it, but what had he said to the best agent Johnson had ever worked with?

Johnson took a step back and raised his right leg just as he heard the sound of a rattling security chain. He lowered his leg and smoothed back his hair. Violence may well not be the answer here, and it didn't hurt to appear friendly and well presented.

The door opened the length of the security chain and a young woman's face peered back at Johnson. A mop of bright red hair sat atop a pale and bony face, and two sunken, world-weary, bloodshot eyes regarded Johnson with contempt. A golden stud sat between her chin and bottom lip, and he noticed the matching tongue piercing the moment she opened her mouth. Her right cheek seemed sore, or perhaps she'd just been resting on it a while.

"I'm not buying what you're selling mate, so jog along."

"I can't do that, Miss. There's something in your home I need to find."

"You what? I don't think so, chum. You should shift before I call the police."

He hadn't time to drag the conversation out, and soon he would have to revert to action. He would try one more time.

"Please, Miss. This is a matter of life and death."

"Yeah, it'll be yours if you don't leg it, pronto. I've got a suped up Taser in the back which will fry your balls and burst your ticker."

A bell rang in Johnson's head.

"I don't think so. Where would you get hold of a gizmo like that?"

"You American's aren't the only ones with the lethal toys mate. My Dad gets all sorts. It's about all the old wanker's good for, other than the rent on this place."

"What's your dad look like? Short, stocky, short straight hair, like mine?"

The woman pulled back a little from the door revealing the full features of her face. Johnson could instantly see the family resemblance beneath the ravages of neglect. "You know my Dad?" she said.

"He's about to wipe out half of Twickenham, you included, if I don't stop him."

"You're Johnson?" she said, unlatching the security chain and opening the door fully. The hall of the flat was in far greater need of a coat of paint than the building's stairwell. Beer cans, bottles and various items of underwear littered the bright pink carpet. She took no more care of her living environment than she did of herself.

"He mentioned me?"

"Yes. We had words and your name came up. He said..."

"I have to be quick," interrupted Johnson. "Did he give you anything?"

His partner's daughter looked offended at Johnson's lack of interest. What was it she didn't get about her father about to wipe out half of Twickenham?

"Stop interrupting, and I'll tell you." She bent over and picked up a briefcase from her left and held it out to Johnson. "He said to give you this and tell you that you were already too late but...? No, that wasn't it." She closed one eye and twisted her head as she thought. As Johnson leaned forward to take the small case, his nostrils were assaulted by the smell of cigarette smoke. "If you're dead, then you're too late... No that's not it... If you're alive, then don't be late... No that's not right." She scratched her head and leaned against the door frame for support. "It's all a bit fuzzy, but he definitely said to give you that."

Johnson dropped to the floor and opened the briefcase. Inside the weapon glinted at him. It was the latest prototype, the gun that Bradshaw had removed from the laboratory. He'd been right to follow his instinct. Wilson didn't have a gun.

"Johnson!" shouted a man's voice.

The agent swivelled round on one foot, pulling his Glock-17 from its holster and prepared to fire, but there were only dark walls and a window in front of him.

"Kinda jumpy aren't you, Johnson?" Kate said.

"Johnson!" came the voice again as the agent instinctively brought his hand up to the earpiece, realising that it was Smith trying to contact him.

"Shut up, I need to listen." Johnson attached the nuclear source to the barrel and trigger mechanism, and it clicked into place. The large handgun emitted a low hum and vibrated softly in his grip. He had held several prototypes before but never actually fired a fully charged version. The power emanating from the lead-lined, cold, steel casing was unimaginable.

"Wilson has gone nuts, you hear me? I've been trying to keep the watch pointed in his direction. He's talking to Fisher out of earshot. We're stuck on a bench next to platform four. You'd better hurry. He's given Fisher the weapon. He's coming, got to go..."

The earpiece went dead again. Then, Wilson's voice: "I told you two, no talking. I'll be with you in one minute."

How could Fisher have the gun when Johnson held it in his hand? There was no time to reason, he needed to move.

"Is that my Dad you're listening to?" said Wilson's daughter, jumping up and down. "Fuck me, he's gone mental. Are you gonna blow his head off? Please blow his fucking head off."

From his crouched position, Johnson set off back down the stairs like a sprinter at the sound of a starter pistol.

"Nice meeting you, Johnson. I'm Kate by the way," she called after him.

Johnson adjusted the dials to narrow beam and medium level as he took each flight of stairs in two strides. The shrill voice continued.

"He said if you're still alive and you're not too late then this should even the odds if you've got the guts to use it. Yes, that was it," screamed the voice from above Johnson. Then even louder, "Before you blow out his fucking brains, Johnson... Do you hear me? Before you shoot that piece of shit between the eyes, tell him that I've always fucking hated him."

No wonder he's planning to take her out, thought Johnson, as he flung open the doors to the building and raced towards the station, but what's he got against the rest of Twickenham? He made a mental note to himself to ask Doctor Meredith if she liked kids before he met up with her in person.

26: Monday 26th September, 12:40

Wilson bent down and forced John Smith's ankle against the wrought iron leg of the bench as he snapped on the cold metal cuffs.

"These will keep you here so we can have a nice chat when Savannah leaves."

John had the distinct feeling that he should have made his move before the cuffs came out, but what it might have been, he had no idea.

"So what's your plan?" John asked as the smiling agent wriggled himself between him and Savannah.

Wilson's smile broadened as he regarded John. There was a look of peace in the man's eyes, like he was in a different place, seeing different things to the rest of the world. "Now you're chained, I suppose there's no harm in it. I plan to be with God. What more can a man hope to achieve?"

Savannah remained quiet at John's earlier request when Wilson had been talking to Fisher. But she could not hide the shock on her face. It was all she could do to stay on the bench. Hang in there Savannah.

So, except for Savannah, they were all sentenced to death. A wave of self-preservation washed over John. If their last ditch plan didn't work, and it wasn't likely to, he was facing death right in the face. He had come so far and survived, it seemed unfair to end up dying chained to a bench. "Can I ask why I have to die? What did I ever do to you?"

The agent nibbled his top lip. "You're no good for Savannah. She's better off without you."

"What if I promised not to see her again?"

Wilson laughed. He was certainly more cheerful since he'd lost his mind.

"Nice try, kid, but I don't think so."

"At least stop calling me kid. It's my last request. All condemned men get a last request, right?"

"Sure," Wilson said, grinning. The lunatic agent had become a regular Samaritan.

"What if I scream, by the way?" John asked. Every avenue seemed worth exploring. "If you make one sound or gesture, I'll put a bullet in Savannah's head, and her blood will be on your hands."

So it was down to the last ditch plan again. "You touch one hair on her head and I swear I'll come after you."

A wry smile spread across Wilson's face. "We're about to be blown sky high. The only direction we're going in is up where I can be with my Julie and Kate just like the good old days."

John had observed enough of the rogue agent's behaviour around Savannah to doubt that his threats towards his girlfriend carried much weight, but Wilson was deranged, and who could predict what he would do if the chips were down. John had risked Savannah's life enough in the last few days, and he would not try to save his own by jeopardising hers. He felt pretty good about that thought. It was a shame he would die before the new John Smith had a chance to show what he was made of. Agent Johnson was their only hope now, and for all they knew, Wilson may already have killed him. If Johnson was dead or working with Wilson then all was lost.

"Is Johnson with you in all of this?" John asked.

Wilson sniggered. "Johnson? That fool's stuck in traffic on the M25. If he's early, he'll be here in time to join us in the afterlife, otherwise he'll be scraping you off the buildings half a mile away once the dust dies down. I'm betting on the former."

The agent, who until this morning at Justice Investigations had seemed a decent sort, gave a thumbs up signal to Fisher who waited to the right of the inside of the station entrance. There he could presumably keep a lookout as well as pull the trigger on the gun that would obliterate anything in its locality.

It seemed that Fisher was too mixed up and in awe of Wilson to even consider his own thoughts, although it was a toss-up between the two crazies as to which one might cost the most lives. If Fisher made a run for it, with the weapon under his control, who could say how many social workers he blamed for the predicament with his sister. John's father had always maintained that four social workers' lives only equated to one of anybody else's, so he might consider Fisher's retribution the less costly.

John's eyes misted, and an all too familiar lump rose in his throat at the thought of not seeing his family one more time. They had been right about him, he knew that now. Wishing they could have witnessed the new and improved John, he wondered if they would cry at his funeral. He hoped so, just a little. He wiped his eyes before turning to Savannah who forced a smile back at him. Her lovely eyes were sad and tired. Wilson looked on triumphantly. John winked at Savannah. She knew what to do.

"You'll soon forget him, Savannah," Wilson said, leaning back on the bench like he was in a comfy armchair. "From now on, there will be no more bad influences in your life. You can take control again. We'll all be as dead as that useless father of yours." He pointed to an exit on the far side of the station. "Now leave here while there's still time."

John coughed and rubbed his nose frantically, the signal agreed with Savannah.

"What do you know about my father?" Savannah said, standing up and walking over to Wilson. "Who are you to judge my father?"

Wilson stood up. That's it Savannah, keep him distracted. John was just about to reach out and take the gun from the front of the agent's trousers when the big fool stepped out of reach. Damn it, it had been their final gambit. If it wasn't for his ankle being joined to the bench, he could have leapt forward and made a grab for the gun, killed Wilson and then shot Fisher. It had never been a great plan.

"I just meant that you could put everything behind you," Wilson said, caught off guard by Savannah's outburst.

"He was weak, but he was no murderer which is more than I can say for you." Savannah's hands were on her hips, and her face contorted with an anger that flushed her face and flared her nostrils as she took deep breaths. If this was acting, it was the best John had seen.

John used the distraction to move his Earthguard issue Rolex closer to his mouth and whispered, "I'm about to be launched from this bench if you don't move it Johnson. Platform four, Twickenham Rail Station. It's now or never."

He knew it was hopeless, but unless Savannah could back Wilson up a little closer, he had no chance of reaching the exposed gun. He coughed loudly, a real throat clearer to attract her attention, but she was busy laying into Wilson.

"You're about to murder thousands of innocent people. In what way does that qualify you to bad mouth my family?"

The agent's lips flapped like a flag in a strong breeze, but only one word came out, "But... but... but?"

"But nothing." Wilson took another half step back. One more of those and it might just be worth a shot. Just as John's heart accelerated with the adrenalin rush that was hope, Wilson took a step to his left taking him well out of his reach. John slapped his head with both hands.

It was over.

"One break, that's all I was asking." As the words left his lips, John felt the tightness on his ankle release as the cuffs fell away and clinked on the concrete floor below. There was no time for thinking. The plan was already ingrained, having been played over and over in his head. He pushed off from the secured bench with one foot and launched himself at Wilson. For the longest time John seemed airborne, no part of him close to the ground.

Wilson turned to see his attacker, the thick coat swinging open to reveal the pistol only a foot away. John's hand opened to take hold of the pistol. As John's fingers circled the grip of the gun, a huge fist came crashing down onto the back of his neck sending him face first onto the floor. John heard his nose break before the pain registered, but neither worried him as he double rolled to his left leaving a small pool of blood behind him. The plan had failed. He looked up at Wilson to see him draw his own gun from beneath his left armpit.

*

Savannah Jones ran into Wilson at full pelt, like a rugby player hungry for the try line. Instead of sending him flying, the impact merely knocked him off balance. A look of disbelief and hurt appeared on his face. He began to shake his head as he pulled out Fisher's gun from his trousers with his empty hand, flipping it around expertly so that the barrel pointed at him and the grip was extended towards Savannah.

"Is this what you want? This world is over for me anyway but if you'd prefer to do the honours."

She snatched the gun before he had time to reconsider and brought her other hand up to hold the weapon steady.

"Drop the gun," she screamed, looking around her to see that the few travellers in the station were fleeing for the exits. One woman shrieked, and the distant sound of sirens approaching could be heard.

Wilson stared into her eyes. Not an ounce of fear emanated from him.

"I said, drop the gun."

"You're all the same," the agent said, moving towards Savannah as he spoke. "You say you want one thing, and yet when it's put in reach, you want something else."

"Don't come any closer," Savannah backed away as Wilson approached. "Drop the gun, or I'll shoot you."

Wilson stopped and turned towards John who had started to rise.

"Stay on the floor, Smith, or I'll kill the girl in front of your eyes."

John obeyed and slumped back to the ground, his eyes fixed on Wilson and his broken nose pointing to one side, blood dripping steadily onto the ground. Wilson raised his gun and pointed it at Smith's head. His expression was blank, and he spoke like a man without a worry in the world.

"If you want to save this worthless lout, then you'd better shoot me before I shoot him. The safety's off, so you just need to point the Berretta and pull the trigger. The two of you deserve each other. That's the offer. Kill me and you both have time to make it out of here before Fisher pulls the trigger. I'll count down from three, and you can decide what's important to you."

Savannah's hands shook so violently she thought the gun might jump out of her grip.

"Three," began Wilson.

"I'll shoot, Wilson. Put the gun down."

"Two."

"I'm not kidding." Savannah's breathing quickened, her heart hammered so hard it hurt and her knees began to tremble. A wave of dizziness took hold, and she stumbled sideways. She couldn't pass out, not now. The gun pulled her arms down like it was a fifty pound weight.

"One."

Savannah lifted the drooping gun to chest height where her target looked the biggest, and, before the weight could drag her arms back down, she pulled the trigger. The bullet caught Wilson in his right shoulder, twisting him sideways and sending him two steps back. His left hand immediately jumped to the wound before any blood appeared. His mouth opened in a grimace, and his screwed up eyes stared back at Savannah.

The gunshot echoed around the station as Wilson's demeanour took on a menacing appearance, anger surfacing through the pain. He looked like a wounded Pitt Bull Terrier, lips stretched wide and teeth bared in a snarl. The gun echo faded and was replaced by a loud ringing in Savannah's ears. Wilson pulled his hand away from his shoulder, revealing no penetration hole and no blood. At first she thought that her gun was full of blanks, and then her stupidity dawned on her. He had reeled from the impact. It must be the coat. No wonder they wore them all the time.

With a concerted effort, she raised the gun to his head and pulled the trigger once more but the shot missed and he was on her in a second, tearing the gun from her grasp and stuffing it back into his trousers. His top lip curled as he placed his own gun back in its holster and glared at Savannah.

"You're no better than my drug-addicted slag of a daughter." Wilson cocked his huge arm back behind his head and made a fist. "Well, you can die here with us. I'm done with you."

Before the brute of a man could release the blow, John Smith grabbed the tree trunk of an arm from behind with both hands and hung on with every drop of strength he had.

"What the..?" Wilson exclaimed, turning his body round and ripping free from John's grip like his arms were made of paper. John ran at Wilson, but thick arms swatted him away like a bothersome insect. But the insect kept coming, blood pouring from his crumpled nose. Wilson swung and swatted until, with exasperation clear in his face, he raised his fist and unleashed a heavy punch straight into John's nose which soaked up its second bone-shattering blow.

John travelled back several feet before stopping. His eyes glazed over, and he swayed like a flower in a stiff breeze. John's nose erupted like a thick red geyser before he swayed one more time and dropped to the floor as if his legs had lost their bones. Savannah had watched enough boxing with her father to know that John was out cold.

"You bastard." Savannah marched up to Wilson and began swinging her fists like windmills. The agent pushed her away and drew out his gun.

"In heaven you'll see the light just like Kate," he said, aiming the gun at Savannah's head. "God has no use for you on earth." Savannah closed her eyes. It was the end. A high-pitched whistle from her right filled the air, but before she could open her eyes, another shot rang out, and her thigh exploded in pain. She dropped to the ground clutching her leg and screamed.

*

I can't believe what I'm seeing. Wilson is about to die. I am drawn to the conflict and the outcome. Wilson doesn't see Johnson, and the tall agent is closing in fast. What's that he's holding? It's another nuclear gun! It must be the one Bradshaw promised me. What if I could get hold of that one? I wouldn't have to worry about Armageddon every time I fired it. Think of the death and destruction I could cause for years to come.

Johnson positions himself and raises the gun. I feel the excitement I thought Sasha had stolen forever. I realise that I don't crave a cigarette. I am not done by a long shot.

*

Herb Johnson was thirty feet away when he made the shot which hit his partner in the left thigh and went all the way through both legs, leaving a two foot crater in the concrete behind the damaged limbs. The beam had not knocked his partner off balance but had literally cut right through him. He noticed that the closest entry wound was charred and smouldering as Wilson dropped to his knees, a mocking smile on his lips.

There was no debris around the crater. The concrete had disintegrated. He would have taken his partners head off, but he had no idea how far the energy burst would travel at head height and who and what it would go through on its way. There had been barely a sound to accompany the extreme devastation to both flesh and solid station floor.

He looked over to Savannah, who was fast losing consciousness in a growing pool of her own blood. Her screams had reduced to a low intermittent moaning. She needed urgent treatment. As he bent down to check the damage to her leg, he felt a sharp pain as a nine millimetre bullet entered his calf muscle. What an idiot. Never turn your back on a madman until he's dead - he knew that. Wilson was fuelled with insanity. He should have finished him before helping the girl. He turned to Wilson, who grinned at him like he'd just won the lottery.

"It's too late, Herb. Fisher's going to activate the explosion any second. You don't get to save the girl or the day. I'm going to meet my maker, and you're going to Hell."

"What happened to you, Max?" Johnson asked, bending down to pull up his blood-soaked trouser leg and hold his calf tightly to stem the flow of blood. His partner chuckled like an asylum inmate. He was not the man Johnson had known.

Johnson placed the nuclear gun prototype on the ground by his feet and, in one smooth motion, drew out his own Glock and put a bullet between Wilson's eyes, sending the back of his head, along with unthinking brain matter, all over John Smith and the surrounding area. At least Kate would be happy. To the tall agent it was like putting down a rabid dog that had once been a close companion - best for everybody.

Johnson picked up the humming gun and, putting his weight mainly on his good leg, hobbled over to Smith and knelt down beside him.

"Smith, wake up," he said, slapping his face hard.

Smith's eyes opened into narrow slits which fought to focus on Johnson.

"Are we dead?" the prone figure said.

"Where's Fisher? We have to get the other nuclear gun?"

"There are two?"

Johnson slapped him again. "Focus, Smith. Where's Fisher?"

Smith raised his body on his elbows and turned and pointed to the entrance where Fisher had been standing at Wilson's instruction.

"He was there a few minutes ago," Smith said, looking to each side of the entrance. "Maybe he ran off when the bullets started flying."

Johnson grabbed Smith by the lapels of his jacket and sat him upright.

He offered the weapon to Smith. "Take this gun, find and kill him," he said.

Smith's narrow slits widened. "Me? Are you serious?"

Johnson pulled him close until their faces almost touched.

"My leg's useless. There's no time to argue. Find him and kill him or we're all dead and that includes Savannah."

John Smith stood up bit by bit on shaking legs, and the world around him shimmered like a desert mirage. He blinked his eyes and twisted his head from side to side. Focus returned to his vision. He took the heavy weapon from Johnson's outstretched hand. He wrapped his fingers around the grip and felt the pulsating tingle from the destructive power inside.

"Go man," Johnson said, crawling on hands and knees towards Savannah, who lay curled in a foetal position in a worryingly large circle of red goo. "I'll take care of her. Go, for God's sake man, go."

John stumbled towards the entrance as fast as his legs would carry him. There was an eerie silence in the station and not a soul in sight near the entrance. He saw a movement to the right and, leaping unsteadily sideways, took shelter behind a large green bin. John poked his head out and waited for the right moment to make his move.

*

Wilson is dead. I wish I'd killed him. I hear sirens and poke my head out of the glass doors. Blue and red flashing lights approach. I elect to entrust my future to chance and adjust the gun's dials. A car's tyres squeal as they brake. Two armed officers get out. I turn back to platform four where Johnson is leaning over Smith.

I have to go soon. There is no time to stay and take out Smith. But the thought makes my skin tingle. He is the biggest fraud of them all. I look through the glass doors. The two officers are halfway to the entrance. I want to use the gun, but it will attract Johnson's attention.

I take cover behind a coffee cart. I wait. The gun is heavy. I turn the weapon around. The first officer swings his rifle from side to side. Where do they get these people? His attention shifts to Johnson and Savannah. I can't see Smith.

I raise the heavy gun and rush out in one stride and sideswipe the officer's head. His lower jaw is torn free from its ligaments and is no longer in line with his head. It is not the best blow, but now my eye is in and I finish the job. He looks like an extra from a zombie movie. I duck back behind the stand. His partner comes over to attend to him. He looks my way, but I am too quick. I have always been too quick. While he calls on his radio, I circle back round the stand and creep up behind him. It is too easy.

"Look out," Smith screams.

Where did he come from? I bring the gun down four times until the officer's shoulders and neck are broken. I can kill anyone. Protective helmets are not designed against my attacks. Smith looks sickened and as pale as me. He has the other gun. It is my lucky day after all.

*

ETHAN JUSTICE: ORIGINS • 230

John turned to face Fisher, who stood, legs slightly apart, glinting gun pointing downwards, behind the dead body of an armed police officer. Fisher had killed two men before his very eyes, and now John was in the open facing death again. Why hadn't he shot from behind the bin? There was only ten feet between the two men.

Fisher was SAS trained. What chance did John have? He was at the other man's mercy. As John stared into Fisher's eyes, he could see the man's facial tics dancing across his face. They were not so obvious when he spoke.

"I'm not going to blow up the station, Smith. I was never going to. As soon as I'd killed Wilson, I was going to get myself up to York. All that soldier crap, who was he trying to kid? Shame Johnson had to steal all my fun."

John had talked himself out of trouble before, and other than an old fashioned gun draw contest, it was his only option. Reinforcements would be coming soon. "You're going after the social workers?"

"Exactly. I'm going to hunt them down and kill every one of them."

"Can't you hear the sirens? They'll be swarming this place within minutes."

"Not before I kill you. Besides, they're no match for me."

"You're that good?"

Fisher brought his hand away from his head and looked at his gun. "Have you felt the power humming from these things? I think I'll take my chances. If I get cornered, I'll just take them all with me. Are you ready to die, Smith?"

John studied the man in front of him as he considered his choices. He was no match for an elite soldier in a gun fight. He recalled an Oprah Winfrey rerun on a wet Sunday afternoon when they had suggested that running was the best option. Chances were that the gunman would miss, especially if you ran in a zig-zag motion. John's legs didn't feel like there was a single zig left in them, although running did seem appealing in light of the alternative.

Using both hands, Fisher levelled the large shiny barrelled gun at John.

John felt his breath stop. He couldn't die without defending himself. He had to think of something. "Do you know who the social workers were?" he said.

"What?"

"How do know who to kill?"

"I'll kill everyone in the York office."

"What if some have moved or retired or changed vocation?"

Fisher lowered the gun. "I'll find them and kill them one by one."

"You're well and truly on the radar now. You get one chance, and then you're jailed for life."

As Fisher considered John's remark, his attention left John momentarily, his eyes darting about the station.

"What about your sister?" John said. "What will she think?"

Fisher's gaze returned to John with added intensity. "What do I care what she thinks? She's made her feelings clear."

"Maybe if you acted like her brother and stopped trying to hit on her she might feel differently."

Checking behind him first, Fisher stepped over the lifeless body at his feet, raised the gun and levelled it at John's chest. His face was undulating with tics and twitches. "You heard our conversation." It wasn't a question.

John could hear Oprah telling him to run. "Only the bit about you wanting her to talk dirty while you played with yourself," he said.

Fisher's face flushed beetroot red as he hung his head, dropped his arms to his sides and started talking to himself. "No-one can know. It wasn't my fault, it was ... my father. Who else knows?"

John looked around for signs of the cavalry, but other than Johnson tending to Savannah's injury, there was no other movement in the station.

"I said who else knows?" Fisher shrieked, his face still staring at his own feet like he was... Like he was what?

Ashamed. That was it. The twitching maniac was ashamed that others knew about his sordid secret. He was so ashamed that he couldn't look John in the face. John seized the moment and raised his gun.

"Put the weapon down, Fisher."

"Who else knows?" Fisher repeated, his head jerking like a nodding dog on a car dashboard as he refused to look up at John. "Tell me who else knows. They all ... have to die."

It was John's chance. The man was lost in his own world of crazy. So why couldn't he pull the trigger?

"Put the gun down," John repeated at the top of his voice.

Fisher looked up, and shock spread across his face. His enemy had turned the tables. John was transfixed by the writhing face whose cheeks, lips, eyelids and nose convulsed. At the last moment, he saw Fisher's arms raise the gun. John didn't feel himself pull the trigger. A piercing whine sounded, and a half inch circular hole appeared in the centre of Fisher's forehead.

For the briefest of moments, John could see through the hole to the newsstand and another hole beyond before blood and brains filled the space, blocking the view and Fisher's body crumpled to the hard floor. A wisp of smoke floated from the hole in Fisher's head as the brain matter oozed out behind it.

"That's for Mark, you sick bastard," John said, marching towards the dead body. He bent down and removed the gun from Fisher's hand. As he pulled the grip clear of the barrel and firing mechanism, he noticed that both dials were set to maximum. He might not have died alone if Fisher had fired first.

John looked across to Savannah where two members of an ambulance crew were seeing to her wound. When did they turn up? She was sat up and talking to them. He could see Johnson talking to an armed police officer. Before he could make a move, a burly police officer snapped handcuffs on him from behind. John looked up to the ceiling of the station but aimed his annoyance at the heavens beyond.

"Oh come on!" he yelled as he was dragged backwards and into a caged van.

27: Monday 26th September, 19:20

In a basement, in the bowels of London, at the Earthguard hospital, exact location unknown, John Smith was sitting on Savannah Jones's bed. Savannah, with the aid of the high-tech bed, was sitting up dressed in plain, light blue pyjamas supplied by Earthguard. John wondered if they were bullet proof, like the coats.

The large private ward, complete with fridge, large flat screen television and room service, put the private healthcare service to shame. John, after minor nose surgery to move a small piece of bone back into place, had his nostrils stuffed with gauze.

"You look ridiculous, Smith," Savannah said, taking his hand and squeezing it.

John squeezed back and spoke like he had a cold. "It's only for today. How's the leg?"

"Fine, the doctor said that if it wasn't for Johnson using his belt as a tourniquet, then I'd be dead."

"Yeah, he's quite the hero."

"You are," Savannah said, stroking his cheek. "You saved Twickenham from destruction."

He blushed. "I think that was Johnson again. Besides you had your fair share of selfless action."

John, who had been longing to kiss Savannah since he had left surgery and taken up residence in her room, leaned forward and pecked her on the lips.

She smiled as he drew his head back. "Is that the best you can do, Smith?"

His mouth returned to hers. His tongue's entry was eagerly accepted by her parted lips. The sound of a closing door stopped them in their tracks. The deep growl of a man's throat clearing alerted them to another's presence in the room. Surprised, John rotated his neck and caught his nose on Savannah's, sending spasms of pain through the recently straightened appendage.

A few choice swear words hovered on his lips as he automatically brought up his hand to cover his nose. Agent Johnson was standing in the centre of the private room with the aid of two crutches, wearing pale blue pyjamas and a dark blue dressing gown. John was amazed at how little noise the agent's crutches had made. Was it the Earthguard training, or had John's mind been lost in the kiss? He suspected it was a little of both.

"You'd better watch what you do with that or it'll need resetting," the Earthguard agent said, his lips squeezed together in a poor attempt to keep a snigger at bay.

"Very funny," John said, still wincing in pain. "Did they take out the wires from your lips while removing the bullet so that you can manage a smile now?"

"I didn't recognise you without your coat," Savannah added, laughing. "Won't they let you wear it in here?"

Johnson's mouth resisted, twitching at the edges, before widening into an enormous grin.

"Look, I'd put my hands up and surrender, but I'd probably fall to the floor so I'll just say that you guys win. Any room on that bed for me?"

Savannah patted the left side of the bed by her injured leg. "Of course, it's not often a girl gets to have two heroes on her bed."

In two swings on the crutches Johnson was at the bedside, lowering himself next to Savannah, taking great care to avoid her damaged leg.

"Sorry to interrupt you lovebirds, but I was getting bored with the TV in my room and thought I'd check up on you both." Johnson placed his hand on Savannah's lower leg away from the injury. "I might have known that

Justice would be here trying to take advantage of your inability to run away."

Savannah laughed so much that the bed started to shake.

"Stop it, you're making my leg hurt," Savannah complained, teardrops congregating at the corners of her big brown eyes.

John began to laugh too, but the tears which welled in *his* eyes were from the pain in his nose which didn't react well to the rhythmic head movement. The change in Johnson's demeanour was beyond dramatic. With a smile on his face and no long dark coat, he was barely recognisable as the man who had guided them through their ordeal of the last three days. It dawned on John that he would miss the tall man, especially since he had gained a sense of humour.

"So it's all over now? You don't need us anymore?" John asked.

"Yes and no," Johnson said. "Yes, it's over. Both guns are safely in our hands and scheduled for destruction." The agent narrowed his eyes and picked at the bedcover as he seemed to run through his thoughts. John and Savannah's interests were heightened by the pause. "As far as needing you anymore, I have a proposition for you both."

John and Savannah looked at each other.

"Go on," John said, keeping his eyes firmly on Savannah's.

"I have persuaded the agency that Ethan here..."

"Please don't call me that."

"It's your name from now on. All records for John Smith have been erased, never to return."

"I rather like it. It's very manly," Savannah said, eyes wide and excited. "Go on, Herb."

"Manly ... really?" John said, not convinced.

"For now, you'll have to get used to it. Anyway, as I was saying, the agency has agreed to fund your own detective agency and put you through full agent training."

"To be your partner?"

"Not at this point, and it's unlikely to happen with your family ties. You can run your own private investigations and make some good money along the way. We will provide you with all the equipment you need which will put you way ahead of any rival agencies, and when I need your assistance, you can help me out... Fully paid of course."

"And Savannah?"

Johnson turned to Savannah who was clearly thrilled about her role in all of this. "You can work for Justice Investigations and assist Ethan if you want."

Savannah tugged at John's white t-shirt, another gift from Earthguard Health Services. "Can we John? I mean Ethan?"

Her eyes pleaded with him, but it was a big decision, and he didn't want to be rushed. She would always be impulsive. It was obviously part of her make up. There was no doubt in John's mind that she would get him into more scrapes before long. There would be a lot of excitement too.

"I'd like to talk to Savannah alone and then run it by my family, if that's okay?"

"Sure, I'll leave you in peace now. But before you turn me down, I'd just like to say that I've never seen anyone more naturally gifted and suited to this type of work."

John regarded the agent closely but saw no signs of a joke at his expense. He looked at Savannah who shrugged her shoulders. If he agreed to Johnson's offer, he would ask the agent to repeat those words to his parents.

"I'm not kidding, Justice. You were made for this. Just give it plenty of thought, that's all I'm asking."

John admired his suped up Rolex. "Can I keep the watch?"

"Yeah and one of our trademark coats that I know you've been hankering for. I'll rustle another watch up for Savannah if you agree. Are you a Cartier or a Rolex kind of gal? We don't have as many female operatives and so there's less of a choice for the ladies."

"I was a Timex kind of gal actually, so either's good."

"No problem." With the aid of his crutches, Johnson stood up and bent over to kiss Savannah on the cheek. "Sorry for what we put you through, and good luck getting back on your feet."

Savannah punched his arm playfully.

"Forget it. I had the time of my life. Smith ... I mean Justice did too. He just won't admit it."

So much trouble, thought John.

Johnson, resting his elbow on the crutch, extended his hand half way to John. John jumped off the bed and walked round to the side where Johnson stood. He grabbed the agent's hand and shook it hard.

"Whatever I decide, it's been ... well ... something else," John said.

"Yeah, I know. There's nothing quite like it, is there?" Johnson withdrew his hand. "I'd better get going. I'm expecting a visit from Susan Meredith, Fisher's psychologist."

"Do I sense a little romance blooming?" Savannah asked, both rows of teeth exposed by her grin.

"More like some long overdue head work I would imagine," John said.

"We'll see. Have to get myself a suitable mask first, if you know what I mean. First date in a while."

John didn't and Savannah appeared similarly baffled. Before either could ask, Johnson turned and left just as quietly as he had arrived. John returned to sit on Savannah's bed when a knock came at the door, and a white coated doctor in his late forties with thick grey hair entered with a clip board and pen.

"Ah, there you are, Mr Justice," he said, comparing his notes to the ones at the foot of the bed. "I was told I'd find you here. Might as well check you both together."

John cringed at the sound of his new name. It would take a lot of getting used to. How was he going to explain the change to his parents?

"Miss Jones, you are doing just fine, and we'll have you back on your feet before you know it." The doctor walked up to John, grabbed his chin and proceeded to gaze at his nose from several angles, his facial expression changing with each viewpoint. "Better than the original I'd say, Mr Justice," he finished, making a note on a separate form. "I'll leave you both in peace now."

The doctor made his way to the door and turned back to face them just before he reached it. "Third button on the top right of the bed remote locks this door if you'd like some privacy."

"Thank you, Doctor," Savannah said. The door clicked shut. She took hold of John's hand again. "So what do you want to do about Johnson's offer?"

John really had no idea. "There's no rush, right?"

"If you say yes ..." She picked up the remote control for the bed and locked the door, "... and you speak to me with your Russian accent..."

"Yes?" John said, liking where this was going.

"I'll let you see what's under my pyjamas."

Savannah pushed John off the bed and lifted the covers to reveal matching bottoms to the pyjamas. One leg had been removed to allow easy access to the wound which was heavily bandaged.

"What's it to be, Justice?" she asked, undoing the buttons on her pyjama top.

"You can call me Dmitri," said Ethan Justice. "Get ready for famous Moscow manoeuvre."

The End

Thank You

I greatly appreciate you taking the time to read my book. I hope you enjoyed it and would love to hear your feedback.

Please contact me via:
My website: SimonJenner.com
Facebook: Facebook.com/SimonJennerAuthor
Twitter: Twitter.com/simonrjenner

While on my website, why not sign up to get updates on new releases, deals, giveaways, exclusive content and my personal recommendations for other great thrillers?

One last thing, if you believe the book is worth sharing, please take a few seconds to let your friends know about it and to leave a quick review on Amazon. Your efforts are much appreciated.

All the best,
Simon

Other Action Thrillers by Simon Jenner

Ethan Justice: Relentless

Printed in Great Britain
by Amazon.co.uk, Ltd.,
Marston Gate.